The Magic of Miramare

With best wishes,

Soulla

x

Soulla Christodoulou

KINGSLEY
PUBLISHERS

First published in South Africa by Kingsley Publishers, 2024
Copyright © Soulla Christodoulou, 2024

The right of Soulla Christodoulou to be identified as author
of this work has been asserted.

Kingsley Publishers
Pretoria, South Africa
www.kingsleypublishers.com

A catalogue copy of this book will be available from the
National Library of South Africa

Paperback ISBN: 978-1-7764837-3-0
eBook ISBN: 978-1-7764837-2-3

Also by Soulla Christodoulou

A Palette of Magpies
The Village House
Alexander & Maria
The Summer Will Come
Broken Pieces of Tomorrow

Dedicated to my family who I shared the most wonderful summer holiday with, on the island of Kefalonia, in August 2014. To my mamma and baba, Alan, Christian, Alexei, Angelo, Lia, Darren, Elisia, Jojo, Reece, Maria, Lee, Sofia and Zach. The best holiday ever.

November 2022

Stella

Stella snuggled on the sofa, she leaned into her lover trying to get comfortable but the sinking feeling in her tummy took hold and she could neither get comfy nor relax. Suddenly conscious of her bare breasts she tugged at her kimono, pulling it around her; vulnerability pushing down on her, the night sky through the window seamlessly staining midnight blue to charcoal black.

'Almost time for me to go,' Anton said through a stifled yawn, but he made no effort to get up. He slipped his hand under the kimono's silky fabric and caressed her left breast, his hand hot against her cool skin and he leaned in, kissing her on the forehead.

The minutes ticked by, closing in on her, smothering, claustrophobic. She wanted to scream don't go but that's not how it worked, not how this relationship did things.

He shifted, pushing her away as he extricated himself from their embrace. He stretched one of his arms, out to his side and then up over his head, and yawned again, this time a full, wide yawn which he closed his eyes to and shook against.

She watched him through glazed eyes, caught his yawn, and stood up. She wished things could be different. Every evening they had together ended the same way, and now with the same familiar dragging nausea in the pit of her stomach. A growing agitation engulfed her as the clock ticked, seemingly getting faster and faster, louder, and louder, mocking her, as it approached ten o'clock. He would jump up any moment now and announce it was getting late, he had to get home.

As if he had read her mind, he pushed her gently off him and stood up, stretching upwards, his hands almost touching the low ceiling of her two-bedroom cottage.

'Let me do the washing up before I go,' he said, clearing their dinner plates from the glass coffee table where they had, only three hours earlier, eaten a takeaway of Pad Thai noodles, green chicken curry and coconut rice. They had eaten both portions of rice and then burnt it off. The food and the sex a kind of ritual, had, over the years, become a way to express themselves, define their relationship. The food staved off her feelings their relationship was about the sex, the need to be physical, a hunger which they both satiated for each other.

His offer to clear up grated on her nerves, stretched like taut bowstrings. *Why doesn't he spend the last few minutes with me?*

***

Stella had spent the day in London in a meeting with her publishers who had, in not so many words, given her an ultimatum: Write the next book and hand in the manuscript within the next six weeks or they would regrettably have no alternative but to terminate her contract. She had left their offices deflated and the excitement she had held in her about going away for the summer, for the first time in her relationship with Anton, had quickly faded, leaving a tight knot of anxiety deep in the pit of her stomach.

She would write the book. She would give them their blasted manuscript and then she would terminate the contract with them. Ha. They wouldn't see that coming, would they? She had stopped off at the express supermarket and picked up the ingredients to cook Anton's favourite meal. He was coming over that evening and she wanted to make it special for him. Special for them both. They had been together for almost twenty years.

Years of clandestine dinners, lunchtime sex, hotel rooms and room service so they could spend as much time as possible in bed together. The years had drifted by in a surreal way, a fantasy bubble far-removed from the realities of both their lives, but it worked, and Stella had always focused on the time they had together and not the time they didn't, grateful to have found her soul mate.

She got in, after standing all the way home on the train, getting pushed and shoved by men in wet, steaming overcoats, sopping umbrellas, and heavy briefcases. The drive home from the station proved treacherous, a car accident had left a tailback three miles long on one of the main thoroughfares back to the village. Only a few miles up the M1, the motorway led north from London and brought her home within half an hour but not today.

She began to prepare dinner and halfway through peeling and slicing potatoes to make the chunky wedges Anton loved, having already trimmed the mushrooms, and chopped the onions, she looked at the clock, and decided to order his favourite takeout instead. He would be here within the next hour. Tired on her feet, intolerably footsore, she made a mug of tea, lit a cigarette, and sat in front of the TV, switching it on from the remote by the sofa. She could really do with a foot massage.

Without realising it, the time ticked by, and it was seven o'clock. She got up to place the Thai food order when her mobile buzzed on the kitchen counter. She grabbed it, all smiles. 'Hello, my darling. I'm about to order your favourite Thai.'

'I'm sorry, Stella but I won't be able to make it.'

'No worries,' she said, with forced joviality.

'I can't talk now. A family emergency. Will try to text later. Love you.'

'Love you,' she said, but he was already gone, and her words fell into the silent abyss of the closed line between them. She shook off a shiver of irritation, unlike her, and reached for her cigarettes, her hand shaking as she plucked one from the packet.

She packaged the chopped vegetables into plastic containers and arranged them neatly in the fridge. She had lost her appetite. She took a semi-hot shower, the water barely warming her skin under its spray and went to bed early, full of irritation. With her laptop open, balanced on her lap as she sat with her legs stretched out under the duvet, she tried to focus but couldn't concentrate, and her glass of wine did nothing to appease her temperament.

She couldn't remember the last time she had felt this disappointed, and it not only upset her, but an unrecognisable anger welled up like a volcano waiting to erupt. She was exhausted, fed up. She convinced herself it was the meeting with her publisher; it had left a lasting ill feeling. That's what it was.

The following morning Anton didn't call or message, a habit over the years, and it discombobulated her. *What was going on?* She didn't message or try to call him, unsure of what she should do in the situation. That's not the way their relationship rolled but all the same she was edgy all day. A group of yummy mummies occupied her usual spot in the local coffee shop and their toddlers sucking on yoghurt smoothies and crumbling oaty bites all over the floor and across the tables. The noisy babies crying, and snuffling newborns snuggled int their mothers' soft milky breasts, forced her decision not to stay.

She ordered her favourite latte, extra sweet, to go. She had booked one of the hot desks at her publisher's premises to write from mid-morning, but the coffee did nothing to make her feel better or ignite her writing mojo. The day dragged. The other two authors there, kept themselves to themselves, much younger than her, giggling and looking down at their phones every few minutes, and she wasn't in the mood for conversation anyway.

Stella spent most of the stretched-out hours not writing but gazing out of the room's rain-spattered windows, grimy with pollution, onto the wet street, passers by rushing past the steamy windows holding umbrellas at different angles to avoid the rain hitting them. It poured grey and wet and drizzly all day.

Inspiration did not come, and she barely added another

two paragraphs to her writing. She browsed Instagram and liked a few posts, noticing how the last dozen or so posts by her publisher had not mentioned her forthcoming book; not surprising though when she didn't even have a solid idea for her next story. Her procrastination continued and then social media swallowed her up.

At half past four, desperate to escape and for a cigarette, she decided to make a run to the Underground. She finally got to the station, soaked; her umbrella unable to withstand the incessant rain and the force of the wind which came with it. She stopped off to grab another cup of her favourite coffee before collecting her car from the station car park at the other end and driving home. The drink's usually welcome caramel sweetness didn't reduce her irritability. She had not heard from Anton all day again. She hoped he was okay. Hoped nothing serious was keeping him from making contact.

Finally at home, she shook off the rain, now softer like the sound of fountains, unwrapped the steak and cooked one sirloin for herself. She ate it with a one-portion packet of instant mash and the peas which she boiled for three minutes in the microwave. Anton hated her using the microwave, but he wasn't there to tell her off. By eleven o'clock she was about to give up on him when her phone buzzed. She picked it up and read his message:

Sorry not been in touch. Brandon had an accident at work. Still at the hospital.
Will call when I can.

There was no miss you or love you. No kiss or heart emoji.

The fleeting fire in her heart that he had remembered her fizzled out like a snowflake in sunshine and guilt quickly replaced it, consumed her. Brandon, his son, was twenty-two and had recently started his first post-graduate position with a high-profile engineering company. *Anton must have been worried sick.*

She went to bed reasoning Anton was stressed; he would otherwise have said I love you. She begrudged her own feelings and wanted to be more compassionate, but she couldn't. She tried to push the situation out of her mind, but she couldn't. A selfishness consumed her. This was different. This was a time she needed his support, his presence. With her writing not forthcoming and the stress of her publishers pushing deadlines at her she needed him. Needed to talk to him, share her feelings of inadequacy with him. But it wasn't like her to be needy. She knew what their relationship entailed. This wasn't the first time Anton had not turned up or been enticed with family stuff going on.

Pull yourself together, she said, *you'll see him tomorrow.* And in only a few short months they would be on their holiday abroad. Together. For the first time.

Melody

Melody's hazel eyes moved around the room as she sat on the sofa; from the deep-pile rug, which was hoovered and fluffed up all the way under the coffee table, to the three framed photographs on the wall which hung perfectly aligned and then to two vases on the side tables facing each other perpendicularly.

She didn't lean back in the sofa, not wanting to squash the five plump cushions arranged in a regularly interspaced pattern across the back of the deep velvet couch. She had spent the better part of half an hour arranging and rearranging them until she was happy with the way they looked.

She took a deep breath and tugged at the hem of her flowing mid-length skirt which brushed her calves. She looked over towards the clock on the oak mantelpiece above the gas-lit real-affect fire; it was 5.26pm. She suddenly stood up. She walked into the small oblong kitchen at the back of the semi-detached house she shared with her husband of eight years and re-arranged the plates and cutlery already laid out on the ditsy flower-print cloth covering the kitchen table. She moved them a millimetre here and a millimetre there.

The weak sun, masked by the sheet of slate rain, filtered through the small square window overlooking the garden with its old-fashioned crazy-paved patio area, meandering path, and neat borders. On a brighter day, light bounced around the kitchen highlighting the buttermilk walls and gloss finish of the skirtings and door jambs but today the mocking greyness further numbed her senses and filled her stomach, making her nauseous.

On hearing the slam of the car door on the drive she silently walked back from the kitchen to the sitting room through the downstairs hallway and perched on the edge of the three-seater. The silence closed in around her; her ears full of the palpitations of her racing heart. She wanted Luke to be glad to be home, to be home with her. She wanted things to be alright between them again.

She heard the key at the front door, preceded by the habitual wiggle of the key on the lock, followed by the grating screech of the rusted hinges as Luke pushed it open. Then came the slam as he kicked it shut with his foot. She counted the seconds in her head. One, two, three, four... in time with the sound of his footsteps. She took shallow breaths to calm herself, biting on her thumb nail and pulling at the red-raw skin around the short, bitten-down nail. The clock said 5.30pm. It always did. It never said anything different. Her life was accounted for by the ticking minutes of the clock; she had created a gilded cage around her, clipped her own wings since resigning from her job. But what other choice did she have? She had hemmed herself into a corner.

'I work with a bunch of complete morons,' called Luke from the hallway; she caught his agitation, heard him kick off his shoes and dump his briefcase down with a bang onto the highly polished parquet. Melody responded, 'At least you're home now.'

'It's been a shit day, Mel.'

'Dinner's ready. You can relax now,' Melody said, a bird-like cheep in her voice, as she made the effort to diffuse his agitation. Things had to get better. She had to find a way to bring them back to a place of love and understanding.

'Is that all you've got to say? These twenty somethings, think they know it all, but don't know their backsides from their elbows.'

'It's lucky they have you to keep them in line. Keep things ticking over,' she said lightly.

'Ticking over? Ticking over?'

'Well…'

'Is that what you think I do all bloody day? Keep things ticking over?' he ranted.

Luke was of average height, of average build. He had average size nine feet and an average shirt collar of fifteen and a half inches. Everything about him was average. Quite ordinary and it had been the quiet mystique rippling under his ordinariness that had attracted her to him. His ordinary smile which fell slightly lopsided and tugged at her heartstrings, the flop of his fair hair over his left eye. But all that seemed like it belonged to someone else's life now. And it was all her fault.

He slipped off his suit jacket, undid his tie and dropped it on top of his jacket on the sofa next to her.

Melody instantly sprung to her feet to hang the jacket on the coat stand in the hallway.

'Leave it love,' he said.

'It'll get creased,' she said, smoothing it out as she held it from the collar. She disappeared and hung it up, carefully.

'Dinner ready?'

'Yes, table's laid. The lasagne is ready, and I've made

a salad. And there's bread in the basket,' she said, as they both moved to the kitchen.

'Alright, alright. I don't need a running commentary love. I get enough of that at work. Those immature, straight-out-of-college secretaries gossiping all day,' he sighed.

'I just want everything to be okay between us.'

'It is, Meli. It's all okay. Just don't keep reminding me it isn't.'

'How many times do you want me to say sorry?'

'I don't know. I'm still reeling from the shock. You hurt me. You hurt our relationship. Destroyed the trust we have always had between us.'

Luke uncorked a bottle of red wine. He sat stiffly; his legs spread like planks under the table, taking up all the space underneath it. He held his glass with one hand while the other drummed on the table, the sound muffled by the table covering. Melody moved swiftly, yet she could almost feel the waft of his disappointment as she opened the oven door. Leaning in she pulled out the blue Denby oven dish using the padded oven glove and placed it carefully onto the cork mat in the middle of the table.

She took the salad out of the fridge and drizzled it with a shop-bought dressing, before placing it on the table next to the main course. She had already filled the breadbasket with thick slices of ciabatta she bought earlier in the day from the local bakery.

Melody carefully cut into the layers of mince and pasta sheets careful not to dribble any béchamel sauce onto the tablecloth and passed the plate to Luke. The aroma of tomatoes, onions and garlic hung in the air; as if trying to stir things up for her, stuffing her nostrils with their intensity.

'Smells good,' he said, smiling for the first time since getting home.

'Thank you,' she said, and she allowed herself to smile.

Melody swallowed and forked up a slice of tomato and red onion into her mouth.

'Aren't you eating?' he asked, pausing before shovelling another forkful of the pasta into his mouth.

'Sorry. I don't feel hungry.' She rarely was around Luke nowadays. Her own deceit, her own lies, ate her from the inside, taken up by the heaviness of her own guilt, leaving no space for food.

'You're always sorry about something… all I get from you… every… blasted… day.'

'But it's true. I am sorry. I want to make up for what I did. I can't stand your pain.'

'You can't!' He threw his fist down onto the table. The table shook and the wine glass toppled. Melody jumped up and grabbed a wet cloth from the sink, almost knocking over a jug set on a trivet next to it. She straightened up the wine glass and dabbed at the red mark which had spread across the starched white cloth like the red-hot flush seeping up from her neck and across her face.

'I'm sorry, Luke. Please,' she begged.

'Don't tell me you're sorry again. I don't want to hear it. Leave it. Sit down. Try and eat something.'

Melody sat down; the soaked dishcloth in her lap dripping through the fabric of her skirt. She tugged at her long ponytail and then folded her hands in her lap and sat up straight; like a troublemaker being reprimanded by the head teacher. She bit hard on her lower lip to stop herself from crying. She looked down at her hands, wishing to avoid the hurt which filled Luke's brown-black eyes, and inside her head she counted to ten slowly to calm her jangling, frayed nerves. She was desperate to bite her nails but forced her hands to remain where they were.

He poured another glass of wine and slurped at it noisily. His lips left greasy smears on the glass. He ate the lasagne cutting into it roughly and stabbed viciously at the salad. A drop of dressing dripped from the end of his fork and plopped onto the edge of his plate, missing the front of his shirt. Melody watched him as if watching a movie. This wasn't her life, this was somebody else's. He appeared calm on the outside, but his gestures told a different story. He was tormented.

'That was a great dinner, love,' he said with forced joviality, setting his knife and fork across the plate diagonally.

He pushed his chair back across the floor tiles, scraping them carelessly, and stood up. Melody almost felt relieved. She wanted to be with him but seeing him in so much pain after all this time was unbearable.

'I'm going to watch TV.'

'I'll wash up and then bring you in a cup of coffee.'

She heard the TV click into life with a cacophony of sounds as he flicked through the channels. She imagined him sitting in the middle of the sofa, squashing her perfectly arranged cushions.

Melody hand washed the dishes and spooned the

rest of the lasagne into a Tupperware for Luke's lunch the next day. She then filled a washing bowl with stain remover and soaked the tablecloth. She gave it a little dunk and a quick rub before leaving it on the counter to soak overnight. She could sort it in the morning.

She sloshed some bleach around the sink before rinsing it. She made Luke's coffee and carried the tray with the coffee and a plate of biscuits into the lounge. She placed it on the coffee table and put his mug next to him on the side table.

'Come and sit here love. Emmerdale is starting. Can't believe it's your favourite soap series after all these years.' Melody sat next to him. He was trying. 'I'll take a shower after this,' he said.

For the next half hour Melody couldn't focus on what used to be her favourite soap. Every word of their ongoing arguments filling her head, round and round like a washing machine stuck on the same wash cycle.

She dried the washing up and put away the dinner plates while Luke had his shower.

Her mind wandered to her painting. She had begun to paint the past few weeks having met a volunteer art teacher at the library one week as she stood in the queue to return her books; Books were her saviour; her sanity; her escape. Art, a longing to be creative, beckoned her too.

Her scrapbook overflowed with a collection of old letters and postcards collected over the years; she had stapled together coloured sheets of paper to make the book like she used to when she played "teachers" as a girl with her older sister. The gift of cash she had received as part of her leaving present, was still in an envelope next to the bed. She wanted to buy some more art materials but felt guilty finding enjoyment in this new situation of her own making when Luke was hurting so much. She had made him like this. It was all her fault.

He had kindly marvelled at her artwork when she showed him her first attempt at painting and since then she had kept her drawings from him, tucked away behind her vanity case at the back of her wardrobe. She wasn't looking for compliments. Painting gave her a place of refuge; a place where her thoughts and imagination were set free, but she didn't want him to see her making the most of not working when he was suffering. An animal still wounded, still in pain. Mirroring her own pain too.

'You not drinking your coffee, love?'

'Yes,' she said and offered him a biscuit, which he declined. She sat with both hands wrapped around her favourite mug; Emma Bridgewater with pink hearts all over it; a gift from her older sister four Christmases before. Her current read, a romance novel by one of her favourite authors lay next to her.

Later, closer to eleven o'clock and after a perfunctory session in bed, Melody fell asleep, exhausted but relieved they had at least made love; small steps, there was no hurry.

He had become a different person to the one she had fallen in love with. Overnight he changed from being an attentive, loving man to one who demanded and controlled and had a temper. She had thrown all of it away, had slowly succumbed to her own guilty, smothering feelings, her ego. Despite all of it, she held onto the belief they could be close again. They would find a way through this mess of two fragile hearts. She hoped it wasn't too late. Their relationship had reached a critical point, but hopefully not that of no return.

Melody thought back to all the rushing around of the classroom, trying to tidy up before the bell rang for the next lesson. She used to will the time to pass, to get through one more lesson, to finally be able to rush home. As a Teaching Assistant in an oversubscribed and widely diverse three-form entry primary school Melody was underpaid, overworked, and exhausted every day. As tiring as she found it, it had been her haven too; given her space, freedom, and choices, though at the time she had taken all those things for granted, had not appreciated them. But she ruined it all and had to suffer the consequences. It had been the right thing to do, though humiliating, embarrassing. The only choice she had to save her marriage.

She thought about the holiday booking Luke had surprised her with the week before. She looked forward to spending some time away from everything which didn't work between them anymore, hoping to inject a new lease of life into their strained, failing relationship.

Over the weeks that followed, he came home later and later, and Melody slowly but guiltily relished being able to paint for longer, while a part of her missed spending time with her husband.

She hoped and prayed the holiday would go a long way to making things right between them again. That's all she wanted.

Eliana

'Come on, babe,' called Eliana.

'I'm coming, woman. Always nagging at me. Non-stop… nag, nag, nag.'

Eliana rolled her eyes. Dean, trailed behind her; lagging like he usually did nowadays.

She knew his knee was hurting more than usual but she couldn't be bothered to console him; he always wanted her attention. Moscow, their easy-going, playful Labrador, pulled on his lead, keen to be released from its hold. As soon as she got through the park gate, Eliana unclipped him and off he lolloped, his tail wagging as he bounded, like an athlete running the marathon, towards another dog and his owner, his heading bobbing furiously.

Eliana dawdled by the gate, keeping an eye on Moscow, containing her impatience with Dean by focusing on the first buds of pink blossom pushing out of the tree ahead of her. A few seconds later, Dean pushed the gate open, and she put her arm through his, partly to appease him and partly to extinguish her irritation with him.

'He's so happy,' she beamed.

'Shame you're not as concerned about my happiness,' he said.

'For goodness' sake. You're a grown man. It's like I'm married to an old codger.'

'My knee's stiff. It's the cold.'

'It's because you've put on weight. It all puts extra pressure on your knee.'

'You think you know it all.'

'I do,' she said, with a cheeky grin. 'Now come on, babe. Before he disappears or gets into trouble,' she said, pulling at Dean to get a move on.

An hour later, with Dean habitually lagging behind Eliana, they arrived back home.

'Gosh it was nippy out there today,' she said, pulling off her gloves and blowing into her hands as Dean shut the front door behind him. 'So much for spring being in the air.'

'I'll light the fire. Take the chill out of the air,' said Dean, as Eliana, already in the kitchen, flicked on the kettle to make them a cuppa.

'Biscuits would be good,' he said, taking the steaming mug from her a few minutes later.

'You can have two, no more. You're putting on weight…' She disappeared back into the kitchen, calling back to him, 'which is why you're all aches and pains. You have to be careful Dean.'

'I hope you're not going to be like this on holiday. I've paid a fortune for this place. It's out of the way, exclusive.'

Reminded of his generosity she returned with two custard creams on a plate for him, having softened under his pleading puppy-dog eyes.

'I can't wait to lie in the sun all day. But you'll have to be careful. I don't want you looking like a burnt lobster.' She laughed at her own joke, remembering the absolute nightmare of a holiday in Tenerife the year before.

'I've got the factor 30,' he said, talking and chewing, a whole biscuit in his mouth.

'More like factor seventy. You need the extra slap-on protection all the mums buy for their toddlers,' said Eliana.

He slurped his tea, dunked his second biscuit, and stuffed it, whole and soggy, into his mouth. Eliana shook her head, pulling a face. She hated dunking biscuits. She hated the way the biscuit went floppy and limp.

After watching a couple of recorded programmes, Dean disappeared upstairs singing, "*When you're in love with a beautiful woman, you know it's hard, it's hard, you know it gets so hard...*" When he hadn't come back down fifteen minutes later Eliana went up to see what he was doing, though she already guessed what would be waiting for her. Dean was anything if not predictable.

'You took your time,' he said, as she opened the bedroom door to find him spreadeagled and naked on the bed.

Eliana gave a sigh, then succumbed to a half laugh. 'I knew you were up to something, babe. Every time you sing that song...'

'Don't look so surprised then.'

'Now's not the time, Dean. One track mind.'

'Come on. I'll warm you up.'

'Put down the sheet first. I don't want the duvet getting stained,' she succumbed eventually.

Dean didn't need telling again. He sprung off the bed, almost tripping over his discarded clothes on the floor, and opened the drawer at the bottom of the wardrobe. He took out their love-making sheet. He threw back the duvet, shook out the cotton sheet and, spread it over the bed's silk under sheets, smoothing out its creases.

Eliana, not in the mood, did her best to hide her tepid enthusiasm. She made the breathy gasps and noises she thought sounded sexy, like she was enjoying sex with him and then, finally spent, Dean rolled over; hot, sweaty, breathing hard. She turned her back on him; Dean reached out and patted her bottom and she quietly lay there suffocating in frustration.

They didn't speak. It was like this most of the time. She wondered how many of her friends felt the same. They didn't ever talk about their sex lives, but it wasn't anything like in the movies; not for her. It was a chore. Something she did to keep the peace. Sex wasn't a priority. She didn't want it. She didn't need it. This was her grey, shadowy truth; unable to voice it, unable to obliterate it, unable to embrace it.

Everything else in her life was good without it, and her life was a good life.

Dean had money, worked long hours and this gave her the time and space to do her own thing most of the time.

'About time you made an honest woman out of her,' her mother had said, not knowing all the years they had spent unmarried had been her daughter's choice all along. The wedding breakfast for fifty guests, the epitome of Instagrammable luxuriousness, left nothing to chance and, she had to admit, mirrored her dream of unforgettable, amazing perfection.

Their meeting had not been anything fancy or memorable. They had met online; she at home in her loungewear, hair tied up loosely in a bun, with her cup of coffee for company. He had clicked on her profile accidentally. But they hit it off and their online chat became a habit, filling their lonely, empty nights for the next few weeks until they finally agreed to meet in person.

He made her laugh out loud. He thought she was sexy. And sex was all he seemed to want from her. It was easy, at first, non-committal, unencumbered and automatic. The online conversations phone conversations, late into the night, with the fullness of the moon glimpsing into her room through the gap in the curtains, dwindled over time. Eliana quickly discovered withholding sex gave her the upper hand, the treat-them-mean, keep-them-keen scenario, worked eventually.

Dean, always talking about sex, kept himself entertained, satiated, most of the time with all his fantasising. She knew he was too vocal, often crude, sometimes embarrassing, yet she loved him. He was good for her, and she knew he loved her despite his silly banter about other women and what a stud muffin they all thought he was.

After a few years of dating, he had finally moved in with her and they had tied the knot; a small, private ceremony with their closest friends and family present. The wedding, the getting married was something she could have done without, but Dean covered all the expenses, and her parents were thrilled. She had to admit it was lovely.

She turned to face him. 'Did you speak to your mum about looking after Moscow when we're away?'

'It's too soon. She'll forget. You know what she's like,' said Dean, twisting and untwisting her hair around his fingers.

'She needs plenty of warning. You know she's always busy. I'll get up in the morning and take Moscow for his morning walk and then drop him to her by ten o'clock. We can then leave for the airport by eleven.'

'I suppose that'll save her having to take him out in the morning and us enough time to check in, grab some lunch.'

'Why don't you eat before we set off. We don't have to eat at the airport. We would only have just had breakfast.'

'It'll be my treat,' he said.

'It's your money, so if you want to spend it without any thought for tomorrow, you go ahead. I need a new perfume too. We can stop at the Duty-Free on the way to the gate.'

'Here we go again. Spending my money but as soon as I want a bit of loving…'

'Shut up. I'll show you a good time,' she said, swiping him across the arm playfully, already dreaming about their holiday.

July 2023

Chapter 1

In the warm glow of the gathering dusk; a picture-postcard image of single storey, whitewashed buildings, pretty with their traditional charm, peppered the hillside overlooking glorious emerald waters. The holiday brochure had described Kefalonia's landscape perfectly. The island was regarded as the most romantic in the Ionian Sea.

Stella pondered on her journey from the small airport, however, the phrase not-so-idyllic punctuated her thoughts. The driver, of the not-so-modern or comfortable coach, had made three stops already and each time a slightly less picturesque building greeted its new guests. Stella wondered whether that was a coincidence; whether her own bijou hotel, when she eventually arrived, would be the least attractive, the most basic. She hoped her usually keen senses, her instinctual powers were wrong, that the unfolding downward trend would be broken.

The transfer bus had already disappointingly not been

what the website promised, and she wondered whether, had this been the UK, the transport would have been roadworthy, despite it making its way determinedly on and on. The earlier enchantment she welcomed now evaporated.

She glanced at her watch: 7.32. There were no markers on the horizon, nor along the road, to indicate they were any closer to their destination. The transfer bus trundled to the top of the mountain, more peacefully now most of the holidaymakers with young children had alighted.

The rugged beauty of the mountainous terrain, with its sheer sloping sides a patchwork of earthy greens and browns and tall, majestic pines, evoked a sense of calmness, of change, in the evening's seam of half-light.

In the distance a neat row of golden bee hives dotted the natural landscape. Stella imagined the buzz of the bees as they worked tirelessly all day collecting from the wild heather and lavender. She remembered her visit to a beekeeper in Somerset where she researched bee keeping for one of her novels; the sweet smells and the most delicious nectar.

The trees faded and merged; a compost of majesty and simplicity. Stella could not help but succumb to the feeling of something mystical and magnetic, a lightness in the air, flirting with her, inviting her to play. For a moment, she shivered, not against the sensation but gliding along with it, its playfulness like a mischievous nymph out in the woods.

The driver, as if wanting to prove her ease wrong, negotiated a hairpin bend with a screech. A thud reverberated through the quiet. He slammed on the brakes. The tyres dragged across the road, sending rolling clouds of dust against the coach windows. He mumbled an apology, passengers were thrust forward, and then his tone changed. Stella imagined the list of expletives he spat out in quick succession, one Greek word after another, as his mouth worked quickly spilling out the words. The patter familiar but indistinct.

She gripped the edge of her seat as the bus skidded around the sharp bend, for a split-second wishing Anton was with her. Her breath caught in her throat and her hand rested over her chest, her beating heart pushing against it with force. 'Hope he hasn't been drinking,' Stella said under her breath eventually. She pushed her belongings back into her bag, launched out of it with the force, her face reddening when a tampon rolled under the seat in front of her.

Thankfully, it disappeared and stayed wherever it had lodged. She turned towards a commotion at the back of the coach. Another couple sitting three rows across from her seemed to be having a disagreement, their voices grew louder and more animated, sending her into the midst of the last time she saw Anton; something she didn't want to think about now. Not at the start of her holiday and at the start of what could quite possibly be a new beginning. At least that's what she told herself to stop going back over everything. The words pulled her back into the present.

'Dean? Oh my God, you're bleeding.'

'It's nothing, El.'

'How can you say it's nothing. You slammed into the seat in front of you. Your head's bleeding.'

'Stop fussing. It's either all or nothing with you.'

Stella looked back; her sudden melancholy replaced with a rising panic. She fumbled in her bag until she found what she was looking for. 'Excuse me, do you need these?' she asked and reaching out pushed a packet of antiseptic wipes towards the woman whose pale face looked back at her.

'Thank you. That's really kind.'

'I'm fine,' said Dean and not wanting to intrude, Stella turned away, but not before giving the woman a half-smile.

Oblivious to Dean's injury, the now not-so-calm driver apologised with a sheepish look and accelerated as he took off again, navigating the skinniest of roads, mostly dirt tracks, the light of his headlamps guiding the way along the final twist. He turned on the radio and Stella squeezed her eyes against the crackling and hissing until it cleared; a Greek tune, slow, folksy rolled over the speakers and she listened as the driver sang along, his voice deep, drawling.

'Hopefully we'll be there soon,' said Eliana, wiping her tired eyes, her eye makeup now smudged.

'I thought the worst of it would be falling asleep but the driver's going to kill us first by the looks of it.' Stella smiled half-heartedly as the words of the woman reached her; she felt the same way.

Stella watched as the driver yanked hard on the brake's mechanical hand lever, pressed a red button on the scratched dash and, for the fourth time that evening, the front exit door sprung open with a clank. Simultaneously the recessed bulbs came on and bathed the coach in an unwelcome, harsh light. Stella lowered her head, scrunched her eyes against the brightness.

The driver reached for a worn hand towel and mopped his sweating forehead. He unfastened his clip board from a hook on the dashboard and ran his finger down the list.

She glanced out of the partly curtained window; a sign read: Miramare. A large blue arrow, hand-painted beneath it, pointed in the direction of an uphill path.

Seconds later, she fanned herself with her magazine as a solid sheet of stifling air claustrophobed the bus's interior; the temperature rocketed, the space seemed to shrink; the rush of heat rolling in. The atmosphere charged her yo-yoing explosive mood further.

'Cleverly, Walker, Bowen and Handley.' The name Bowen mocked her and reminded her she was here alone, but determined to make the most of it, she shook away the negativity threatening to burrow into her. 'Miramare awaits,' the driver called out towards the back of the coach, his heavy Greek accent making the British names sound more mysterious and unusual than they were. He slowly raised himself from the driver's seat, pressed another switch, which glowed green, and disembarked, ahead of the passengers. He stopped in front of the raised door of the coach's underhold. Stella could see the top of his head beyond the heavy raised door.

Further along the front of the coach a man nudged a woman. 'Come on, Melody.'

'Okay, let me—'

'We've been on this bus long enough. I can't feel my legs. They're numb.'

'Let me get my bag, Luke,' she said, and her head

disappeared below the head rest as she reached for her bag on the floor under the seat in front of her.

'You get up. I'll get it,' he said, his voice raised a notch in agitation. Melody got up and waited in the aisle for Luke as he scrambled for the bag.

Luke edged out of the row. They ambled down towards the front of the coach, but not before Stella noticed Luke pushing Melody in the back. Stella averted her eyes but shook her head and sighed. *Some men can be such bullies.*

Stella plucked out her compact and opened it; a soft light flicked on behind the mirror. She sighed and quickly ran the bright pink lipstick, bought at Duty Free that morning, across her dry, thirsty lips. She puckered and rubbed them together to even out the coverage and snapped her compact shut. She popped it back in her bag, zipping it closed with care. She ran her hands over her long hair, the blond waves limp after the hours of travelling covered in a day.

She squeezed out of her seat and a man knocked into her, almost pushing her off balance. 'I'm sorry,' she said automatically.

'Get moving,' said the man, his voice gruff, surly. 'We haven't got all night, El. We need to get off here.' Stella, too stunned to say anything more, inched to the side to make room for his bulky frame, easily over six-foot tall, to pass. She recognised him as Dean, the man who had been injured.

'I'm coming,' mouthed the tall slim woman lagging a couple of paces behind him. 'He's a bit tetchy after the long drive,' she said, as if in apology.

'You coming, El?' Stella heard his booming voice from the front of the coach and glimpsed the back of his cropped hair as he descended the two steps to the outside.

'Sorry again,' the woman mouthed in Stella's direction as he repeated his words.

His wife, Stella noticed her gold wedding band and diamond ring, tutted and an overpowering relief flooded Stella. She was glad the woman stood up for herself.

Stella got up, gathered her belongings; she needed to claim her luggage before the driver shut up the hold and trapped her on the bus for another three hours.

Chapter 2

Outside, the air was fresh; the warm breeze brought with it the sea and a hint of saltiness. It coated Stella's tongue as she took in a deep breath. They found their suitcases by the light of the torch the driver directed into the hold. He reached in, his hands leathery brown and calloused, as the holidaymakers pointed out their luggage in turn. Without any effort at all he heaved out their cases and placed them onto the dry, dusty roadside. Eliana held onto her handbag and the Duty-Free bags; they looked like they weighed too much for her slim arms and Stella espied two bottles of vodka poking out the top.

Stella looked around and noticed the other couple standing a few feet away from her. She lit a cigarette, took a long drag, and exhaled slowly, glad to be out in the open. She tried to catch the other woman's eye, but she didn't look up or towards her at any point, so Stella eventually gave up. The couple kept their distance. Stella noticed how neither of them spoke, either to each other or to Eliana and Dean who were standing closer to them.

The driver wished them a hurried farewell, gave them a salute by way of an adieu and climbing back behind the wheel navigated a tight three-point turn on the narrow road before disappearing, leaving them coughing as they waved away a choking cloud of dust.

'Wait,' called Eliana. 'We're missing a suitcase.' She ran after the bus, but it was long gone, the taillights glittering red pinpricks like a predator's eyes in the night.

Stella fought the tickle in her throat and flapped at the heavy fumes. 'Hopefully the hotel staff can get in touch with him for you,' said Stella, as she ground her cigarette butt into the dry hard earth.

'You don't concentrate, woman,' said Dean, his voice sharp, accusatory, as he turned on Eliana. 'How can you not notice your own case wasn't here?'

Stella winced as Eliana's cheeks flushed scarlet with obvious embarrassment or was it defiance.

'Why didn't you notice? You've been standing here too,' she said back, but more quietly. Dean sighed, his anger to all appearances dissipating as quickly as it had come.

They bickered, and all Stella wanted was to sleep. This was not the relaxing start to her holiday she had envisaged.

Stella counted the five of them now making their way, somewhat cautiously in the dimming light, towards the silhouette of the partly lit, growing shape of the building ahead. The uneven track, full of tiny rocks and pebbles, lead them towards the walled entrance of the small, exclusive hotel complex; twinkling coloured lights like festoons of tiny fruit garlanded the outer wall and along the meandering path, smoother now and paved, which guided them to the hotel's main foyer.

'The fresh smell in the air. So fruity, sweet... like nectar,' said Stella, to no one in particular. She listened; ribbons of nocturnal sounds threaded their way through her: a tz tz tz tz tz that came from the trees, a flutter of wings as a night bird flew nestled in the branches, the soft whistling of the almost-still air.

She quickly realised, despite the heat and exhaustion, an expectant excitement filled her. Her mind flew to the pictures of the hotel as she trudged along, the bright full moon peering down at her as if waiting for her to look up at it and say: 'Hello Mr Moon,' like she used to as a young girl. She hoped the location and décor of the family-run resort, lived up to its description: *Traditionally furnished, in a simple, local style with no fancy modern amenities... immediate landscape and promise of home-grown produce used in the culinary delights of your generous host, sure to be an absolute taste adventure...*

Chapter 3

Stella lagged a little behind Eliana and her partner and the other couple. If anyone spied them, they would see a line of slightly dishevelled travellers with bowed heads struggling to carry the overstuffed suitcases, hard-shell vanity cases and bulging holdalls. They continued, towards the entrance. Their home for the next two weeks came into their periphery; a crowning purple pearl against the backdrop of the shimmering sky.

'Thank goodness it looks decent,' said Luke, letting out a low whistle.

'Exactly like the brochure,' said Eliana.

'The website didn't lie.' Melody said, stifling a yawn.

'Let's hope it's worth the money,' said Luke.

'This had better be worth it, woman,' said Dean and turning to Stella said, 'Almost there. Here, let me take the case from you. You won't be able to get it up those steps.'

'Thank you so much,' Stella said, a little embarrassed at her obvious struggle she welcomed his old-fashioned thoughtfulness and chivalry.

Dean took the case from Stella, and she gave him a thankful smile. She flexed her hand to relieve the strain in her fingers and walked up the six wide steps, sprightlier than she felt.

'We're like hard working ants,' said Eliana, half to herself, half out loud. 'All shuffling along weighted down with all this luggage.'

'Only some of us,' said Dean, and Stella caught him giving Eliana a look. Maybe not as forgiving as he was chivalrous.

'Give it a rest, babe,' said Eliana, and she let out a loud huff.

'Oh, wow!' said Stella, breaking the ice as the hotel came into view.

The lobby, a metamorphic stage of sandy-coloured marble with an M laid out in soft white pebbles at its centre, welcomed them. It opened out into a semi-circle which housed a solid reception desk made of the same crystalline stone.

The hotel was small; bijou was the word used to describe it in the brochure yet the reception area with its soft recessed lighting hidden in the ceiling's plasterwork, created the impression of a much grander space. The sweet scent of jasmine filled the space. A tall glass vase overflowing with the creamy blooms; their soft shade reminded Stella of her mother's pearls.

A man looked up from behind the oversized desk. He was casually dressed in a dark blue shirt. His smile was instant, and his brilliant white teeth shone out against his tanned, leathery skin. His black hairy moustache jiggled as he spoke, and his dark eyes sparkled.

'*Kalispera*. Good evening and welcome friends. I am Prodromos. Welcome to Miramare and our jewel of a hotel.'

'Good evening,' they chimed, and Stella noticed how Melody avoided eye contact with any of them, especially the men. She was younger than the others in their small group. She was just shy, reserved.

Their host instantly disappeared behind the reception desk and through a door before he magically re-appeared seconds later, via a different door, with a tray of juice-filled tumblers.

'Welcome. Please. Have some apricot juice. Fresh from the fruits of the trees here in the hotel grounds.' His steps echoed around the reception as his crumpled linen trousers, the colour of cinnamon, made a soft swish as he moved. The marbled flooring, provocatively glossy under his feet, echoed his dancing shadow which followed him. Stella already liked him.

Everyone reached out for a glass, one after the other, as he passed between them with the loaded metal tray. Dean promptly downed his drink in one and took another as murmurs of thank you and pleased to meet you littered the hotel's serenity and everyone smiled. Stella, however, noted again how Melody withdrew into herself, stared at the floor.

Stella wondered how comfortable she would be too with the other guests; they seemed friendly, but they were all younger and attached. She found herself second guessing how much of them she could put up with and realised the place was much smaller than she had anticipated, and she was alone. The word alone hit her again, like a stone from a catapult.

'You're welcome. Take your time,' the hotel owner chattered on. 'Your accommodation is ready and Yiannis will show you to your rooms as soon as you have checked in.' A tall man, with a boyish face, late twenties, appeared, his jet-black hair flopping over his eyes, his sinewy arms dangling at his sides, almost reaching his knees. 'Say hello, Yiannis,' urged Prodromos.

'Hello,' said Yiannis shyly, but seconds later, Stella caught him looking at her from under his dark lashes.

She shook off a current of electricity which shot through her like flames to a brandy-soaked pudding. She forced herself to think about Anton. Then quickly replaced that thought with the incredible time she was going to have writing; her first writing-retreat holiday though it hadn't been planned this way, the writing rebranding quickly replacing the romantic holiday originally imagined. Then, within minutes, she was staring at Yiannis, and he looked straight at her, unwavering in his fevered gaze.

Dean and Eliana were the first couple to check in; a seamless procedure, and Prodromos, with firm assurance, promised to have Eliana's suitcase delivered to the hotel by the following afternoon. Bidding the rest of the guests a polite good night, Dean shuffled off, clearly still in some pain, trying to keep up with Eliana and Yiannis.

They disappeared outside, past the pool, which was clothed in darkness and shadows, and down another small set of steps. Stella watched them go. She took in the view across the outside area with its neat row of sunbeds. An almond-white painted canopy, heavy with jewel-bright pink blooms clung onto twisting green boughs and interwoven woody branches.

'I have check-in papers for Cleverly,' announced Prodromos, now behind the desk where he was arranging documents in a black folder. He placed a pen there, turned the pages around ready to be filled in.

'That's us,' said Luke. He stepped forward, grabbing Melody by the arm awkwardly. Stella winced. Melody flinched so quickly, Stella thought she had imagined it, but the woman's tormented face told Stella she had not.

Stella waited patiently; she made herself comfortable on one of the wooden framed two seaters in the lobby pushed up against the wall opposite the front desk. The whitewashed walls were bare apart from a painting of a still-life; a bowl of purple figs, a carafe of blood-red wine and a simple village loaf on a blue and white chequered tablecloth with white tassel fringing around the edge.

Stella smiled at Prodromos, but her smile vacant of energy, gave way to a wave of tiredness. Her bones were heavy, and her hair no longer conveyed the bounce it had first thing in the morning, after the dragging hours of travelling. She traipsed closer to the open doors which lead to the pool and immaculately kept gardens.

A stooped silhouette with a rake, the gardener perhaps, in the distance, made her stretch out her back and push her shoulders out. She lit a cigarette; she inhaled deeply and blew out the smoke slowly, deliberately, watching as the little rings disappeared into the night air.

Stella watched as Luke and Melody followed Yiannis

round the other side of the pool and disappeared through a door, painted a powdery blue. Yiannis' dark hair shone under the glow of the wall lanterns. She forced her mind firmly back to the blue door; she liked the colour and was hoping to paint her wooden planters back home the very same shade ready for the summer; though it depended on whether they got a summer long enough to enjoy the outdoors. She wondered about the woman. Her writer's imagination beginning to work.

'Now Mr Bowen and Miss Handley?'

'Oh, yes…' Stella said, hesitating for a split second.

'Please this won't take long, and you can get some sleep, eh?'

'Thank you. The travelling has really taken it out of me,' said Stella, a little flustered at his annunciation of Miss and, moreover, because hearing her and Anton's surnames side by side, like this, on show, yet shrouded in their not-so-open relationship, seemed dangerous, a risky flirtation with their illicitness in the open. 'Mr Bowen, I'm afraid didn't make it.' She cringed as two other guests walked through the reception. Their arms were linked, and the woman's flirtatious laugh taunted her. She was sure the man's fleeting glance in Stella's direction was one of pity.

She smiled hesitantly and stumped out her cigarette in the free-standing cigarette bin at the end of the counter before moving silently back to where Prodromos waited behind the desk. She jutted up against the reception desk's cool marble facade, subconsciously wanting to protect herself and then berated herself. She took a step back. No one would recognise her here. She could relax.

She filled in the paperwork with speed and watched Prodromos' hand scribbling furiously from one section to the next on another sheet.

'I hope all is well. Will Mr Bowen be joining you later?'

'I'm sure he will contact you should that be the case.'

Prodromos continued, 'Your room is incredibly quiet. You will like it, I hope. Breakfast, should you wish to join us, is from eight o'clock to ten o'clock by the poolside. If you require breakfast in your room, it will be served after ten o'clock but before midday.'

She wanted to get to her room as quickly as possible, and before she knew it, she followed Yiannis, already returned and leading the way, to her quarters.

'Thank you and goodnight,' said Stella as she closed the door behind Yiannis but not before giving him a tip and not before Yiannis caught Stella's eye again, for the third time that evening.

The luxury double room, open plan with a spacious sitting area and a balcony overlooking the gardens was situated on the first floor, with an elevated view across the grassy sloping banks at the rear of the hotel. It was perfect. The intermittent shaft of light from the solar lanterns shone across the expanse and created the impression of an emerald, green carpet; the grass looked soft. The thick blades sparkled from the zig-zag tell-tale of coppery sprinklers which automatically hydrated them.

The garden was scattered with a handful of baby olive trees and a trio of waving palms, and a climbing jasmine twisted and turned itself along the periphery wall, its rough-edged boulders stacked on top of each other, exquisitely haphazard. In its shade, a tabby cat, her belly distended with unborn kittens, lay stretched out.

The holiday, this room, this view, had cost them a small fortune, his words, not hers, and considerable juggling of his finances to avoid detection, but he had assured her she was worth the risk. *Hardly the romantic gesture.* But, in the end, not enough for him to be with her.

Stella focused on the here and now, not wanting to dwell on what might have been. She unpacked, had a quick shower, and sunk into the squidgy mattress of the double bed; her wet hair splayed across the pillow like a puddle. She vowed to draft the best story ever.

Chapter 4

Stella stayed up late, sleep evading her, the twinkle of the stars beckoning her... billions of light years away and yet bright enough and deceivingly near enough she might reach up and pluck one from the sky. A universe of stories past, present and future, waiting to unravel, to find their voice, to be heard.

She brushed her long blond hair, her brush tangled with loose strands; she should cut it short. She was, two years shy of fifty now and storytelling, some might argue, were too far in the past for her. Her long hair felt too youthful for her in so many ways too, despite Anton insisting she keep it long. *He wishes I were still his thirty-something mistress*, thought Stella, then brushed the thought away. What did she care what he thought?

Anton, their relationship, heady emotion, and uncontrollable want, seemed like an exceedingly long time ago; she was a different woman. She remembered the details of how a casual, but lusty, passionate affair, had turned into a two decades-long relationship with a wife in the picture and a grown-up son. Two strangers. Two people she would pass in the street and not recognise.

Life had not been what she expected; in some ways it had given her so much more, but equally it had stopped her from having so much else. *Always up and down on those scales of life,* she thought. *If I'm up, he's down. If I'm down, he's up. Life is a constant synchronising of energies, priorities, and vision.*

Her crashing thoughts invaded her calm space and she tried to shake them off and instead listened to the sounds of the island as night fell and wrapped itself around her like the familiar softness of a long-forgotten summer shawl, transporting her to a place of peaceful privacy, composed calm. Words fought for space in her mind: would she be okay without Anton, had she been kidding herself, maybe this was all too much to expect him to drop everything and be with her, she needed time alone, this was just what she needed.

A gentle ease enveloped her and the tiredness of earlier fell away. She thought about her life's choices and wondered whether that was her lot now or whether life was going to surprise her. After all this trip to Kefalonia, the materialisation of the confirmation email, had come as a huge surprise after Anton had insisted that they wouldn't get the chance to go away together and yet, here she was. Here alone.

No Anton.

No lovers' dream holiday.

But in that there were possibilities. She momentarily

forgot Anton.

New beginnings.

Adventures.

A few weeks before, Stella had panicked about planning a holiday with Anton, abandoning her routine, risking holidaying with him.

'Kefalonia,' he had drooled.

'Kefalonia. Captain Corelli's Mandolin,' she had enthused. And, quite out of character, she had dreamed about meeting a dark and handsome Greek to sweep her off to that same white beach and offer her a whole new world of romance.

Perhaps she had pre-empted Anton's last-minute cancellation. Perhaps the universe had read her mind and offered her a taste of what life might be without him. It was never too late for new beginnings. She hoped this turned out to be just that and didn't leave her with regrets.

She smiled at first supressing her glee, and then letting her joy below from deep within her belly, laughed. She tittered at the thought and felt her face flush from its silliness. At her age. How ridiculous. After all the time she had invested in this relationship with Anton. Relationship. Perhaps she was kidding herself. Perhaps she had to face up to it simply being an affair. A long, stretched-out affair. But her acceptance of her relationship's sudden, changed status, shockingly and admittedly didn't worry her.

Her mobile beeped and she instantly picked it up; a message telling her she had arrived in Greece and was now connected to the local network flashed across her screen. No message from Anton. She scrolled through some of his past messages and smiled, but she felt empty, tired of all the effort needed to make it all work.

She took out her laptop, determination coming at her, and opened a new document. *A Love Story (Working Title)*, she typed and with a wrinkled brow, focused intently on the screen in front of her. She would welcome the inspiration this magnificent island would bring. Despite being alone, she secretly craved the unknown, the uncertainty of her future here. She willed it to be something mystical. Something good had to come out of this blasted disaster of a trip.

Chapter 5

Stella yawned and reached for her mobile. Half past eight; that would make it half past six in the UK. She pushed her arm out, across the double bed, spanning the empty space. It reminded her Anton hadn't made it.

She strained her ears and was surprised to hear... nothing. No braying donkeys, no barking dogs, and no dawning rooster calls. It was monumentally quiet, and she lay there in the semi-darkness wondering whether to get up. She tried to recall what the breakfast serving time was but guessed it wouldn't be too far off now.

Eventually, she got up and switched on the room's ceiling fan, which gently hummed into life, circulating the too warm air around the room. She padded over to the shuttered doors; the bedroom tiles cool underfoot. She ceremoniously unbolted the latch; the ironmongery made a clatter as she pushed the doors wide. The early morning sun cast a warm glow across the room, and the heat rose around her like warm honey as she stepped out, her skin already sticky with sweat. She squeezed her eyes tight and slowly opened them trying to filter the brightness of the vast, crystal-blue sky.

Out on the square verandah, she smiled to herself. 'Oh my! What a bright morning.' She breathed deeply, stretched her arms over her head, held the pose and then flopped forward towards her ankles, her arms dangling. She repeated the stretch ten times, fostering an energetic wakefulness in her.

She tapped out a cigarette from the soft packet, bought from the airport on arrival. She surveyed the immaculate lawns of the hotel grounds and the scraggly, dry mountains beyond.

She re-focused her eyes adjusting to the glare of the Kefalonian sun, a radiating crown, mocking a happiness drained from her over the outcomes of the past forty-eight hours. The strike of the lighter broke the peacefulness. She lit her cigarette and took a long drag. She filled her lungs and blew out a long puff of smoke through rounded, puckered lips. It quickly disappeared into the balmy air and as she inhaled again a calmness came to her. Her phone vibrated on the table:

Enjoy yourself my darling. Love you, Mum x
PS: Your dad won the allotment competition for biggest marrow.

Stella smiled. Still no message from Anton. She started tapping out a message to him:

I've landed, it's beautiful. Wish you were here. S x

She deleted it. Turned her phone face down on the small iron table. She would call her mum later.

Maybe her thoughts had manifested this whole situation.

'You get what you put out there, darling,' her mum said, as she poured out the coffee from the silver coffee pot, the last time Stella had visited her. 'If you want to meet someone, then you need to manifest it. Imagine you're already with him. Already a couple.'

'When did you become so out there?' asked Stella, feeling guilty about her secret lover.

'Stop it, Stella. All this manifesting your dreams is nothing new. It's been out there for years. I was young once.'

'Mum! Did you manifest your relationship with Dad?'

'Maybe... yes.'

'I can't believe we've never talked about this before. You always said you and Dad met at a charity bingo night.'

'We did. But the bumping into each other after that and the going out for dinner was all of my own making. I made that happen.'

'Oh Mum...'

'There's no oh Mum about it. Really. Try it.'

And since then, Anton had been on her mind floating in a different realm, a different context to that which he had always been... in her mind there had been a niggling, twitchy doubt these last few months... a tiny ticking time bomb... most men went back to their wives in the end. It was only a matter of time even if that time was years later.

She had played the scene over in her head so many times that she could see every second of every moment. He would leave her for his wife and never come back, not give her a moment's thought. Men could compartmentalise. Anton had aways been good at keeping his two lives separate.

Stella finished her cigarette and unpacked, hanging her dresses, and shaking out the creases in the hope some of the deeper ones would fall out with the humidity. She threw on a sundress, grabbed her devices, sunglasses, and bag, slipped on her flipflops, and ventured out, her stomach rumbling. Breakfast was calling.

Chapter 6

Stella sat drinking her morning coffee, reading the email from her publisher; the deadlines, on the timeline for her next release, shouting at her in bold capitals. *They didn't waste any time.* She read it again, wanting to imprint the most imminent deadline into her brain.

She had exactly eighteen days to get the synopsis emailed over and six weeks for the first draft meeting with her editor. The publisher's online booking schedule flashed on and off, prompting her to schedule a date and time for the meeting on the company's appointment calendar. She opened a Word document in another tab, let out a sigh.

'Hope all is well,' said Prodromos, as he worked his way around the breakfast tables, clearing and resetting them.

'Yes, thank you. It's work.'

'You must leave work and lose yourself in what is

alluring about being away from home,

being away from your day-to-day existence,' he said.

'I'm relying on that very thing,' she said. 'A story of love and magic on a Greek island.'

She took another sip of her coffee and heard voices coming from the meandering path around the pool's periphery. She took in a deep whistly breath, the sweet scent of the jasmine which clung to the wall behind her filling her. She recognised the couple, as they came into view, from the night before. The man walked with a limp, negligible, but there all the same and Eliana walked haughtily ahead of him.

'You never wait,' he moaned at her. 'You know my knee hurts. The damage from the mining accident isn't going to disappear.'

'Over thirty years ago, Dean. Change the record.'

'Wait for one second.'

'For God's sake, babe. What do I need to wait for? You're not a baby. You're not going to get lost, are you?' Eliana cocked her head proudly, in defiance, and continued at a pace.

As they approached the breakfast area by the pool side, close to where Stella sat, she doubted her earlier thoughts this would be the place for love and magic. *This couple don't appear to have either of those in their aura,* she thought.

Prodromos, like a magician on stage, appeared from behind the bar, adorning a white apron to match his gleaming smile.

'*Kalimera*, good morning, Mr Walker and Mrs Jones-Walker, my friends. I hope you slept well... your first night in Kefalonia,' he said.

'Good morning,' Eliana and Dean, responded in unison, with forced smiles.

'Yes, thank you,' said Eliana, and distracted she irritably swatting a fly from her arm.

'*Kalimera*. Sit wherever you like.' He gestured with a sweep of his arm towards the small cluster of tables each artfully arranged with a small glass vase of wildflowers, folded napkins in a raffia holder, and a cutlery tray.

Dean immediately shifted one of the small white plastic tables in the cooler more shaded area under the arbour shrouded in dazzling pink flowers. The noise punctuated the solitary peace like screeching brakes on tarmac, and Stella winced.

'I want to be in the sun,' announced Eliana and she picked up a fallen petal, already browning round the edges, and rubbed it between her forefinger and thumb, its pink staining her fingers and releasing a gentle sweet scent.

'The sun's not going anywhere for Christ's sake woman,' said Dean as he sat down heavily in the chair, its hinged. It creaked against his weight as he leaned into the seat back. 'We're here for two whole weeks. It's not going to disappear.'

Eliana withdrew the paisley print wrap from around her shoulders and placed it in her lap as she sat down opposite him, facing the glittering pool, the sunlight bouncing off its still surface. She tutted and adjusted the twisted strap of her summer dress, which was poking out from under her pashmina, the soft fabric slipped down over her arms to her elbow. 'I want to make the most of it,' she said, and Stella picked up the tone of a petulant child in her.

'And we will. We're in for a treat here. Hope you appreciate the money I've spent.' The mention of money reminded Stella of Anton's words and she grimaced at how most men took all the romance out of life by mentioning the cost of everything.

'Babe! Do you think that means you're going to be getting it the whole holiday? Is that what you think this is all about?' Eliana whined, lowering her voice.

'Well, yes, I'm not an idiot. But you deserve the best and… and I'm going to get my wicked way with you this holiday…' He reached over and took her slim hand in his big, fleshy hand and squeezed it. 'I love you. Stupid woman that you are,' Dean said.

'I know Dean. Now stop it. You know it's not about that. You're not going to get what you want because you've brought me on holiday.'

'For God's sake. What do I need to do?'

'Stop going on, that's what. You're doing my head in.'

Dean caught Stella's eye but Stella, looked away, not wanting to attract their attention, or be drawn into their bickering. She listened as they threw words at each other, thoughtless, random, out of nowhere and by the end of it their words had nothing to do with what had started their disagreement. She knew there was much more that the words carried: trauma, anger, disappointment, lies. Every word seemed weighed down with pain. She focused on the notes in her notebook and in her perfect cursive handwriting she wrote down the words: *love, romance, modern relationships, striking a balance, give and take, not all it seems, behind closed doors.*

Prodromos, back again, interrupted the couple's bickering without hesitation, as if not noticing it.

'Please help yourselves from the bar. Fresh peach juice from our own fruit trees. Or fresh lemonade prepared by my good lady wife's hands this morning. I will bring your breakfast shortly.'

'Thank you,' said Eliana.

'What d'you want?' asked Dean as he placed their room key with the heavy brass tag, shaped like a seashell, onto the table next to his sunglasses and mobile phone.

'I'll get it myself.'

'For Christ's sake, let me get it. You're so awkward about everything.'

'All right. No need to have a fit. Peach please.'

Dean got up, noisily again, scraping his chair across the tiled flooring. Stella flinched at the sharp, invasive sound, lowered her eyes, not wanting to be dragged into their argument. Dean seemed like a spoilt child wanting his own way. An echo of flip-flopping bounced against the whitewashed walls of the hotel buildings. Stella suppressed a smile, as he walked over to the bar; an inviting focal point, draped in a colourfully embroidered cloth and filled with rows of glasses of the peach juice and *lemonada*, traditionally made lemonade from the freshly squeezed juice of lemons.

Eliana, sat sulkily, hiding behind her Prada sunglasses as she played with the links of her Tag Heuer watch. She looked down at Dean's phone and seemed suddenly annoyed.

'Damn it,' she said and then to Stella, 'Oops, sorry.

I've left my mobile charging by the bed.'

'Funny how we rely on our phones. Lost without them.'

'Yeah. And Dean's not much company when he's in a mood.'

'How's his head, this morning?'

'His head?'

'That bump on the bus, yesterday. Quite a nasty knock.'

'He's fine. His big head can take it,' said Eliana.

'Men. One minute they're all tough and the next minute they want all the undivided attention of new-born twins,' said Stella.

'You're right there. He revels in it. Only he moans enough for two sets of twins and more. A whole class of toddlers.' Eliana laughed but sounded burdened.

Stella smiled politely and then diverted her attention back to her writing, continued working. She refocused, trying to repel the couple's obvious tetchy mood with each other, not wanting their issues to upset her holiday vibes, her internal equilibrium. The last thing she needed was to get dragged into their disagreement; she was here to relax and write. And forget about men which was difficult when she was a romance author; boy meets girl, girl meets boy, they fall in love, happy-ever-after ending.

'Good morning,' said Eliana, her cheery voice, now calmer than a few moments before, cutting into Stella's thoughts.

Stella looked up again to see the other couple, who had checked in the night before, approaching.

The woman, Melody, smiled as she introduced herself,

'And this is Luke, my husband,' she said.

'Eliana.'

Stella noticed Eliana keeping her eyes on Dean from behind her shades; he picked up three glasses from the breakfast bar and returned with them, spilling a little as he shuffled back, the juice running down through his fingers and dripping onto the tiled floor.

'This is Dean,' said Eliana. He placed the glasses on the table, bid good morning to the couple. 'This is Melody and Luke. They were on the coach with us.'

'Pleased to meet you mate,' said Dean, leaning over to shake hands with Luke. 'Excuse the sticky fingers,' he said, wiping them on the front of his shorts. Dean leaned in and kissed Melody on the cheek, Stella noticed, squeezing her a bit too tightly as he said, 'Come 'ere, drop one in then.' Eliana rolled her eyes and let out a sigh. Eliana gave him a look, but he ignored her, sat down. Stella noted how cock sure and confident, brash, he was.

'Who's the other juice for?' asked Eliana.

'Two for me, one for you,' he said. 'I mean look at the size of these glasses. Anybody would think they were playing toddlers.'

'Stops wastage, I guess,' said Luke.

'Nothing's ever wasted with Dean,' said Eliana. 'He's like a human food waste disposal. He'll eat anything.'

Luke shifted in his seat. 'Holidays are a good time to indulge in the local cuisine.'

'I'm here for the painting, the landscape is stunning,' said Eliana.

'Me too,' said Melody, remembering how nervous she

had been at first, mentioning the painting to Luke. He had surprised her by saying it was good she had something new to focus on, something away from school.

'I've brought my painting stuff with me,' said Eliana. 'Perhaps we could paint together one afternoon.'

'I'd love to,' said Melody.

'I can see you two are going to get on like a house on fire. Don't forget to come up for air, eh?' said Dean.

'She's not an expert, so don't get too excited,' chuckled Luke and Stella noticed Melody shrink with his words. A second later, as if Luke realised his hurtful remark said, 'But she's got a lot of passion…'

'I bet she does! Not like my bird,' said Dean.

Stella wondered what Luke and Dean meant. Melody seemed to curl in on herself, Eliana thumped Dean on the arm.

'I was a teaching assistant at our local primary school and loved the art lessons. I really want to give it a go,' said Melody, biting on her thumbnail, nibbling at the torn skin around it. Her dark eyes squinted against the sun; a few loose strands of black hair fell in messy waves, like running water, across her bare shoulders. The elastic of the top of her dress cut into the top of her breasts and Stella noticed a birthmark under her arm, near the softness of her pit, and she looked away when Melody caught her looking. She snapped her arm down and Stella focused instead on the long flowing, shushing skirt of her multi-coloured floor-length dress.

'He means we'll be talking non-stop,' chipped in Eliana, by way of explaining Dean's remark.

'Oh right,' said Melody her confusion leaving her

face scrunched up, her other thumb inserted into her downturned mouth as she continued gnawing at the rough skin around her bitten down nail.

'Nothing wrong with that. It's good to have hobbies… things to syphon you away from the norm, don't you think? I know I feel happier since tapping into my creativity full time.' They all looked round to see Stella closing her laptop. She wasn't going to get any more work done with them all talking so she might as well join in.

'You paint too? This is great,' said Eliana again.

'No, not paint. I write. I'm an author. Romance,' said Stella.

'Romance?' said Eliana.

'Yes… messy, real, love.'

'Give me a good romance novel any day,' said Melody, and her cheeks reddened, as if embarrassed by her admittance.

'Is that what you're doing here? Are you working on a new story now?' asked Eliana, tilting her head in the direction of Stella's laptop open on the table.

'Yes, and no. But I'm hoping to find some much-needed inspiration. Under pressure from my publisher to produce something soon,' she said, looking down at her plain nails compared to Eliana's whose finger and toenails were painted magenta.

'Perfect place to be inspired. Looks like we're all going to get on so well. It's great meeting like-minded people,' said Eliana. 'You can write while we paint. We can set up somewhere the three of us. I'm sure we could find a fantastic location around here.'

'Join us for breakfast?' With the introductions and polite chit-chat out the way, Stella was persuaded by Dean to join them.

'Thank you, that's great,' she said, though she immediately regretted it realising she would be the fifth cog in the wheel, the odd one out.

'I'm sure Prodromos won't mind,' said Dean, winking at her.

Dean and Luke repositioned the plastic tables, jutting them up against each other. Stella, watched on, drawn to the huge mirror, partly hidden from view by the blossom-filled tendrils of the bougainvillea cascading down it. The old mirror had an energy, a real pull and she stepped back, fighting against its attraction. The opal, antique glass smoky.

'Are you okay?' asked Eliana.

'Sorry. Miles away. That mirror's gorgeous, isn't it? I wonder how old it is,' said Stella.

'Not old at all. It's made to look old with a squirt of oven cleaner and a splash of bleach,' said Dean.

'You've obliterated all the mystery and wonder,' said Stella.

'He's as clumsy with his words as he is in life,' said Eliana, laughing.

'Actually, one of my mate's wives has a furniture reclamation business, she adds centuries onto the ugliest of furniture with a smear of this and a dash of that and then sells it for four times the price to the big-bucks investors sinking their money into all the property in Kensington and Knightsbridge.'

'Kind of takes away all the romance,' said Stella,

partly intrigued by his knowledge, but also a little put out by not being able to have this conversation with Anton. He had always appreciated her romantic side. But then again, it wasn't him sitting here opposite her.

'Who needs romance when you've got a sexy bod like mine,' guffawed Dean, thrusting his pelvis in and out.

'See what I mean?' said Eliana. 'He's an absolute idiot.'

'Life's gotta be about having a laugh, right?' said Dean, his cheeks flushed, and he reached up to wipe a build up of sweat from his wrinkled brow.

'You're the only one laughing, babe,' said Eliana which had everyone in stitches.

Prodromos watched as the *Angloi*, the English, pushed the tables together and arranged themselves around them. He openly boasted about how he loved it when his guests made a connection with the Greek *philoxenia*, translated as hospitality in its most basic form. He had a good feeling about them all, though wondered why Stella's partner had not travelled with her, and whether he would be arriving at all. He didn't want to press her... she looked a little sad, lost even.

But there was a spark of energy stirring in the still air of the mountain tops with the shimmering sea far below. Something magical but he didn't know what it was, not yet, but over the next two weeks he was sure something would be revealed. Something that even he might not understand... he had watched it and experienced its power every year.

Prodromos, as a little boy, had listened to his yiayia's

tales, wide-eyed, and often late into the night. He would hold onto his scuffed knees, feel the heat of his sunburnt cheeks, and his tussle of black curls kissing the backs of his ears.

He had witnessed such miracles happening ever since he had taken over the hotel business. His *yiayia* had chuckled and told him not to question, just to believe.

'Believe there will always be something greater, more powerful than us mere beings,' his yiayia repeated. He remembered her smile, and her bright white teeth, which, in the end, were too young for her puckered, wrinkled lips.

He was sure the couples would reveal their innermost secrets not only to him but to each other. There was something about the hilltop location of Miramare that did that to people. He had seen it happen year in, year out. Couples would arrive at the resort, tense and distant with one another, their guard up and their secrets hidden but after a few days something would shift.

He knew this was the mystical charm of Miramare with its lemon groves and fir-covered mountains on one side and the crystal waters of the blue Ionian Sea on the other. When the opposing winds of nature met, there was an untouchable magic, music in the air, which some people absorbed unknowingly. Yet, over the years, Prodromos had come to realise it was always those who needed the magic in their lives the most who felt it, were open to welcoming it into their souls. They were the ones who danced when no one else could hear the music.

He would catch their conversations, carried by the cooling sea's evening breeze, as they sat in deep conversation, their faces illuminated by the soft glow of the brassy moon, talking for hours. They would talk, sharing their hopes and dreams, their deepest fears grinding them down like herbs being pummelled, and their mishmash of insecurities scraping their insides sore, until finally, they would emerge stronger and more in love with themselves, or each other, than ever before.

It was one of the things that made running the hotel so rewarding. He knew he was helping people connect in a deeper, more meaningful way, and he took pride in that. Love was everything, in all its shapes and forms. Love blessed those with a gentle obedience, a divine intervention.

There was a magical whisper in the salty fresh air, something that danced on the breeze and gently confettied itself over everyone as they slept, like the most striking snowflakes, as they breathed in the charm of the air.

He disappeared into the kitchens with a twinkle in his eye, a light bounce to his stride. It was already happening. He could feel it. He had to tell Andri.

Chapter 7

Within ten minutes, Prodromos and Yiannis came out carrying two huge trays, visibly trembling under the weight of all the food. They settled the trays onto two tables next to their guests who were now chatting amiably, becoming acquainted with each other, their conversation punctuated with booming laughter and whoops of joy.

'This is wonderful. Thank you Prodromos,' said Stella. 'And what beautiful music.' Prodromos froze for a few seconds, a stillness rendering him speechless. 'Where's it coming from?' asked Stella, the others busy tucking in.

'The music can always be heard by those who are in tune with their souls, be heard by those who welcome its energy,' Prodromos answered eventually, avoiding Stella's eye. Stella waited for a further explanation, but he offered none.

'It makes you feel alive. Who's playing it?' Stella

insisted, but the blank faces around the mishmash of tables revealed no-one had heard it or tuned into it. Maybe their chatter was drowning the sound. She felt a little tingle run along her spine and instead of shaking it off, she welcomed it, leaned into it, smiling to herself, though a little embarrassed. Was she hearing things? She looked expectantly at Prodromos.

Prodromos concurred knowingly as he continued to load the table with abundantly filled hand-painted plates and blue-glazed bowls and lop-sided baskets. Stella observed him. *He can hear it too*; she surmised but decided not to mention it again.

Something magical, unexplained yet present in the air, danced and played out here in Miramare and she hoped it would inspire her, fill her up with an abundance of creativity.

Breakfast was a tantalising, colourful banquet: fresh figs, fleshy and dark purple, glistened in a round basket lined with a crocheted napkin, thickly sliced bread and sesame coated bread sticks as well as darker rye rolls the size of small dough balls filled an oval basket and wrinkled black olives and fresh tomatoes over-filled miniature scallop-edged bowls.

'Good enough for the gods,' said Dean.

'Looks so enticing,' said Eliana.

'Ambrosia,' said Dean.

'What?' said Eliana.

'Ambrosia. Food of the gods.'

'Yes, you are right,' said Prodromos. 'Believed to bring long life and immortality to anyone who consumed it.'

'I'm sure the scientists will find a way to make immortality a reality one day,' said Dean. 'But not in our lifetime.'

'Love makes us immortal,' said Prodromos, a fleeting wistfulness crossing his face. 'Now eat.'

'You don't have to ask me twice. I'm starving,' said Dean, giving Eliana a cocky grin. He rubbed his rotund belly in exaggerated circular motions and reached out for not one but two thick hunks of warm bread. 'Still hot.'

'Those tomatoes. Nothing like home grown is there?' said Stella, pushing the tomato up to her nose and breathing in deeply.

'These smell way better than ours. The dirt must be different out here,' said Dean.

'You mean the soil, Dean. The dirt. What does the dirt even mean, babe?' Eliana smiled, pretending she was only teasing, but Stella could see how annoyed she had become and couldn't understand why she reacted to Dean the way she did. Impatient. Dismissive.

'You grow your own?' asked Luke, breaking the atmosphere.

'My dad and I started an allotment together. Now it's just me: green beans, potatoes, lettuce, carrots, garlic. I give it a go and rotate year on year, but it's hit and miss really. It's only a small allotment but it keeps me busy when the pain in my knee's not too much,' said Dean.

'Bet it does. Good for you,' said Stella, and leaning across the table plucked a tomato, bit into it. 'Nothing like that earthy smell of home-grown, organic veggies. It's something we don't often experience at home.

Those so-called vine-grown tomatoes you get in the supermarket never taste this good.'

'Good to see someone appreciating the merits of organic veg,' said Dean.

Prodromos re-arranged the dishes to fit in plates of boiled eggs and salami. Yiannis appeared with a platter of thick-cut wedges of watermelon and slender slices of honey melon. He placed it down opposite Stella, sucked on his finger, dripping with the pink juice of the watermelon, all the while holding Stella's gaze. Stella suddenly didn't feel like eating, it was as if Yiannis had swallowed her appetite whole and she fought against a flutter tickling her insides.

'You enjoy breakfast the Greek way, my friends,' said Prodromos.

'Thank you, Prodromos,' echoed the group as they tucked in, oohs and aahs filling the air every few seconds as they chewed and tasted the appetising food.

They conversed politely at first and then towards the end of breakfast were laughing, and joking, like reacquainted old friends, sharing anecdotes and revealing titbits of information about themselves through their common experiences.

Prodromos left them to it, until a few minutes later, puffing out his chest, he came back and made an announcement. 'Your suitcase has been found,' he said, with a flurry of his hand.

'What a relief. Thank you,' said Eliana, reaching for it.

'Thanks mate. Saved me hundreds in having to buy her new clothes,' said Dean.

'Not at all. Here for anything you need.'

'You're going to regret that. She's always forgetting something,' snorted Dean, thanking Prodromos all the same.

'No, I'm not. Enough, Dean.'

'Well, thanks mate. That's saved me a few hundred euros in new tops and bikinis.'

'You'll only find good honest people here on our island,' said Prodromos.

Stella, listened on, and though she was the odd one out, sitting there with no partner, felt at ease with these two couples and their wonderful host. She welcomed how liberating it felt not to be answering questions about her history or the unexpected disastrousness of her dream holiday.

She vowed to focus on moving forward with her writing and if Anton turned up, as his last voice message promised, she would be able to enjoy the time they had left on the island together. But even without him, Kefalonia was waiting, like something mysterious in the wings, and she had a good feeling about it.

Prodromos looked on from the sidelines where he enjoyed his demi-tasse of Greek coffee and a sesame bread stick. Prodromos was happy the new guests seemed satisfied with their breakfast feast. His wife, Andri, sat in the shade under the awning, silhouetted against the white stone wall. Her favourite spot to take a minute, to sit with him. Andri, her feet propped up on a little stool with a raffia seat, sipped at her Greek coffee too.

'I know what you're thinking Prodromos,' she whispered.

'You do?'

'Yes, I do. And I'm telling you to stay out of it.'

'I am in no way in control of any of this.'

'Then you'll have no problem taking heed and stepping back,' said Andri, as she tipped her coffee cup over and let it sit upside down on the tiny saucer. He imagined the coffee dregs already making patterns as they trickled down the inside of the cup as it rested there.

'But the energy of Miramare, the magic, is already at work.'

'Enough,' said Andri. 'Leave the couples alone. They are here to enjoy themselves. They don't need you meddling.'

'The meddling is out of my hands,' he said. 'It's on the breeze, in the hands of the Gods.'

'It's all in your head,' she tutted, but gave him a smile all the same.

Prodromos imagined the sun was setting behind the ancient temple on the site not even ten kilometres from where they sat. Casting a warm glow over the ornate pillars and carved statues that stood guard over the sacred site, the legend was as old as time itself, and he couldn't help but wonder what would happen next. He could feel her dark eyes on him, and he looked up and smiled back.

'Their fate is out of your hands.'

He closed his eyes and whispered a prayer to the Gods. 'The meddling is out of my hands, you're right my dearest Andri. It's on the breeze, in the hands of the Gods,' he said, snapping his eyes open.

Andri said, 'My darling. You're such a dreamer. A romantic. But not everyone is.'

'Says the woman who reads coffee.'

'That's different. That's a tradition, a skill, passed down through the generations.'

'That may well be, but you know as well as I do, this is beyond my control, yet it touches me too. Touches my soul, sure and subtle. I feel it. They will feel it. Whether I dream or not these people will not leave the island the same as they arrived.'

'Love will find a way,' whispered Andri.

Chapter 8

After breakfast, the group broke up from around the hub of tables, now scattered with empty bowls and platters, scrunched up napkins and lip-smeared glasses.

'I think we're staying round the pool today. First day and all that... plenty of time for exploring,' said Luke. Melody, like a nodding dog, bobbed her head in agreement.

'I think we'll do the same,' said Dean, reaching for Eliana's suitcase while looking for a word of confirmation from Eliana, but she wasn't listening as she zipped closed her clutch bag and wedged it under her arm.

'I might see you later then,' said Stella. 'I'm going to take a stroll. Check out Fiskardo, the harbour's meant to be pretty.

'The landscape... the deserted clay-beaten beach, the wondrous mountains, the apiary of bee hives, the peaceful lone trails... so much to see and do here,' said

Luke, surprising Stella with his poetic descriptions, until she noticed he was looking down at an app on his phone.

'Ooh, yes to all of it but that will take more planning time… and energy,' said Stella.

'There's an amazing system of caves to explore – both underwater and on foot,' said Dean. 'There's a leaflet in reception. Ask our host. I'm sure he'll set you off in the right direction.'

'Yeah, definitely, thanks Dean,' said Stella and then, *I have to find out where the music is coming from,* she thought.

She bid them farewell, and they all gave her a smile.

Stella caught up with Prodromos on her way to her room to freshen up. 'All is well?' asked Prodromos.

'They seem nice,' said Stella.

'They are nice people.'

'And breakfast was delicious. Thank you.'

'I think you're going to get on well together,' Prodromos said, his head bobbing up and down with confirmation.

'I hope so. I'm looking for inspiration. That's what I need the most.'

Prodromos, looked out towards a bird sitting on a lowly branch and said, 'If you cannot find inspiration in Kefalonia then you won't find it anywhere.'

'I can already see it might be true. I'm going to grab what I need before heading off on what I hope will be an adventurous day to fill me with all the inspiration I'm counting on.'

Prodromos acceded knowingly and they continued to walk in the same direction. They passed a big mirror, like the one near the breakfast area; set flush into the plastered, whitewashed wall. Stella paused. It had a dull gold frame, chipped in places, and faded where the gild had worn away from years of polishing and cleaning. The mirror was smoky; patches of light spots and ripples mottled her reflection. She caught her face in it... mirrors and music she thought. And love. And freckles, she laughed. She felt someone behind her. She turned but no-one was there.

'I bet this could tell so many stories,' said Stella.

'Indeed. Love and romance,' said Prodromos. Their eyes met in the mirror.

'Not sure I can comment. Not anymore. Or maybe I never could.'

'Miss Stella?'

'Nothing. Ignore me. Love and romance are what I'm looking for. My publisher is waiting.'

'Ah, yes. You are a writer, a magician who turns memories and words into stories.'

'Something like that,' laughed Stella, blushing.

'The Greek poet, Eftychia Panayiotou, stayed here two years ago. Such a wonderful young woman. She talked of creating a desirable life out of simplicity: love, friendship, knowledge, art,' said Prodromos.

'I believe we mustn't accept what life brings to us each day as our reality. It's more about what you want your life to look like and then going out to make that life picture a reality,' said Stella dreamily.

'Of course, but with all those things, no?'

'Truly inspirational. That is what I hope to evoke in my writing, the words I choose, the stories I share.'

'Look her up. I think you will like her poems,' said Prodromos.

'I will and I'm hoping your homeland will inspire me.'

They passed a cluster of miniature potted lemon trees, the fuzzy citrus aroma filling her nostrils as she brushed past, the overhanging branches heavy with fat, dimpled ovals. Beyond the wall, fully grown lemon and peach trees filled the vibrant oasis of the orchard, contrasted by the surrounding arid countryside. The rows and rows stretched out as far as Stella could see, each one bursting with bright, juicy lemons that glowed like miniature suns against the dark green foliage and velvety plump peaches reminding her of summer carefree days. They seemed a long time ago, perhaps she was remembering them through rose-tinted glasses. She smiled at Prodromos.

As if reading her mind, Prodromos said, 'The tangy scent. It's incredibly punchy.'

'The trees look alive, each with their own personality, gnarled and twisted, their branches bowed under the weight of their own heavy bounty.'

'You're a poet too,' he said.

They both stopped and marvelled at the view and the distant thrum of the cicadas suddenly became louder, their cries ear splitting, as they sang in unison, breaking the magic. Yet amid the chaos, Stella stood, gazing over the orchard, with a sense of peace and contentment sitting softly in her. She could lose herself here in the simple beauty of nature and forget her worries; the lemon tree orchard was a true wonder of the natural world, a testament to the power and beauty of the earth, and a symbol of the enduring cycle of life and renewal.

She bid Prodromos a good day and followed the path of wide grey flagstones before they disappeared giving way to a section of still wet, recently mopped, concrete floor as she took the last few steps to her room.

She scrolled to her mum's home number and pressed call on her mobile.

'Hello darling,' her mum answered on the third ring. 'How are you getting on?'

'Hi Mum. It's great here. You should come with Dad. So idyllic.'

'I'm sure we would darling, but you know your dad can't travel with all his health complications. Have some fun for us, won't you?'

'Of course, I will Mum. Send Dad my love and congratulate him on his prize marrow. What did you make with it?'

'I've frozen some of the pumpkin and quinoa pies I made. You can pick some up when you're back.'

'I will, thanks Mum. Look I better go. The mobile charges are ridiculous from out here, but I will call as soon as I'm back.'

'Okay, darling. You take care and remember to enjoy yourself. Life is not all about work, work, work. Look at where it's got your dad.'

'I know Mum. Love you.'

'Love you too.'

Stella put the phone down and thought about her parents and the incredible relationship they had. They had never had a cross word, always gave what they could and would ask the other to make it up until they could give 100% again. She remembered their conversations...

'I've had a tough day today, so my energy level is at 45%. My battery's running low.'

'Don't worry love,' her mum would say, 'I will give an extra 55% tonight make it up to 100% for you. I've got your back.'

Another night her mum would say, 'I've only got 75% patience and my concentration is at 65%.'

'Don't worry love, we can leave the paperwork for another night and save finishing the jigsaw with Stella until tomorrow. You rest up.'

She never really understood it or how it worked and didn't ever ask either. It was just her mum and dad. Their way of talking about things but, looking back, she realised how they considered each other on every level. They stepped up to help each other at times of need, whether because they lacked energy, humour, drive, patience, or concentration. That was a real relationship. A commitment to be there for each other always and Stella reflected why she had failed so miserably to have that in her life too.

Chapter 9

Stella strolled past the pool, the sunlight glittering on the water, and gave a wave to the others who had claimed their sunbeds, already soaking up the morning sun. Eliana, in a crystal-encrusted white bikini, lay statuesque-like on her perfectly arranged sunbed, already catching the sun's rays. A table next to her was arranged with her designer leather holdall and matching toiletry bag.

Melody wearing an all in one, turquoise with seashells and anchors all over it, in contrast, sat upright, with her legs folded into her chest, her beach bag dropped haphazardly on the tiles between the two loungers. Her towel had been carelessly thrown on the lounger, its edges sweeping the tiles. A paperback, on the floor next to her kept company with a tube of sun cream and bottle of water propped next to it.

Dean, though handsome, looked like he had seen fitter days; his muffin top spilled over the elasticated waistband of his trunks and he was already getting sunburnt. She smiled though, he was quite a character, and she wasn't judging him. Luke, in contrast, was slim but equally as red as a sundried tomato in a pair of grey non-descript trunks and bright red patches across his belly and forehead forming already.

Stella, conscious of her not-so-perfect older body suddenly felt better. She was going to be okay in her swimwear in front of them. Her scars, a part of her, told a story and she was not going to hide them behind layers of fabric, she would show them off like a trophy. Without them, she might not be here.

As ambassador to the charity *All Bodies Are Beautiful*, she knew how a positive body image impacted on the mental and physical well-being of young girls and women, and in recent years of boys and men of all ages. She had met some incredible women through her work with the charity, which came about thirty years after her own brush with body dysmorphia at the age of seventeen.

She grabbed what she needed and ambled back through reception and Prodromos, now behind the check-in desk, gave her a big smile and rested his eyes for a second too long on Stella's cleavage. She smiled back, in amusement. She was used to that, but it had taken her a long time to accept her bigger-than-average breasts. The chief editor at the publishing house she used to work at spent the entire time talking to her boobs whenever they met. She smiled again remembering how many times she was tempted to tilt his chin up to look her in the eyes instead. But she never did. He had been harmless, though had she been the same person she had been in her teens his reaction would have sent her over the edge and triggered her self-harming, a downward spiral of self-hate and loathing. Now she accepted her body was hers and it didn't matter what anyone else's looked like. Her concern was her own and her own was as good as anyone else's.

'Have a good day,' said Prodromos.

'I'm going to discover the delight that is Fiskardo,' said Stella, and she hoisted her bag up onto her shoulder. 'I need to see and feel the culture of the Greek people and be surrounded by some Kefalonian colour and traditions.'

'Walk to the bottom of the path and then turn left. Take the bus. The stop is signposted with a red letter Λ.' He drew the Greek letter on a sheet of paper; the letter stood for *Λεοforeío*, bus in Greek. 'It's painted on the abandoned tyre there. Catch the bus into the town square and from there you take another bus. Look for the harbour name on the front.'

'Sounds easy enough. Thank you.'

'You'll find everything you need there. I am sure of it. A quaint coffee shop run by my friend Andros and three shops down from there, a small restaurant, traditional cuisine, my cousin Giorgos, and his wife Cleo run it during the summer months. The rest of the year he works his farm with his two sons. Be sure to stop and say hello. Tell him you are staying here with me.'

'I will,' she assured him and headed out with more confidence than she felt.

There was no traffic and looking at how narrow and steep the road was Stella questioned how the transfer bus had safely brought them to the hotel the night before. There were no streetlamps or safety barriers against the steep drop to the cavernous valley below. The mountainside was a patchwork of dry olive trees, low walls made of boulders and stones. Small wooden huts, shelter for the shepherds, looked miniature. The dots of goats and sheep, hid in clusters under the shade of the bigger, larger trees.

She walked past a tree dripping in flashes of red: ribbons and twisted string, rags, and faded pieces of cloth. The scarlet created sparkling streams and flashes of colour against the dusty background.

Stella recalled the tradition, *martis,* where threads were used to protect children and youths from evil spirits and witchcraft. It pleased her to see the tradition firsthand. She reached up to touch one of the fluttering ribbons, lightly blowing in the spiky branches, and the tinny jingle of the bells tied around the flocks' necks permeated the air. Stella puzzled over whether the bells could have been the music she had heard earlier.

She walked further along the main road, careful not to step too close to the path's edge on one side, littered with empty water bottles and crisp packets. Overgrown brambles and wild shrubs threatened to scratch her bare legs; grey-brown bark flaked back to reveal reddish brown bark underneath. On the outer edge of the path, she had to dodge the oncoming traffic which came perilously close to her. An old man, unfazed by the whoosh of fast-moving cars and trucks, trotted by on the back of a donkey. Dressed in traditional pleated baggy trousers to the knees, secured around the waist with a black rope and tassels and a cheesecloth shirt, Stella thought he looked like someone from a bygone era.

'*Kalimera*,' he greeted her, with a toothless grin, his eyes sparkling, telling of a younger, much-fulfilled life.

'*Kalimera*,' she waved, her words dragged away by the speed of another oncoming vehicle. The old man went on his way, not a care in the world, his donkey weighed down with two raffia baskets; woody olive branches poked out of them, and black olives stared out at her like beady eyes.

Further along two old women, clad from head to foot in black clothing, their heads wrapped in black scarves and almost touching as they sat on the opposite side of the road, surveyed her as she walked past smiling. They muttered something in her direction and continued chatting, their smiles suspicious.

With no pavements the road, nothing more than a steep winding dirt track, seemed dangerous and dwindled the initial happiness associated with a leisurely walk to that of a knotty ball of angst. She jumped when two sweat-drenched torsos, no more than four years old, rose from behind an overgrown bush. The boys grinned revealing two missing front teeth, and then bent over again, collected whatever treasures they hunted for. Their giggling dissipated her unrealistic fear, replacing the heaviness in the air with a tinkle of joy and playfulness. A woman deeper into the overgrowth, called and waved at them to come to her.

By the time she reached the end of the winding road her feet were grey with dust, and she could feel the sweat circles under her arms. She waved the bus down with relief, glad to be sitting down at last and out of the onslaught of the traffic. The air-conditioning cooled her, and she pressed her face against the cool glass of the window; its orange curtains tied back with a straggly piece of string. The hum of the bus engine swallowing up the outside traffic and the hum of people talking around her cushioning her ears against it too.

Eventually, her stomach rolling uncomfortably after the bumpy bus ride, she arrived feeling a little relieved if a little discombobulated too.

Fiskardo did not disappoint her; the unique, picturesque harbour village, with its original Venetian buildings intact, presented itself as breathtakingly quaint and the Greek equivalent of English chocolate-box country villages.

She strolled by the buildings, one after the other, one painted a sky blue with butter-painted windows and a door with a carved portico above it. The next one, bright white and three-floors tall, had blue-painted windows, a white lace curtain caught in its opening.

A cat sat lazily on the stone sill, shaded by the boughs of grapevines, abundant with shiny long-stems and a mass of heart-shaped leaves which nodded ever so gently in the faint breeze. Each building, unique, stood tall facing the crystal waters of the little harbour, and the beauty of the seaside village captured Stella's attention, mesmerising her with its splendour.

After stopping to buy a wide-brimmed sun hat, Stella happier to be shading her face from the prickling heat of the sun, chastised herself for not bringing her suncream. She stopped at a building with peach-coloured walls and white-shuttered windows, its window boxes a burst of colour; two butterflies danced around the blooms and a beetle as black and as shiny as an obsidian jewel scurried across the ledge. She absorbed the array of racks and turning displays flowing out onto the walkway; sapphire glass evil eye décor, crocheted placemats, key rings, leather handbags and an assortment of sunglasses.

The place buzzed with throngs of tourists and local peddlers selling their wares, restaurateurs in white shirts and silk waistcoats and waiters posing in blue t-shirts emblazoned with eatery names. Everyone smiled freely and warmly here. They practised their English, enticing clientele to sit in their tavernas and eat-in patisseries with proffered laminated menus, restaurants with pretty-clothed tables and promises of fresh fish and home-made pastries.

She stumbled upon the coffee shop Prodromos had told her about. He had described it perfectly: blushing pink terra cotta walls, windows framed with typically Greek blue shutters and blue and white tablecloths covering the square tables surrounded by sets of wooden chairs stained the limitless blue of the summer sky.

She took a seat at the last table, facing the harbour, and a tall, lean man with a huge black jiggling moustache and hazel green eyes, appeared and pressed a blue-and-white menu into her hands. He smiled widely.

'You must be Miss Stella,' he said.

'When did I become so famous?' she smiled, smoothing out a tiny crease in the tablecloth, thinking about how to navigate the surrealness of fame, even if only here in a tiny fishing port on a Greek island.

'Prodromos called ahead to say you might be passing through.'

'Oh my, that was very good of him.'

'I'm glad to make your acquaintance. I'm Andros.'

'I'm pleased to meet you. I won't ask how he described me,' said Stella, a little taken aback by the man's piercing gaze.

'He was most accurate.'

'What an exquisite spot,' Stella said, moving the subject away from herself and breathing in the sea breeze as it wafted across from the harbour. She took in the sound of the water, let it wash over her, as it lapped against the harbour side and up against the rounded bows of the colourful moored fishing boats.

'Welcome and thank you kindly for saying so. It's busier than most days today, the fishing boats are already back and those who were here early enough, were able to buy freshly caught fish straight from the fishermen's catch.'

'How wonderful.'

'You must have fish for lunch. Today is one of the best days to have it.'

'I will,' said Stella, realising his patter had been learnt off-by-heart to attract the tourists.

'The others moored alongside them are the visitors' yachts. These luxurious boats are here only during the summer,' he said, following Stella's idle gaze.

'I can see that. Busy, indeed and your coffee shop is so pretty.'

'It is small, but we are proud of our little business and our homemade desserts are most popular. In fact, the best you will find on the whole island,' he said, leaning in towards her conspiratorially. Stella beamed at his obvious exaggeration, liking his cheeky personality. 'Let me get you a glass of water while you decide what delight you would like.'

Andros disappeared in a flurry and Stella studied the menu. She decided on the *mandolato,* a soft nougat traditionally prepared with a light meringue base enriched with honey, sugar, and almonds. She remembered the sticky bars she used to eat back as a child and suddenly yearned for simpler days, days with no responsibility and no worries about tomorrow.

She was having second thoughts about ordering it wanting to save room for lunch but licked her lips in anticipation all the same. She took out her notebook and pen. She pressed open its pages, wiping its edges. She chewed on the end of the biro... this was quite a view and inspiration seeped into her. She quickly inked words, one after the other, onto the pages; *acid-bright dresses, metallic hues, a sequined gold shirt, a blue sky, damp air, a blast of sea air...*

The *mandolato,* sweet and sticky, satiated her tastebuds as did the coffee, rich and creamy. She dreamily licked the tips of her fingers and brushed away the drip of coffee staining the page of her open pad. She could see why Prodromos was proud to direct his guests to his friend's café; the ambiance and location, overlooking the harbour were delightful and the delicacies were delicious.

With Andros' permission she sat a little longer. Her thoughts took her into an abyss of note making and storytelling as she continued to write, her pen gliding over the pages of the small notepad she balanced on her lap, her legs crossed, her skirt flowing like the wings of a moth in the catch of a slight breeze.

Intermittently, she put down her pen and with a sidelong glance people watched; older couples ambling by arm in arm, groups of university-age students chatting animatedly, a group of sun-kissed youths carrying backpacks, and the locals going about their business. The space around her flooded with smiling, tanned patrons. She was glad to be here.

'*Yeia sou, Yiannis*,' greeted Andros. Yiannis appeared, his motorcycle helmet under his arm.

'Hello,' Yiannis said to Stella.

'Yiannis. What an unexpected coincidence,' she said, struggling to hide her obvious pleasure at seeing him.

'May I?' he asked, pointing to the chair opposite her.

'Yes, please do,' she said, closing her notebook with its permanent words inked neatly. She fiddled around, placing it with the pen into her bag, suddenly feeling exposed, out of her depth.

'Should I call you Theodora?' Stella scrunched up her face in puzzlement. 'According to mythology, *mandolato* was considered an aphrodisiac and used by Emperor Justinianus to plan secret trysts and entice Empress Theodora with.'

'What a wonderful tale,' said Stella, not quite sure how to react.

'Prodromos was worried you may not find this place, so he sent me to look for you,' Yiannis said, tipping back in his chair.

'He's a kind man, but as you can see, I'm fine and

Andros has looked after me well.'

'You like it here?' Yiannis asked genially.

'It's truly wonderful.'

'You stay here, or you go now? I can give you lift back on my moped,' he said, his words drenched in a soft Greek accent.

'I was hoping to stay and have lunch.'

'For sure. I will wait for you.'

'I don't know how long I will be. I can get the bus back,' said Stella.

'I can wait. No problem.'

'Stella,' called out Eliana, waving from a few feet away.

'Hello,' said Stella, reddening as if she had been caught out doing something illicit. 'You decided to come too.'

Dean and Eliana took a seat next to each other. 'This is perfect,' cooed Eliana. 'The round table and low armchairs, so inviting. They were calling us over to sit and relax in the sun,' she said. 'And the harbour is breathtaking.' Eliana patted the puffy orange cushions and pulled up her sunshades to the top of her head.

Stella relaxed. She looked towards the harbour again; the ocean bobbed with simple fishing boats, painted blue, white, yellow, and black. She read the names: *Anna, Markela, Bella, and Monica.* Each boat dipped up and down on the waves lapping against the harbour wall.

'How amazing it would be to have a little boat to bob about in,' said Eliana.

'Less idyllic than you think. I don't think getting thrashed on the open sea in a little thing like that would be great,' said Dean, pointing to a tiny trawler, its deck piled with a tangled mound of old fishing nets and buoys. 'That one looks like it's been battered to near breaking point.'

He pulled a face which held the expression Stella's mother would have commented on:'Most unattractive' she would have said with distain. With thoughts of her mum popping up in her head she wondered what she would have made of the mess she was in had she confided in her. But she pushed the thought away: There was no way she would ever tell her mother and though she was certain of it, a little dip of melancholy poked her in the chest like a thin accusatory finger.

'No probably not. But that one, over there,' she said, her finger extended towards a shiny yacht in the distance. 'That would be okay.'

'Yeah, if we had a couple of million to spend.'

'One day...' she mused.

'We don't need it,' he said. 'Not when we've got each other.'

Stella felt a stab of something hot in her chest as she realised this man loved this woman very much and she wished she had someone in her life who she didn't ever want to be without.

Then she heard Eliana's retort, 'But the yacht would still be good.'

Stella stifled a giggle, her romanticising punctured, and she turned back to Yiannis. 'Will you join me for lunch?' Stella said, tripping over her words as they tumbled out of her, saying their piece before she had time to check herself.

'Why not?' said Yiannis, not missing a beat.

Stella paid the bill. 'Thank you, Andros for your kind hospitality. I promise to return before I leave for England,' she said and turning back to Eliana and Dean she waved goodbye, promising to see them back at the hotel.

Stella and Yiannis strolled over to the taverna; its canopied dining area on the harbour side, as idyllic as all the other restaurants. She sat opposite Yiannis, a prickle of magic ran up her arm and then, just as suddenly, musical notes reached her. She turned around, looking up and down and then behind her.

'Have you lost something?' asked Yiannis.

'No, it's nothing.'

'You look, what is it you English say, unsettled.'

'I wanted to ask where the music was coming from.'

'Music?'

'I can't be wrong about it again,' Stella said, shaking off the scintillating feeling like ants crawling up and down her arms.

'That's something you must speak to Prodromos about. He is the only one who understands.'

'What do you mean?'

'You are in touch with the magic of Kefalonia if you hear the music,' he said with a twinkle in his eye.

'I heard it at breakfast,' Stella said, and she felt lost in this place, she felt the pull of seductiveness beyond that which she could explain, like leaning against the cheek of God, and she shook off a fleeting flutter of flirtatiousness deep within her, like a butterfly bursting out of its chrysalis.

'*Kalispera*. Welcome,' interrupted a fair-haired man

with an abundance of chest hair sprouting from his open-buttoned shirt. '*Yeia sou, Yiannis.*'

After a short conversation in Greek, Yiannis introduced Stella. With a flick over the menu, she quickly agreed with Yiannis's instinct to trust the owner's recommendation. They dispensed with the menus which were written in Greek anyway.

Within half an hour, the food was laid out in front of them, and Stella began to relax in Yiannis' company, talking like they had known each other a lifetime. Yiannis, easy to talk to, despite his broken English, made Stella warm and fuzzy inside with his tales of growing up in the village.

'My grandparents and old aunt were forever chasing me across the fields. But I was too quick for them. They would try to lure me back with their tales of lost spirits living in the old olive trees, but I was too clever to believe such nonsense.'

'Sounds like you were quite a handful.'

'Once father was gone, he drowned at sea, my mother, she nearly died of a broken heart.'

'So sorry. But the story ends well,' said Stella, searching his eyes.

'Yes, until a visiting stranger fell in love with her and brought her out of mourning and into a life of joy,' he said.

Despite the sadness surrounding his father's death, Yiannis had grown up with huge episodes of love, affection, and attention not only from his mother but her new partner and the entire village.

'Must be nice having so many people looking out for

you,' she said longingly, relishing in the moments of connection between them. We have to think differently about expressing love and pain. We have to be open about our desire for closeness.'

'Greeks, they all care for one another. It's a blessing but also a curse,' he smiled.

'How?'

'The English have the saying too many cooks?'

'Ah, yes, but better too many cooks than none,' said Stella.

'A toast,' he said, 'to too many cooks.'

'To too many cooks,' she laughed and finished her second glass of locally produced wine.

After their main meal of fresh *barbouni,* red mullet, chargrilled and served with chunky cut potatoes finished with oregano and a drizzle of olive oil, Stella hiccupped. She forked a piece of cucumber and a slice of tomato onto her fork and savoured the richness of the olive oil and fresh coriander dressing which zinged with freshly squeezed lemon juice.

'The perfect salad dressing. How do you Greeks do it so well? In fact, how do you do everything with food so well?'

'It is not just food we do well,' said Yiannis.

Stella looked away, picked up her glass and sipped her water, looked back at him.

Yiannis was still looking at her intently. 'There is something not good in your life, Stella,' he said, his dark eyes not leaving hers for a second.

'What makes you say that?' she said, trying to appear calm, cool.

'Your eyes,' he said, still holding her gaze.

'Don't believe my eyes,' she said. 'They're tired.' She looked away suddenly conscious of the half-moons and her darkening freckles.

The church bells rang through the gaps between the roofs of the buildings and Stella glanced at her watch. It was already five o'clock. 'I think you should take me home,' she said, hiccupping and changing the subject, feeling suddenly too exposed and a little vulnerable yet unable to unlock her eyes from his.

'Of course.'

'Let me settle the bill,' she said, taking out her credit card.

'It has been settled,' said Yiannis, and he placed his hand over hers. The shock of his hand on hers sent a fizzing through her and she shifted in her seat. They remained still for a few seconds. Was she imagining these feelings in her? Did he feel them too? He moved his hand away.

'That's too kind, Yiannis. You shouldn't have,' she said automatically, clumsily. And as she said his name, she reached up to hide her flushed face from him. What was happening here? Her phone vibrated and she picked it up off the table. A message from Anton:

I will come out to you as soon as I can. X

A message from Anton usually sent her into a tizzy, wanting to be with him, yearning for his touch. She questioned why she didn't feel like that now. Was it being so far away? Was it the disappointment of being let down by him? Was it him not being with her already when he had promised? She looked up at Yiannis. A prickle of electricity ran through her belly and into her chest. She tried to subdue it, extinguish it, but couldn't. Perhaps she didn't want to.

They walked a few metres to his bike, lined up with another dozen or so against a shaded wall.

'You have a beautiful smile,' said Yiannis, catching her glow.

'You left your bike unlocked and your helmets here,' she said, embarrassed by his compliment.

'No one will steal them,' he chuckled. 'Though someone may steal you.'

'Back home that would be seen as reckless behaviour.'

'Reckless?'

'Yes,' she said, not sure what she was agreeing to, her head and her swelling heart in a flutter.

The word reckless and all it conjured up teased her, and she suddenly wanted to flirt with danger, flirt with the unknown.

Yiannis helped her put on the helmet, pulling most of her hair back from her face, he fastened the strap under her chin. She realised how ridiculous she must look with a helmet on, her hair all over the place under it, but didn't care. This was what being adventurous was all about and it was long overdue. She wanted to turn the pages of this new book and see which page it would fall open at.

Sitting behind Yiannis on his motorbike, with her arms wrapped around his toned waist, she had no choice but to lean into him, take in the smell of the salt in his wildly tangled sea-swept hair, and an erotic clench, out of nowhere, tightened her belly. She had never ridden a motorbike before let alone held onto a man she barely knew.

With her wind-whipped hair across her face, she allowed herself to smile welcoming the glorious, incendiary sensation which rippled through her as they drove back. Yiannis navigated the winding roads with ease and when he approached a wide bend in the road sped up, as if to give her a thrill, and she held onto him tighter. She shivered with a secret pleasure.

She was forty-eight and speeding along the dusty roads of a captivating Greek island on the back of a motorcycle with a man half her age. Waves of longing radiated from her, and she didn't fight them, but rather welcomed them like an old forgotten friend. Life was unbelievably unpredictable, playful. Life was full of the unexpected. It was time she welcomed everything new it brought to her. No more shying away. No more hiding behind a stale, ten-year affair with a married man. A man who wasn't even here with her. She clung onto Yiannis a little tighter still, almost cradling his torso, not bothering to hide her elation.

'Woo-hoo!' she screamed into the air, not caring how crazy she sounded. How crazy it all felt. Her elation caught in her hair and got carried on the breeze. As they whooshed closer to the hotel, she reasoned whether she would be going home a different woman to the woman who had arrived on the island.

As they rounded the last bend in the road, the hotel appeared white on the horizon, a white flag of surrender, thought Stella and she shivered against a tremor of anticipation.

Yiannis stopped a few feet from the path leading up to the hotel's entrance and waited for the longest moment or two before cutting the impatient, idling engine. It was as if he too didn't want their unexpected adventure to end. Stella released her arms from around his waist with reluctance. He swiftly pushed down the kickstart, stood facing her. She felt trapped on the back of the bike, too exposed suddenly.

'I said I would get you home safely.'

'Thank you,' she said, breathless and suddenly claustrophobic with the helmet still on.

'Here, let me help you,' he said, as she fiddled with the strap.

As she lifted the helmet his hand brushed against her face, and she momentarily fought against a swooping sensation around her heart and deep in her belly. 'Thank you,' she managed to say, though inside her a tumble of other words lurked unsaid pushing to be freed.

'Who said a forty-year-old couldn't ride a bike?'

'Forty and the rest,' she laughed, the tension lifting between them. She hoisted her bag over her shoulder and as she walked up the path to the hotel, noticing a pile of wooden crates laden with fresh fruits and vegetables. One of the pomegranates had cracked open, its red juice stained the other fruit packed into the same box. She smiled; the fruit a symbol of life and abundance. With a lightness in her step and a dizzying flutter in her heart, she looked back. Yiannis was watching her. Her heart flipped in her chest.

Chapter 10

Stella tried to block out the buzz coming from Eliana and Dean who were arguing about when to have lunch and what to eat. Sitting under the shade of one of the big umbrellas by the pool, she had her laptop propped on her lap, planning her story, painstakingly slow; the inspiration wasn't there. To get the creative juices flowing, she made notes on what was going on around her. It wasn't working either. Not this time.

'You don't need a full meal again after your indigestion last night. And you ate loads at breakfast.' Dean ignored her. She continued, 'Prodromos has already said he's preparing something special for us all tonight so why d'you have to be so bloody greedy?'

'Right. Well, that's it. You tell me I can't, and I will.' Dean got up, grabbed his wallet.

'For God's sake. You're like a big lump of food, babe. That's all you do. Eat.'

'And you going on isn't going to change anything,' he called back at her. 'Do you fancy a pint?' Dean asked Luke, who, with Melody, was beside them.

'Yeah, why not?' Luke said, hesitantly.

'Leave the women to it,' said Dean, looking towards Melody who was hiding behind her paperback. 'Until later.' Dean gyrated his pelvis in Eliana's direction. Stella stifled a giggle; Dean was quite a character.

'Yeah, yeah,' Eliana said.

The men wandered over to the bar, pulling on their T-shirts as they went.

Eliana and Melody continued to sunbathe not mentioning the embarrassing situation. A few minutes later, Eliana sat up and called Yiannis over. 'Can I have a Coke Zero, with ice, please?'

'Me too,' said Melody from behind the pages of her book.

Yiannis gave a little bow and smiled. 'Thank you, Yiannis,' she said.

'Dean's a laugh, isn't he?' said Melody.

'Sometimes,' said Eliana.

'It's so hot,' said Melody, dabbing at her forehead with the corner of her towel.

'Too hot for anything. He's like a dog on heat but there's no way he's getting it when it's so hot. Yuk. All that sweat.'

'Oh, right,' said Melody, the hot rash spreading across her cheeks giving her away, obviously embarrassed by Eliana's openness.

'Sorry. Too much information. I've been with Dean too long,' she said. 'I don't think the air-con is working in our room either.'

'Oh, right,' said Melody again. 'I guess it's easy to be open with people you don't know well,' said Melody. 'You'd be amazed how many parents spilled the beans about their home life to us at school.'

'You were a teacher?'

'A Teaching Assistant, Level 3, so I was more involved in the classroom than most.'

'Was? You're not anymore?'

'I left. You know, to pursue other things. Painting.'

'Could you not have done both?'

'It was time to leave,' said Melody, ending the conversation, tugging at her thumbnail and the torn skin around it with her fingers and then, shoving the end of her thumb in her mouth, she continued to nip at the ragged skin.

Stella couldn't help but wonder what had forced Melody to leave her job, and her intuition kicked in. Perhaps the mousy teaching assistant had a secret life nobody knew about. Her fingers clicked over the laptop keys: *a secret life no one knows about.*

Eliana nattered on about Moscow and how she was missing him. She took out her mobile and handed Melody the phone.

'Swipe left… Silver Labrador, isn't he adorable?'

'He's gorgeous. Handsome dog. I used to dog-walk for three locals. It was demanding work but kept me fit.'

'If it weren't for Moscow Dean wouldn't move. He'd go from the bed to the couch, eating in between. He says his knee stops him from exercising but it's an excuse. It's because he's overweight and can't move.'

'Who can't move?' asked Dean as he approached with a pint glass in each hand.

'Two?' said Eliana.

'I'm on holiday and Luke insisted,' he said, signalling with a thrust of his chin in Luke's direction.

'Move over, Melody. I'll sit here,' said Luke. She got up and moved to the next sun lounger, one away from where Dean had sat.

'Holidays are all about the sun and sea, food, and drink.'

'And sex,' said Dean.

'Here we go again,' said Eliana, and they both fell about unable to contain their glee, but Stella saw how Luke and Melody remained stony faced.

'We were tempted to go all-inclusive but then I said the last thing we needed was overindulgent international buffets every day and crowds of children and screaming parents. This place is perfect,' said Luke, as he rearranged the back of his lounger into a more upright position.

'Yeah, over excited kids and frazzled parents are not a good combination when all you're looking for is to relax,' said Dean and he slurped the last dregs of his pint.

'Oh, I don't know. It's good to see families spending time together,' said Melody.

'Who made you Minister for Children and Families?' asked Dean, more abruptly than the situation or the comment demanded.

Melody stuck out her chin and answered with an air of stubborn confidence. 'Someone needs to stick up for them. They're always being ignored in favour of the economy. Parents getting pushed to work more hours and longer hours than ever. So many little ones dropped off at breakfast club, shunted into after-school clubs.'

'You're a fine one to talk about family,' said Luke, spitting out the words.

'Not now, Luke. Please,' said Melody, her cheeks colouring, her eyes filling with tears. She leaned over and stroked his arm, but he shrunk back.

'No. not now. Of course not. Let's not spoil the holiday.'

'Looks like you both need a shag,' said Dean, laughing.

'Yeah, mate. You don't know the half of it,' said Luke, and Stella's eyes were on him from the sidelines. *What did he mean?*

They spent the rest of the morning sunbathing and intermittently chatting. Eventually, catching her eye, they called her over to join them for lunch.

'Enough work,' called Dean.

She packed away her laptop and happily joined them for a light meal of Greek salad and charcoal-grilled chicken wraps around the pool which they washed down with chilled freshly squeezed lemonade and ice-cold beers drank straight from the bottles.

Happy to have been invited to join them all, Stella stayed and lay back in the sun for an afternoon siesta, observing her new holiday friends. Dean and Eliana, their loungers pushed together, fell asleep back-to-back. She flicked her eyes over Luke, fast asleep, gripping Melody's hand between their loungers, a possessiveness and intensity about him she couldn't fathom. Stella puzzled over what Melody and Luke's story was.

Chapter 11

'It's a shame none of the guys wanted to come with us,' said Stella, speaking the truth but, deep down, she was curious. She wanted to elicit a reaction from the women about love, wanting to get to the core of their relationships, having observed them for a couple of days. *I'm a romance author ,* she thought. *This can be part of my research.*

'We're better off without them,' said Eliana. 'Dean would only moan after an hour or two about getting back to the bar. This way we can paint, and you can write, for as long as we like.'

'I think Luke wants me back by lunch time,' Melody said hesitantly.

'Doubt it,' said Eliana. 'Once we start, we'll forget the time and the men,' she laughed.

'Luke knows you're with us. I'm sure he'll be okay if you're a bit later getting back,' said Stella.

'I hope so,' said Melody. 'He can be a bit clingy.' And Stella wondered why.

They trudged along the sand-filled path, careful as they navigated the steep slope down to the secluded beach. The mountain climbed up on one side, taking with it its blanket of black firs, tall and majestic, reaching like rockets towards the never-ending blue of the sky. Stella focused on the black; the colour of a promise that might soon be revealed to her.

'Glad, Prodromos told us about this little stretch of beach. Look how quiet it is,' said Stella. She glanced hesitantly in the direction of a family of four. The mother was weighed down with beach bags, towels, and all sorts of swimming paraphernalia while the father walked ahead of her, hands in his pockets, as if without a care in the world. The children, Stella guessed aged five and seven, mock-punched each other the entire time it took to walk from one end of the beach to the area marked Kids Diving Club. They calmed down when the club leader greeted them with high fives. The mother looked relieved to relinquish the responsibility to someone else for a couple of precious hours.

'Not that it's going to be that quiet with us nattering on,' said Eliana.

'Don't you worry. Once we set up and start painting, we'll disappear into our own little world and you won't hear a word,' said Melody. Both women gave her a quizzical look. 'I need to concentrate.'

'Very teacher-like,' said Stella.

'There's something about the quiet, feeling the gentle swoosh of each brushstroke across the page. It's so soothing,' said Melody and she held up her hand, the brush poised like a wand, ready to colour magic onto the page.

'That's how I feel with the pen in my hand as it rushes across the blank space, one word after another, one sentence after the other. Words chasing each other, filling the page. It's like magic,' said Stella. She wiped the sweat off her forehead, and hoisted her bag up onto her shoulder, while struggling to keep a grip of the roll of paper under her other arm at the same time.

'Writing is a different discipline altogether,' said Eliana. 'How do you come up with your stories?'

'Life, observation, listening,' said Stella as she looked out towards the distant blue line of the ocean, feeling the pull of the sea, majestic and calming. 'I seem to notice things that other people don't notice.'

'Like what?'

'The exact colour of a piece of fruit, the way a child looks up at his mother, the light dancing across a street littered with rubbish, the way a drop of wine sits on the rim of a glass and then trickles down the side, the soft green of a fresh bud on a tree, people around me...'

'We'd better watch out Melody. We could end up in one of her books,' said Eliana.

They trudged on. Stella coloured, guilty as charged. The soaring heat of the sun bore into her side and she hid behind her hand shading her eyes against the blazing sun rays, tilting her face away. She looked down pretending to be minding her step, though she had to be careful on the sandy track leading down to the beach.

'Here, let me help you,' said Melody taking the paper

roll from her. 'It's our equipment, after all.'

'They're getting a bit heavy. And I'm not used to walking and talking. It's knackering,' said Stella, stopping to take a breath.

'It'll be worse coming back up,' said Eliana, as she rushed ahead, her steps light in her rubber-soled pumps, her hair tied up in a bun with a velvet ribbon wrapped around it.

Once they reached the sandy beach they trudged across in their shoes, the heat of the sand seeping into their thin-soled sandals and burning the tips of their toes in their flipflops.

'I'm going to set up here, looking over in that direction. I'm going to paint the two fishing boats bobbing over there and hope the anglers loading their nets don't head out before I'm finished,' said Eliana, neatly organising her art materials onto the sand. She popped up her telescopic easel, plunging the tripod base into the sand to make it sturdy.

Stella bent down to pick up a tiny light-brown ammonite and a spiral seashell, its delicate form tinged pink. She plucked away the tangle of seaweed bound to them. 'Peopleless,' she whispered, 'and incredible discoveries.'

'Splendid,' said Melody to Eliana. 'I might tackle a seascape. See how I get on.'

'I'll take the picnic hamper and put it under the shade of the lone clump of trees over there,' said Stella. 'I'm going to sit there too. Give me a shout if you need anything.'

Eliana turned back to her easel. Stella, a few feet

away, patted the ground and settled down, facing the two women. The breeze, Stella guessed, was gentle enough not to blow Eliana's paper around, but Stella watched her clip it down with a couple of bulldog clips all the same.

'This is going to be a good day. I know Dean is taking advantage of me not being with him and will be propping up the bar all day,' Eliana said. 'Keeping Prodromos busy.'

'He'll have Luke's company,' said Melody.

'What's Luke like? There's something intense about him. Those piercing eyes, nervous energy,' said Stella, something pushing her to ask the question, and she took a few steps back towards the women.

Melody hesitated. 'It's good to have some space.'

'From Luke you mean?'

'Yeah, I suppose. Don't get me wrong, he's a good guy.'

'I sense a but coming,' said Eliana.

'We've had some personal stuff which needs ironing out.'

'His or yours?' asked Eliana, and then quickly added, 'Sorry, too nosey. I don't mean to be. I'm not usually this inquisitive.'

Melody shifted from one foot to the other, and called back, 'Actually, it's a relief to have someone to talk to.'

'So?' said Eliana.

'Let's say we both have demons to point our middle finger at.'

'I suppose coming away on holiday seems like the answer but sometimes, our problems follow us back again on the flight home,' said Eliana.

'You and Dean?'

'Oh, no. We're fine. We get on like salt and pepper shakers, side by side, different but the same.'

'You seem like a fun couple, though you do… disagree a lot,' said Melody.

'Do we?'

'I would say so, you seem to clash a lot,' said Stella, appearing behind them. She handed out a can of lemonade to each of the women. 'You always seem a bit prickly with him and he is with you, too.'

'I never noticed,' said Eliana. 'I don't think we're as argumentative as you're implying.'

'Sometimes you don't notice stuff when you're in the thick of it,' said Stella. 'You kind of become immune to your own idiosyncrasies.' Stella thought about her relationship with Anton and how they had become so used to being together on a part-time basis that she lived her life in two parts: with him and without him, the latter being the bigger part, the part she now realised was holding her back, limiting her life, her life's experience.

Eliana said nothing and focused on her art. Stella hoped their comments had not offended her. She surmised Eliana didn't look like the sort of woman who would be easily offended and, thankfully, appeared to be happily engrossed in her painting.

The two women took their positions in front of their easels, the wide-open sea and the deep, broad horizon sitting upon it: a perfect example of God's exquisite creation, nature, the people in it.

Stella, deep in thought, wondered about people and

their relationships. Writing romance, she was interested in relationships, in love, in what kept couples together and what pushed them apart.

It wasn't always what you saw or heard but what was sitting under the surface which nurtured relationships, shaped them, broke them, pieced them back together again. Stella sat, watching, half lost in her own thoughts, half listening to what the breeze was whispering.

Eliana drew a horizontal line across her paper and added a curved line below it. 'The tideline, she said, talking to herself and then, 'Squiggles to show the waves.' *The difficulties of relationships and love* thought Stella, as she looked on for a few more seconds.

'I wouldn't know where to start,' said Stella, watching her outlining the boats, their round-bellied hulls, partly bobbing on the water, partly submerged. *Just like love, sometimes on show and other times so deep we can't touch it.* Stella's thoughts whirled around.

'I can't stop thinking about what you've said,' Eliana said. 'It's not the first time someone has pointed out how tempestuous we are, but I don't see it as negative. Surely, it's better to say how you feel than to keep it all inside.'

'And you love him,' said Stella, joining in. 'Sorry, force of habit bringing up the love word

what with being a romance author.'

'Yes, I do…' she said, but Stella wasn't so sure about that, convinced Eliana was holding back. 'But you don't like being intimate with him?'

'Sometimes, but not as often as he wants it. It's so messy. I mean men are constantly wanting sex, aren't they?'

'Perhaps that's how he equates your love for him and his love for you, through sex and if you don't want it when he does then he thinks you're rejecting him and his love,' said Stella.

'Not thought of it in those terms before. We've not talked about it.'

'Our experiences of love and sex get blurred and what seems normal behaviour for one person may not be normal for another. Think about how you would feel if he rejected your cuddle when you needed one,' said Stella.

'He never does, unless I have rejected him first, I suppose.'

'So, he only does it to lash out at you,' said Stella. 'What were his previous relationships like? Does he talk about them?' Stella couldn't believe she was asking these questions of someone she hardly knew, but somehow the questions kept coming.

'His ex-wife went off with another man. Do you think that's why he needs sex? It's his way of quantifying and feeling love, of managing the rejection by telling himself someone else loves him.'

'Speak to him. Make him understand the sex isn't the most important thing in your love for him and you adore other things about him.'

'Huh, he'd love that. Me telling him. He's got such an ego,' said Eliana.

'You might find his ego isn't as big as you think when you really get talking. Maybe it's your perception of him that's getting in the way.'

Melody nodded and made little sounds as if following

the conversation between Stella and Eliana, but Stella saw how Melody was lost in her painting, her face scrunched in concentration. She had a story too, but Stella couldn't put her finger on it. Being a writer and a Scorpio, she was more intuitive than most.

Melody looked over in Stella's direction and caught her eye. She waved. Stella waved back and promptly looked back down at her pad.

'What are you writing? Are we really going to appear in the pages of your next best-selling novel like Eliana says?'

'If you're lucky, Melody. I've not had a Melody in my books before, so why not?' Stella froze, straining her ears.

'What is it?' asked Melody.

'Tell me you can hear the music,' said Stella, absorbing the waves of the tune, its mellow notes, strangely a part of her.

'The sea is definitely making its own music,' said Eliana.

'Music?' Melody stared blankly at Stella.

'I heard something back at the hotel too and then realised no one else had heard it,' said Stella.

'Maybe there's a wind chime somewhere,' said Melody.

'Not around here. It's deserted,' said Eliana.

Melody breathed in the blue expanse of the canvas above her. 'Perhaps it's your archangel connecting with you if you believe in all that stuff.'

'Maybe,' said Stella.

Changing the subject, Eliana asked Stella to sit with

them a while. 'You can catch the sun a bit too, or you'll go back home as white as you arrived.'

'You sound like my mum,' said Stella. 'She's already asked me for a photo of my white bits, convinced I'm not enjoying it enough.'

'My mum adored the sun in her day. She was a sun goddess. Like me, really,' said Eliana, and she held out her arms to show them how tanned she already was after only a few days.

'You tan quickly,' said Melody. 'It takes me ages, I go through that horrible pink-lobster stage before I turn anything remotely golden and even then, I don't go as dark as you, Eliana. You must have good melanin.'

'Olive skin's my secret weapon. It's in my DNA. My whole family's the same.'

Another hour passed and they decided to have a break, take a dip in the sea. The sparkling waves, silver-crested and reflecting the bright azure of the mesmerising sky above, cooled Stella down for an instant. The further she waded in, the warmer the undercurrents became.

'This is heaven,' said Stella, grabbing the chance to fill her lungs with the clean, fresh air of the open sea.

'It sure is,' said Eliana and splashing around uncharacteristically, splattered Stella's sunglasses. 'Ooh, sorry. I'm not co-ordinated when it comes to swimming. I'm better on the sunbed than in the water,' she laughed. Sella marvelled at how neat and organised she was on land compared to being in water.

'I'm the same but every now and again, and especially in a place like this, all I want is to immerse myself in the depths of the sea, the multitudes of blue,' said Stella.

'Don't let me stop you.'

'Come in,' called Stella to Melody, waving to her.

Eventually, just as Stella accepted Melody wouldn't be joining them, she waded in and Stella caught the smudge of a purple bruise on Melody's thigh, and another on her upper arm but before she could look again, Melody took a plunge headfirst into an oncoming wave.

'Quite the mermaid,' said Eliana.

Melody pushed out of the water a few feet from where they were half-floating half-swimming. 'So good. I love swimming.'

'By far better than us two,' laughed Stella, as she floated on her back, riding the gentle waves as they tossed her up and down.

Melody took another plunge below the surface of the water, a gentle splash followed, and she disappeared again only to reappear a few metres further out. 'I'm going to swim to the raft.' She turned and disappeared, her arms and legs perfectly attune as she breast-stroked out to the floating raft a hundred metres away.

'I'm not going out any deeper,' said Eliana.

'Nor me,' said Stella. She twirled and turned, like a mermaid, and swam a few more feet, before turning back, her eyes laid on the shore. She swam back until the seabed had risen to meet her and then stood up, waded out; the water's edge now beckoned her more than its depths, enticed her back to the beach. Stella sat on the wet sand and looked out to sea; Melody was a tiny dot floating on the line of the blue ocean and the sky, her arms spread like peacock wings.

***

Stella dried off in minutes and brought the picnic over and laid it out on the beach, where they sat. Melody was dripping wet, the water droplets clung to the top of her head like a sparkling tiara. They ate the simple fayre packed for them, greedily and impatiently opening wrapped packages and bags to reveal black olives, thick slices of cheese and homemade spinach parcels, perfect triangles of deliciousness.

'There's even a bottle of wine,' said Eliana.

'Prodromos and Andri seem to be a couple so in love,' said Melody.

'Not seen Andri, but Prodromos seems so in love with her even after all these years,' said Stella. 'She must be an incredible woman.'

'I think she must be shy and her English, I'm guessing, might not be as good as Prodromos' if she hides away from the guests,' said Melody.

They tucked in and lay back, the sun licking at their bare skin, warming them, their skin glowing a soft pink.

'Probably... ouch,' said Stella.

'I got nipped too. Do you think there's little transparent insects in the sand?' Melody scratched at her ankles.

'Maybe. But they've only just appeared. It must be the food,' said Eliana.

'I think we should head back,' said Stella. I don't fancy walking back up covered in a hundred itchy bites,' she said, and Melody stopped to scratch at a fresh nip behind her knee.

'You're right. We can finish the food and the painting

round the pool now that we have our basic outlines done. I took photos too,' said Melody. 'And Luke... made me promise I wouldn't be too long.'

Eliana looked at Stella who shrugged her shoulders.

Stella brooded over why she would have had to make such a promise. It was obvious they were all together and not doing anything considered risqué... surely painting was allowed. Nothing untoward was planned or going to happen. She shook off a shiver and then considered if Anton had been here with her, he too would have at the very least asked what time she would be back.

'Dean didn't bother asking me. Things aren't so great between us,' said Eliana, to herself, but it hit a nerve with Stella. She fleetingly found herself brooding as to whether there would be a message from Anton when she got back.

After they quickly packed the art stuff, and the leftover picnic, they made their way back up to the top of the hill, the sun warming their backs. Stella turned to face the view one last time and then picked up her step to catch up with the others.

***

It was obvious to all; Dean hadn't missed Eliana. He was still at the bar, drinking with a couple of other guests. 'Luke couldn't keep up with us, he went for a siesta.'

Stella saw Eliana give Dean a hug.

'What's that for?' he asked. 'You're not after money again, are you?'

'Don't be like that, babe. Can't I give my man a kiss

hello after being away all day?'

'Of course, you can. Come here,' he said and drew her to him for a kiss.

She instantly pushed him away, the warmth of her initial contact gone. 'I'm going to head back and have a shower,' she said. 'Do you want to follow on or come now?'

'I'll come now. I've missed you,' said Dean, his comment genuine.

'Come on then.'

Eliana put her arm through his and they made their way back to their room. A distinct happiness seemed to explode in Stella's chest like a fresh flower in full bloom and she hoped the simple observation of their behaviour towards each other would iron out their toxicity. Had it really taken someone else to point out how they were towards each other for Eliana to notice it. And what about her own near non-existent relationship with Anton?

Chapter 12

Later that evening, the women, crowded round their cocktails at the pool bar, found their conversation meandering back to the afternoon's topic of Eliana and Dean's relationship.

'This might sound too sicky but this afternoon I didn't complain once about him wanting it,' said Eliana, quietly proud.

'And?' asked Stella.

'It was like a switch changed position. I wanted him.'

Melody stared; gobsmacked. 'No way, really?'

'I liked his usually annoying attention... and the sex wasn't bad either,' Eliana said, with a sing-song tempo, a mischievous glint in her eye.

'And, how about Dean? Did he notice?' asked Stella, not batting an eyelid, a boldness she didn't usually possess pushing her to ask. There was something about this place and the way it spilled treasure chests and revealed secrets.

'Dean said I should go to the beach without him more often.'

'I bet he did,' said Stella.

They all laughed. 'It was the paint fumes and all that sea air,' said Eliana playfully. 'I love Dean and he's a good man. Sex, for him, is a huge part of what a good relationship looks like. I think I understand him more. I've vowed to make it better between us. No more friction between us. It's getting boring, all our rows over sex.'

'Wow! Where did all that come from?' asked Stella, taking the juicy orange slice anchored on the rim of her glass and sucking on it. There was something about this place which got everyone loose lipped. She hoped she didn't start to give too much away.

'I find it hard after being in another…' Eliana changed her mind and stopped.

'Previous abusive relationship?' finished Stella.

Eliana eventually answered, 'Yes… for so long and the last thing I want is to push him away. I don't want to make the same mistakes my mum made either. I promised to try harder from now on and he promised to be more sympathetic to what I need and when I need it.'

'Such good news.'

'He also admitted he's too much like his dad. He called his dad a gruff old git and told me how his parents argued about everything. It was how their relationship worked.'

'Explains a lot,' said Melody.

'We made a pact to try to be nicer to each other. I do love him, but I don't always let it shine through.'

'And now?'

'I don't know if he's going to change. Or if I can. But at least we're going to give it a try, so thank you, both of you.'

'Amazing and brave and brilliant,' said Melody, tears pricking her eyes.

'To you and Dean and happier sex?' said Stella.

'Maybe,' said Eliana and the women clinked their glasses together. The sun, a huge, low-hanging gumdrop ball rested on the mountainside, dipped in slow motion, and then disappeared; a watery scape of a twilight afterglow tinged the huge cloudless sky.

Chapter 13

Late, the following morning, Stella grabbed her bag and mobile and wandered off towards the pool. As she approached, she spied a lone figure, bent over a magazine, silhouetted against the glare of mellow orange, the sun spreading across the sky like orange marmalade, glistening, sweet.

Stella, glad there was peace, she lay back and lathered the sun block in thick layers across her shoulders, arms, and legs, then wriggled around until she was in the right spot, her face in the shade, her body, and limbs in full sun. She closed her eyes and focused on her breathing. Listening to the heaves of her chest up and down as she breathed in and out, deep breath in, long breath out.

In the distance she could hear the rumble of a tractor or some sort of farm equipment, then came the hoot of a car as it sped along the mountainous road above, cut into the mountainside, which lead to the place she had found the handwritten note, or rather where the note had found her. As she sunk deeper into a warm sleep, she thought she heard the flurry of musical notes tinkling in the leaves of the fruit trees in the orchard the other side of the pool. The music a rainbow of colours touching her.

She woke feeling lightheaded and a little disorientated. 'Anton?' she faltered. She blinked her eyes open, and she shuffled further up the lounger, searching for him. She must have been dreaming.

'It's me, Yiannis. I have a message for you.' He handed her a small manilla envelope with the initial S and a kiss on the front of it.

She thanked Yiannis and as she took the note from him his fingers brushed hers leaving tingles like dancing pinpricks where they had touched. Fumbling for her sunglasses, she tore open the envelope. It was from Anton. He had decided to come after all "so as not to prolong the pain of the distance between us" he wrote and finished with "I miss you. See you soon." Her face crumpled and she wiped the tears with the back of her hand. He had made a promise and broken it. Why should she believe he would come now?

She was on her own. She felt suddenly small, alone, vulnerable. She took a deep breath and shook away the doubts and the overwhelming loneliness. I can do this, she told herself.

She sat very still, her mind racing, her heart beating a little too fast, until she willed it to slow, and she let out a quiet whoop. And then another. And then she screamed until she had no more breath in her.

'Stella are you okay?' asked Yiannis, who bounded

back over, his long curly hair flopping over his eyes as he bent over her, a little too close. And then it happened. She drew him to her and kissed him. She felt him freeze, for a split second and then he softened under her lips.

She drew back, panic filling her. Everyone, however far away, would have heard her. Had anyone seen her kiss Yiannis? She didn't care.

'Yiannis, I need you to come to my room,' she said, her words tumbling, her tongue unable to form the words fast enough. He seemed to have understood. His eyes did not leave hers, holding her gaze as if his life depended on it. 'Come in half an hour,' she said and before he could reply she disappeared, quickly, flip flops in one hand and her bag in the other, her steps light, as she ran all the way to her room.

It was a holiday fling. A breakup thing, she assured herself, now laughing uncontrollably as the rising burst of freedom broke from her like a caged bird escaping after years of confinement. She slammed the door behind her, her heart racing. What was she doing? She opened the bottle of wine bought in Fiskardo, the one she was saving to have with Anton. She took a slug, straight from the bottle, the burning a welcome sensation. She screamed again and then cupped her hand over her mouth as a giggle sprung forth like a hopping rabbit. Her heart racing. She knew what she wanted. She had no doubts. She hoped Yiannis would come.

She closed the bedroom shutters, sending the room into semi-darkness with a bang. She switched on the lamp and then, deciding it was too bright, a squabble of colours blinding her, flicked it off again. As she threw back the bedsheets, a knock at the door sent shivers through her. He was here. She hadn't had sex with anyone other than Anton since her thirties. But she had to do this; it was as if a lust-tipped arrow had pierced her heart, filled her with a tormenting longing. She had to break free, and this was the best place to do it. It was now or never. This romantic infatuation whispered to her more plainly than any words Anton could have shared.

She swung the door, stepped back to let him in, a sudden heat darkened his eyes. Part of her hoped no one saw him and yet at the same time she wanted the world to know she had not given up on herself, on her needs. Her breath hitched. Desire pooled in her belly, and she wooed him in, forgetting her modesty. She didn't recognise this impulsive woman.

Yiannis was a smooth and agile, yet clumsy lover, his lack of experience with women evident, but once their bodies melded together, there were no skewed lines, and she guided him, his hands, his lips, groping in the failing light. He made her feel like a goddess. She writhed in unison with him, the swell of new emotions strong and sweet. He slithered down the bed and nudged her legs apart as he buried his face into her. She clawed his back, swallowed his kisses as if she would die of thirst without them and then, spent, they both lay, limbs tangled, sheets twisted under them, as they puffed, their breaths coming in gasps.

'Stella,' he said, his strong, muscly arms outstretched.

She shook her head gently, put a finger to his lips. 'Don't talk,' she said, a clouded stern expression softened only by the tiniest flicker of a smile.

Lying there, under the noisy ceiling fan, she listened to the gentle rhythmic breathing of the young man next to her, a stranger. The light through the slats of the shutters lasered the last crimson gleam of incandescent sunshine beams across the ceiling and down the white-washed walls, across the end of the bed.

She heard the melodious song of a nightingale, and she listened intently as it grew louder and louder. She felt free, released. Her heart though was bruised and broken.

She shook off her sinking melancholy and turned towards him; a show of returning courage and passion. Her heart pounded in anticipation, in disbelief; her boldness surprising her, speaking a language she didn't recognise, had forgotten long ago. Yiannis, sensing her energy, in synchronicity, straddled her in one movement, intertwined his fingers with hers as he pushed her arms above her head, forcing her to rest them on the pillow.

They found their pulse, their beat and when she let out a cry of release, her hands twisting the sheets, a surprising lightness filling her head. He joined her and they both trembled into each other, their bodies wet with sweat, wet with bodily fluids, and wet with ecstasy. Her arms ached, her legs ached, her lips were sore from the kissing and clashing of teeth, but she relished the feeling. She needed to feel something other than hurt. She needed to feel alive, womanly, wanted.

Chapter 14

Two days later, Stella and Yiannis met again, this time late morning, almost getting caught out by the room service attendant, who had knocked and walked in without waiting for a response. Stella clutched the bed sheet around her and called out, 'No service today, thank you,' she giggled while wriggling her way out of Yiannis' embrace.

Yiannis nuzzled her neck with kisses and bit her shoulder, she cried out, a mixture of ecstatic release and longing. She bit down hard on her hand to stop her from alerting the room housekeeper of their presence and when she heard the door bang shut, let out a low moan. They drank fizzy water and Yiannis made mimosas with orange juice and generous measures of white wine. They gorged on the complimentary rusks and fruit for lunch, the crumbs filling the bed and the watermelon juice staining the sheets. Stella didn't care. She threw herself, with wanton abandonment, enjoying the energy and stamina of Yiannis's virile body.

'I must go,' he said eventually.

'If Prodromos says anything, I will tell him you kindly helped me out with something.'

'Thank you, now I must go,' he said, his T-shirt over his head in a flash and his trousers zipped. 'I can't give him fodder to doubt me. I rely on the money. I cannot lose this job. I have so much to prove, not only to myself but to those who have always believed in me when I didn't believe in myself.'

'Go, then. It's fine,' Stella said, not wanting to be needy.

'I will come back soon,' he said, his dark eyes, wide, boring into her.

'I may be going out later, but you might catch me,' she said with a cheeky lilt, yet loved knowing he was already seeking her out.

Stella showered. Her fingers stroked the red marks Yiannis' lips had left on her shoulder blade, on the side of her breast. She dried herself, threw on a pair of shorts, and shimmied into a halter-neck top. She picked up her laptop, grabbed an iced bottle of water from the mini fridge and wandered out onto the verandah where she sat down.

Her story, in reality and on the page, was taking shape and as she breathed in the fresh air, she felt a little twinge of guilt about Anton, but pushed it away like an unwelcome humming in her ears. Whether pride or simply trying to prove she wasn't tied to him any longer, she tried hard to stop thinking about Anton, yet her heart pulled her one way and then the other.

The nights, the black punctuated only by the silver slice of the moon, were for making love, and each time she fell into a fitful dreamlike sleep, images of her in bed; Yiannis on the one side and Anton on the other. She rolled over from one to the other and, filled with joy, faced each of them, yet there was a stench of disloyalty, her lips caked in salt, heavy with lies and half-truths.

Humiliation. Guilt. Pain.

She would wake up and take a shower until her legs ached from the standing. She rubbed at herself with the bar of olive-scented soap to wash herself of Yiannis and his smell, their lovemaking.

In the long stretched out days, continued to write her story… a story of a woman's identity and her battle with memory loss. It wasn't the story she had intended to write but the words kept coming, one word after another, a sentence, two sentences, three sentences, one paragraph followed by another until she had scene after scene and chapter after chapter on her laptop. It was as if all the years of being a mistress had been for this purpose; to write her next best-seller; raw, real, painful, yet with the release of a shining light.

And the story continued to unfold page after page, and she filled her laptop with hopes and dreams, with friends and lovers and dancing and music. Her writing gave her a new lease of life and she wrote with a manic urgency, hurried, rushing, not wanting the thoughts in her head to fade away. The more she wrote the more sex she wanted, the more sex she had the more she wrote.

The cycle became a writing aphrodisiac, she filled

her notebook, her pen moving freely, with sweeps and curves, an energy consumed her and her writing, filling her to the brim and then, repleted, she would refill overnight, after typing up her notes, and start over.

As it continued with Yiannis, she basked in the best sex she had experienced in a long time, new, frenzied, hurried, passionate... until, she realised, she only had four days left and she would be returning home. Returning to her publisher who would be looking for her draft and returning to her flat and a new life as a woman living on her terms for the first time in twenty years.

From a distance, hidden by the low branches of the lemon tree, weighed down with the juicy fat bounty of summer, Prodromos observed Yiannis as he left the English woman's room.

'I knew it would start with her,' he said, turning to Andri, certain she had followed him out to the grove; he could smell a hint of rose perfume, the one she always wore, over the zingy lemons.

She didn't answer, but nodded in agreement, and smiled her wide smile, full of love and it filled him, filled every part of him, until he had to look away, unable to express his love for her. Andri didn't like his tears, always waved them away, saying be happy always, don't waste your energy on lamenting, rejoice and fill your every pore, your every breath, your every heartbeat with happiness.

He looked back towards the lovers' hideout. 'They don't know it yet, but their lives are already changing. The wind whistles, the leaves stir on the trees, and deep beneath our feet the roots push down gasping for more water to sustain them, like a drug, they seek it just as these two seek it from each other.'

'Hope, purity and new beginnings,' whispered Andri.

Prodromos looked back and reached out his hand, to tuck a strand of hair, blowing across her face, behind her ear. He longingly stroked her face and she seemed to disappear, a watery image remaining.

The magic of this place is always here, it is never-fading, always renewing. The scent of lemons hung in the air, refreshing both body and mind, representing the beginning of something new. A goodness surrounded these trees, this place, and Prodromos hung onto it, relishing in its promise. A symbol of hope, happiness, and renewal.

'There is purity here,' he said, his voice shaking, thick with embers of emotion. 'A purity which only those who are worthy can be powerful enough to welcome it into their lives.'

Prodromos ducked behind the trunk of the tree, not wanting Yiannis to see him. He had to trust the magic would work in Yiannis' favour. He had to trust the magic would touch the woman in a way which released both these souls to each other; releasing pain and bringing joy. The joy of newfound love, trust, and happiness. The joy he had always had with Andri, a forever joy deep in his heart, which touched his bones.

Chapter 15

Stella tossed and turned, a veil of moonlight draping the bedroom in a tepid watery blue. A knock at the door, sent Stella's heart thumping.

She ran to the door and swung it wide.

'Anton.'

Heralding an indulgent gift box with Stella's favourite perfume and a bottle of champagne, Anton stood before her with a huge grin.

'I had no idea,' said Stella, afraid her disappointment was showing.

'I wanted to surprise you.'

'You've certainly done that.'

Their conversation was stilted. Thankfully, the journey had exhausted him, and the late hour induced him into sleep quickly.

But the gnawing guilt, the anxiety which enveloped Stella eventually enticed her out of bed. Careful not to wake him, she slipped on her shorts and a top printed with daisies. She draped her favourite crystals around her neck and sneaked out of the room.

It was barely light and the shadows from the lemon trees and the swooping swallows overhead sent a wonderfully soft, gloam to guide her path. Her heart was angry. Her heart was disappointed. Her ego was satisfied. He had come out all this way with only a few days to the end of the holiday. And he should. She was worth it, worth more than that. But she had no idea how this was all going to play out. Eventually, she sat on a wooden bench facing the mountain and gazed out as the sun rose high, a dazzling stain of yellow across the sky. Tears stung her eyes. *What should I do now?*

Eventually, she walked back, her eyes sore, her mouth dry and her stomach rumbling.

'You were gone a long time,' said Anton, pulling her to him and kissing her. 'You okay?'

'I forgot my sunglasses. The sun's so bright out there now,' she said, turning away from him lest he see her pools of tears.

'You should have woken me.'

'You were in such a deep sleep.' He hooked his fingers over the waistband of her shorts and tugged her closer still. He pressed against her with hunger; she felt his arousal. Stella released his fingers from her waist and stepped away, not sure how she felt, in the light of day. 'I'm not sure why you bothered Anton.'

'Don't be grouchy with me. I promised I would come, didn't I?'

'Yes, but…'

'Not quite the reaction I imagined.'

'Sorry…'

'Are you not pleased to see me?'

Stella looked away from him, pretending to study the art on the adjacent wall. 'Of course, I am. I told you last night, didn't I?' she said eventually, her heart beating fast at the lie.

Anton sat back and pushed into the two-seater sofa. 'This is a magnificent space, simple yet so inviting. I'm not disappointed. Not at all. Worth the long transfer here,' said Anton.

Did he really think it was okay to just turn up? And since when was it not okay? This was not how it was meant to be.

'You chose well. Thank you,' she said, shying away from him, suddenly unsure of the feelings playing inside her.

'It's lovely. It's more than lovely. It's beautiful.' Anton came up behind her and planted a row of kisses up and down her neck, his hot breath fanned over her skin sending shivers through her. 'God, you're gorgeous.'

'Stop it Anton, you're scratching me with your day-old stubble.'

'I remember when you used to like my bristle. You said it was sexy,' he said, lines crinkling his face, fanning around his eyes.

'Did I? Must be a long time ago. I don't remember.'

'A lifetime ago… I'll have a shave later.'

'It's fine, sorry. I wasn't expecting you.'

'I suppose I do have a sexy Adonis look about me.'

'Don't be too sure Anton. You're not a young man

anymore,' she teased, and he pulled her into a tight hug and kissed her.

He reached out for her hand and kissed it, nibbled her fingers gently and she giggled, but at the same time she shook off a shiver, her insides fizzing with pure joy and want.

In one swoop, he slipped off her top, and led her to the bedroom. Stella didn't hesitate. She followed him. He had taken his T-shirt off before they reached the bed, their shorts discarded at the foot of the bedstead.

'So, you little minx... enticing me into your lair,' he said, gently pulling her by the multi-strand necklace still adorning her neck. Breathless, he kissed her, cupped her breasts, grazed her nipples.

'I think it's you who enticed me,' she said, caught up in the headiness of the moment, and then she screamed, 'Oh, yeah, baby.' Her scream pierced the silence, and she hoped the panic she felt didn't carry with it. But Anton, it seemed, interpreted it as joyful.

Anton took her in his arms, the earth trembled as she convulsed with desire, and she in turn satisfied him. They fell in each other's arms, spent, and satisfied, their vivacious eyes shimmering with desire for each other, and gently drifted off, exhaustion and heat lulling them into a dreamy sleep.

***

Stella woke, filled with an unnerving shift in her love for the man lying next to her, his jarring snores echoing in her ears. Guilt crept over her, a prickling sensation like ants, running over her skin, and she feared where she might be heading.

Hot and sticky from their lovemaking she got up and wandered over to the kitchenette, where she opened a bottle of water and drank straight from the bottle.

'Good morning... again... you sexy, gorgeous woman. You'll be needing these,' said Anton, passing her sunglasses.

'*Kalimera*, good morning.'

'Did you sleep well?' he asked.

'I think I did. Yes. What time is it?' she asked, yawning. She sensed him stretching, stifling a yawn too, before putting his arms around her waist and nuzzling her neck with a kiss.

'Not sure. My phone's dead but I think it's early. There's no-one round the pool and there's wet puddles where someone's had a scrub at the slabs.' Anton remained behind her, and she could feel him peering over her shoulder in the same direction as her; towards the fig trees a few metres from their balcony, the waft of sweetness delicious, the big green leaves shining under the streams of light finding their way through the trees' heavy canopies.

'The pool looks heavenly this morning,' she said.

'We could go for a dip before breakfast,' he suggested.

'I think we have missed breakfast. But yes, to a dip then. I need it. I'm all sticky.'

'You are, are you?'

'Stop it, Anton,' she said, wriggling free from his embrace.

'That's why we've paid over the odds to stay at an

adult-only resort. We don't have to fight with the belly-flopping screeching kids and their show-off dads. It will be quiet.'

'That's such a generalisation,' Stella said, rolling her eyes in an exaggerated manner.

'But true. I'm looking forward to the quiet and peace and relaxing.'

'I'm jumping in for a quick shower and then I think we should go for a dip before something to eat. And we don't want to miss Prodromos' famous breakfast feast.'

'Don't worry about the time Stella. We're here to get away from the ties of the ticking clock.'

'Time… such a constraint on life… on everything really,' she whispered.

'But we have all the time we want here. Let's enjoy it. Let's focus on each other,' he said.

She shimmied back into the bedroom, not caring the open doors were like a camera lens on her to anyone watching.

She didn't plan to do it. She just needed him. She let her negligee fall to the floor, a puddle of blue silk pooled around her feet like a glistening ocean. She stood for a split second like the Statue of the Naked Lady at Henley's Corner back home, waiting for Anton's reaction. In the distance, from behind a huge, lush palm, two eyes were watching.

'You look like an angel with your blue eyes and sun-bleached hair. Come here…' he beckoned to her. She swept across to him. He sat on the bed, adjusting the plump pillow behind him, one hand under his boxer shorts rubbing at his obvious excitement.

Stella laughed. 'I'm no angel Anton Bowen and you know it.' She winked at him and smiled her sexy smile; the one she knew weakened him instantly into a schoolchild sucking on a gobstopper. She walked across the room swaying her naked bottom. She disappeared into the bathroom, leaving the door slightly ajar on purpose… he can look at me from a distance, she thought.

She knew how to play him. She knew every button to press, and she always did it exactly right. How else would they have remained lovers for so long? But for a split second she wondered whether this might be the last time they would be like this together. *The first and the last.*

Anton pushed the bathroom door open. He ran his eyes over her from the doorway and she turned away from him, but not before she glimpsed him swallow her up with a deep longing. He had a way of taking her whole; her full, voluptuous figure, her physical body being devoured with his eyes. She turned around trying to hide the scars on her otherwise perfectly unblemished belly, but Anton turned her round to face him.

'God, I can't resist you, you're so gorgeous. More gorgeous than ever, you know that?'

'No. Tell me. I need to know. I need to know you still want me Anton…' she said, confusion knotting her heart as she thought about Yiannis, about their lovemaking. She knew she wasn't being fair but none of this was fair.

Stella lost the energy to stand and slumped down onto the cool marble tiles of the shower enclosure. She revelled in the fresh, splash of the soft water as it run over her like a silk scarf. She had her eyes closed and quietly congratulated herself on being manipulative of Anton's desires. Maybe things between them weren't as bad as she had begun to fear. He was here with her and not at home with his wife. The first time she had ever been abroad with him. That had to count for something. Yiannis was a fling. That's all.

Chapter 16

'Hello,' said Stella, recognising Eliana even though she was lying on her front. 'Mind if I join you?'

'Hi,' said Eliana, twisting round onto her back, holding onto her bikini top which she had undone to avoid strap marks. She tied it up, took off her sunglasses and positioned them with precision on her head.

'On your own?'

'Dean was complaining it was too hot. Then we rowed because I wouldn't go back to our room with him after breakfast.'

'The heat can be draining, can't it?'

'Correction. Dean can be draining,' said Eliana.

'Things okay between you?'

'Things are always like this. It's how we are. I don't think anything will ever change.'

'Don't you ever want something different?'

'What do you mean? How?'

'Something less conflicting?' said Stella.

'This is us. It might not look great from the outside but from the inside, from here, as Dean says,' she said tapping her heart, 'it's good. I don't think there's anything wrong with the way we are, the way he is. If it changes, then there's no us left.'

'Glad you made up,' said Stella. 'Anton's turned up. Out the blue. No message.'

'No way. And?'

'And nothing. It's the holiday we planned but we're starting a few days late.'

'Quite romantic, him swooning in like Romeo.'

'I guess so. Yes. Right, I'm going for a dip,' said Stella, not sure what to say. She executed a perfect dive into the pool and swam underwater across the width of the pool until she came up at the other side.

'You're a great swimmer,' clapped Eliana, when Stella swam back and forth a couple of times and then climbed out of the water in front of their sunbeds. She grabbed the bright pink towel and patted herself dry.

Stella proceeded to rub sun lotion onto her legs and abdomen and then her arms. 'Thanks.'

'Where is Anton then?'

'I've left him snoring. Men, eh?'

'Dean guessed you weren't married. No ring on your wedding finger. Though not everyone wears one nowadays,' she said, pointing to her own ring-less finger.

Stella hesitated. 'Feels like it though… we've been together a long time.'

'Dean and I have been together thirteen years. Married for five. But you look like the marrying type.'

'What does the marrying type look like?'

'You know, settled, happy, connected…'

'We were, I mean are, all of those things,' said Stella.

'I sense a but…'

Stella hesitated and then throwing caution to the wind, said, 'Anton has a wife. So, marriage is not an option.'

'He might think him being committed elsewhere, being married, works for you. No commitment. No constraints,' said Eliana.

'I suppose so,' said Stella.

'If it's lasted. I'm not going to judge.'

'It works. Changing it would spoil what we have.'

'I would never have guessed that about you. How did you meet?'

'At my first ever book signing. He was there with his wife. She had dragged him along fighting and kicking, he's not a reader. They arrived late; interrupted my reading, which I was so nervous about. I remember looking up, hardly noticing him, annoyed for stopping my flow. After the reading, she bounced over with her copy of "Marriage Vows Broken" and talked her way into getting an invitation to the after party, which he took advantage of, free-flowing Prosecco and posh finger food.

A call from the sitter, they have a son, all grown up now, dragged her away, leaving him behind. We got talking, I was high on the attention from all the media and literary critics there, I got overwhelmed, we sneaked off, we got drunk…' she stopped talking as Yiannis approached with a metal tray and two tall glasses.

'Ladies,' said Yiannis. '*Lemonada*, freshly made, with

a dash of raki, with Prodromos' best wishes.'

'So sweet, thank you,' chirruped Eliana.

'Thank you,' said Stella, a strawberry blush creeping across her decolletage and up her neck, as she too almost fell out of her bikini top. 'Damn,' she blurted, taking a sip, trying not to look at Yiannis.

'The best lemonade I've ever tasted,' said Eliana.

'Please send our thanks to him,' Stella said, more composed than she felt in his presence. Stella chinked her glass against Eliana's and swirled the zesty yellow liquid expertly, coating the sides, taking in its scent.

'What were we saying?'

'How I met Anton,' said Stella, stirring her drink with the paper straw, looking round to see if Yiannis was close enough to hear their conversation.

'A proper *Mills and Boon* story,' said Eliana. 'Cheers.'

'I guess so,' said Stella, taking a long swig of the cool drink, the fast-melting ice cubes tinkling against the rim of the glass. Her second novel, *When an Affair is Forever* was based on her own illicit relationship and both stories had stood the test of time, both best sellers in over eighteen different countries.

'So, you were the author?' said Eliana, as if Stella's account of how they meet had only just fallen into place for her.

'Yes,' said Stella, as she dragged on her cigarette, tingling with the nicotine rush.

'O.M.G. Your book? Your reading?' Eliana jumped up and whooped. 'Still can't quite believe I've met a real author. A real author.' Stella blushed at Eliana's obvious awe and excitement. 'I'll have to look up your books when we get back home.'

Stella chose not to reveal her author pseudonym. The last thing she needed was a PR disaster or media scandal. She had said too much, her tongue loosened by the warmth of the sun and the complimentary boozy afternoon drink.

'Why don't you ever pick up your phone?' cut in Dean.

'Because I'm having a chat with a real author,' said Eliana, tossing her long ponytail over her shoulder and rolling her eyes. 'Stella is the real deal.'

'Hi, Dean,' said Stella, crushing her cigarette in the metal ashtray.

'Hi. She won't stop going on about you now, you do know that.'

'Good siesta, babe?' asked Eliana but Dean ignored her and made busy repositioning one of the loungers under the sun umbrella.

'Stroppy git,' said Eliana.

'I can hear you,' he called across the ten-foot space between them.

'Good. At least you're not deaf,' she said, taking a slurp of her lemonade.

Chapter 17

She couldn't wait to shower and after, clad in her bikini, she took out her laptop, an urgency to write coming at her which she had not felt in a long time. She wanted to capture the feeling in her, her despondency giving way to excitement. There was a story here in this out-of-the-way place. She could feel it and she wanted to harness the inspiration.

Her writing was taking her attention away from Anton and she welcomed it, liberating her from the shackles she had allowed to tighten around her these past years.

She tapped away, the whirr of the ceiling fan, pushing warm air around the room, offering little relief and unaware of the time passing until she noticed the time on her screen; she had been working for two hours. She had totally lost herself in the story pouring out of her like water from a mountain crevice; full of energy and clarity, love, and hope. This was going to turn out to be the best inspiration and the most she had experienced in a long time. This was sure to be the start of her next best seller.

She pondered over the words best seller and felt a tug at her heartstrings. She had never gone into the world of writing to be an award-winning author but her first story had grabbed the attention of an industry professional and since then, now almost seven years ago, she was writing to a schedule, and she wasn't sure she liked it. Gone were the days of writing for herself. For her own enjoyment and reward. Now it was all word counts and deadlines, writing to market, editing, and marketing. She didn't like it.

She pushed her laptop to the side and stretched. She thought about whether any of the other couples would be round the pool. She was hot and needed to stretch; a few laps of the pool would cool her down and soothe her aching bones. Either it was the freedom of not having to clock watch or the freedom of being away, but Anton had been particularly agile in his lovemaking. She stepped out onto the balcony and saw Eliana already soaking up the sun, relaxing on her lounger. Grabbing her beach bag, mobile phone and suncream, she left a message for Anton and exited the room. This time it would be him waking up on his own in bed with a scribbled note for company.

She felt strange walking away from him when all along all she had ever wanted was to wake up beside him and be together.

Chapter 18

Stella was already at the pool side propped under the shade with her laptop. Melody was busy setting up with her easel. Stella smiled when she saw her screwing her face up in concentration as she painted, the tubes of oil paint scattered across the sun lounger next to her.

It was mid-morning before Eliana made it to the pool. 'You started early,' said Eliana, assessing the progress Melody had made with her painting.

'Yeah. Prodromos printed up my photos so I can get a clearer idea of the colours.'

'Great idea,' said Eliana, lining her colours along the easel's sill: Burnt Umber, Payne Grey, Prussian Blue, India Red and Linen White. 'He's such a generous host. Honestly, this place has been amazing,' said Melody.

'It's been wonderful so far,' said Stella, looking up from her laptop. 'Nothing is too much for him. The real hospitality of Greece oozing from his every pore. Unlike any other you'll find.'

'You're right,' said Melody. 'Go and get your pics printed,' she said to Eliana. 'I'm sure he won't mind, and I did mention it to him. He'll be expecting you.'

'Thanks, I will,' said Eliana.

Back within a few minutes, Eliana announced, 'I had another chat with Dean last night. We sat, in the dark, on the balcony and talked into the early hours as we both witnessed the most beautiful of sun rises.'

'That's the one thing I was looking forward to this holiday… catching the glorious sunrises, the early morning dew on the grass sparkling like scattered diamonds.'

'The view seemed to calm us,' said Eliana.

'Oh, yeah?' said Stella, her ears pricking up.

'You know, the way we are with each other. We talked, a bit, well, a lot and I told him what you said.'

'Again?'

'No, not about the sex. About us bickering, always at each other.'

'Sorry. I didn't mean to criticise. It was an observation.'

'That's okay.'

'Sometimes we're too close to something to notice it, to see what's going on,' said Stella.

'And? What did he say?'

'We're going to try and be nicer to each other,' Eliana said.

'The hashtag #kindnessmatters is always making its way around social media so that's a good place to start. I'm really pleased for you, Eliana. I really am.'

'Me too,' said Melody. 'It's good to sort things out and

there's nothing like a holiday to get everything out in the air, to have the time to talk properly.'

'Thank you. And sorry. For making it awkward,' said Eliana.

'Don't worry about it. We're on holiday. It's not like we're stuck here forever, but it does get a bit cringey sometimes.'

'You're being nice now, but anyway we are going to start anew. This place has really opened my eyes and I hope it has his too. But he really does have to stop eating all the time and do more exercise.' Stella noted how their conversation seemed to have made no difference to Eliana's attitude.

'Thought things were changing?'

'Oh yeah,' said Eliana and Melody rolled her eyes.

'Somehow I don't think you're going to change anything,' said Melody and Eliana bristled. Perhaps she was too far set in her ways to change. Perhaps this is how she was. And that's how he was too.

They painted for a couple of hours and stood back to marvel at each other's masterpieces.

'You are amazing. Look at the reflection on the water. You've captured that perfectly.'

'Thanks. Eliana. Not bad for someone who doesn't have much confidence.'

'It's brilliant. Don't underestimate yourself.'

'And yours is good too. Look at those boats. They're jumping off the page.'

'It's been good painting out here.'

'We should do a mountain landscape next. Are you up for it?'

'I am.'

'Me too,' said Dean. 'I'm always up for it.'

Eliana and Melody burst out laughing, tears streaming down their faces, Melody doubled over on the lounger.

'Say no more,' Eliana eventually managed to say through a hearty bark of laughter.

'Say no more,' giggled Melody.

'Have you two been drinking cocktails again?' Dean asked.

And they both fell about unable to control themselves, until eventually Eliana said, 'So much for in with the new!' and it sent them both into raucous glee again.

'What are you all laughing at?' Luke came up behind Dean. 'Didn't realise painting was this much fun.'

'Is it too early for a beer?'

'Na,' said Luke. 'But need something inside me first.'

'You missed breakfast,' said Melody. 'But I saved you a couple of rolls and some cheese.' She took out a napkin and unrolling it thrust the package towards him.

'Looks a bit sad, but thanks anyway,' Luke said.

'I'm sure Prodromos will rustle something up for us. An omelette or toastie. That'll line our stomachs alright,' said Dean. 'We don't need much.' He tapped his protruding belly with pride.

'You need food more than you care to admit. Food's all you think about,' said Eliana.

'And sex. Don't forget the sex. I can't help it if you make me horny every time, I'm with you.'

'The only thing you can be sure of getting is the food because Prodromos is a good guy, as for the sex you can bog off. One-bloody-track mind,' said Eliana and this time she rolled her eyes at Melody, but Melody didn't join in her laughter.

'What's up?'

'You're arguing again.'

'We're not arguing. It's banter, as the kids say.'

'Whatever, Eliana. But you two aren't going to change, are you?'

'Maybe not. But we're okay like this.'

'As long as you are,' said Melody, an uncertain look on her face.

'You're a bit hyper-sensitive.'

'Maybe.'

'We are fine, honestly. Now let's get this put away and we can get tanning.'

'I think I might continue for a bit. The Summer Art Competition is coming up and I would like to enter this. Do you think it will be good enough?'

'Are you joking? It's brilliant. You're good you know.'

'If you win one of the prizes, we will all go out to celebrate,' said Dean.

'You hit on my wife?' asked Luke, his eyes blazing.

'No, course he's not,' said Eliana, jumping in to defend Dean.

Dean scoffed and walked away. 'What's eating him?' Stella heard him mutter as Eliana dragged him away, obvious she didn't want to create a scene.

'For God's sake, Dean. Keep your gob shut.'

'Be quiet woman. Let me say what I want. Telling me to shut up. No, I won't.'

Stella watched them as they continued to argue, Dean spitting feathers and Eliana getting self-assertive, yet

obvious they were a solid couple ready to stick up for
each other when the situation needed it.

Chapter 19

Stella hogged two sun beds on the far side of the pool, closest to the Spa Bar. Her morning of writing, bent over the laptop had strained her shoulders and neck. She slipped off her kaftan and flip flops and dived into the pool.

'Perfect dive,' said Anton. He dived in behind her and burst out of the water, his face almost touching hers.

'Thank you,' she said. 'That water feels so good against my shoulders.'

Stella turned away. She swam a few lengths of the pool until her breathing became laboured and she pushed out of the pool; she was fit and strong and liked the shape her body was now she had put some weight back on after losing too much a few months before.

'Looks like it's going to be busy round here this afternoon,' Anton said, pointing towards the collection of sun loungers. Most were taken up; some with sun-tanned bodies and others marked out as being occupied with beach towels, flip flops and empty beach bags piled on them.

'I guess so.'

'Would have preferred to have you all to myself,' he said, his eyes taking in her body greedily.

'No chance! I will have to introduce you to Eliana and Dean and Melody and Luke… you'll like them.'

Anton raised his eyebrows. 'Made friends already?'

'It's not so big here and there's only one pool so, yeah, I reckon so. They checked in on the same night.'

'Right.'

'They seemed nice,' said Stella, though she felt a stab of annoyance at having to justify her new friendships.

'Am I not enough for you? I was hoping we could be alone together. Make the most of it.'

'Of course, you are, but we don't want to come across as unsocial.'

'We don't want to get to know them too well,' he said, pulling her in for a kiss. 'I want you to myself.' Stella smiled, then furrowed her brows in concentration. 'You okay? You look thoughtful.'

'Just remembered something. Did you hear music this morning?' asked Stella.

'Music? No can't say I did.'

'It was Greek, I think, kind of romantic… happy but sad at the same time.'

'I definitely didn't hear any music.'

'No?'

'No. Unless it was a radio, and someone switched it off.'

'I don't think so. I could hear it the whole time. It was like a twinkling on the breeze like… like wind-chimes, soft, gentle, joyful metal, but exciting too. Like a sweet fairy. Do you think they have fairies on the island?'

'Sounds perfect. Just like you, my gorgeous Stella.' Anton gave her a cheeky grin and pinched her bottom.

Stella wasted no time in introducing the friends to Anton. He made polite conversation, laughed at Dean's joke about Anton not being able to keep away and put up with Eliana teasing Dean about how much food he stuffed down at lunch.

Then, obvious to Stella but not the others, unable to extend his patience any longer, Anton took Stella by the hand and lead her along the semi-shaded walkway back towards their room.

***

Anton pushed open the wooden shutters and unlatched them, the doors flung open onto the balcony. Light flooded the room, letting in the hot afternoon. Stella kicked off her diamond-studded flip-flops and threw herself onto the bed. She closed her eyes and stretched her arms above her head.

'I ate too much. I feel uncomfortable.'

'Hard not to, the food's delicious.'

'Sun too much for you?' said Stella, knowing the answer already.

'There's no way I could have been around the pool with them all today. Glad we're going out exploring,' said Anton.

'Didn't you like them?' she teased.

'I'm not here to make friends. I'm here to be with you,' he said.

'Even though the other women were slimmer than me?'

'Don't be silly. You're gorgeous. And anyway, did you see Melody and those hairy armpits. Must be one of those natural hippy girls.'

'What were you doing looking at her?'

'You could hardly miss the bushes under her arms.'

'I know, but she's sweet.'

'Luke seemed like a nice guy. Quiet but chatty.'

'A bit different to Dean. He's like a bull in a China shop. What was he saying about the back doors. I didn't get what he was going on about.'

'You don't want to know.'

'So, he was being dirty?'

'Yeah.'

'How embarrassing. Eliana didn't seem to mind, did she?'

'She's used to it. He said they've been together for thirteen years.'

'He wouldn't get past one with me.'

'Well, he's not with you. I am and nothing's gonna change on that score. I promise.'

He walked over to her and stared into her eyes, and planted a long, deep kiss on her lips.

'Right. Let's get organised if we're going out. We don't want to be out in the middle of the afternoon. It'll be far too hot, and we'll burn however much sun cream we plaster on.'

'Okay. Loo and then I'm ready.'

She lay on the bed and closed her eyes again. Within seconds she could hear the music... the same music she had heard during breakfast. She jumped up and went out onto the balcony. She leaned onto the wooden balustrade and leant out towards the openness of the hotel grounds. She strained her ears and her eyes. She could see nothing to suggest someone was playing it. She rolled her shoulders back and felt a prickle on the back of her neck. She pushed her hand under her long hair to rub at it.

'Ready?'

'Can you hear the music now Anton?'

He stopped still and quietened his breathing. 'No.'

'There, now...'

'No, I can't.'

Chapter 20

Even with Anton here now, Stella kept thinking about Yiannis, their bodies entwined, her bare skin up against Yiannis' lean, muscular back, her arms tight around his waist. She had to deal with it and work out what to do.

Prodromos promised to cook a special meal to honour Prodromos's name day. She could not avoid going with Anton and part of her dreaded seeing Yiannis and worried about his reaction to seeing her with Anton. Stella had avoided Yiannis since Anton's arrival. She knew she had deceived them both; at the celebration evening she would be unable to avoid Yiannis any longer.

'It will be a meal fit for the gods,' Prodromos sang. 'You are all invited.'

'Where there's food, and something to sup on, you can count me in,' Dean said.

A chorus of thank yous filled the air and a group of twenty somethings cheered, 'Will there be alcohol?'

Later that evening, Stella and Anton joined Eliana and Dean and Melody and Luke as they gathered by the pool bar for a round of pre-dinner drinks. Dressed up for a night of celebration, the men in summer shirts and the women in pretty summer dresses, Stella looked forward to being showered with Prodromos' warm hospitality. The air was electric, and Stella, though ecstatically joyful on the outside, fought a mixture of nerves and guilty emotions as she caught sight of Yiannis. She gave him a smile, and he beamed back at her, but his smile didn't reach his eyes. His eyes were fixed on Anton's proximity to her; Anton's arm brushing hers as he commented on the smells already wafting into the open air from the kitchen's tiny open window, their mouths salivating, licking their lips.

Her attention was diverted by a smattering of early-bird diners, who, dressed up to the nines were planning their night out, having already finished their meals. They called goodnight to Yiannis and Prodromos and noisily chatted about the club they would be dancing the night away in. Stella suddenly wanted to be away from the obvious excitement but continued to listen as the conversation buzzed around her.

'Glad we're not in England. Nothing but rain,' said Eliana. 'The dog walker said Moscow was covered in mud after his walk, stuck to his fur like clay. Look.' She passed round her mobile with a snapshot of her beloved dog.

'He's getting more exercise than I am,' said Dean.

'The walk around Fiskardo was most enjoyable. Nice bars and restaurants. You can always go for another stroll. It's not too far from here if you want the exercise. Prodromos' recommendations were perfect,' said Stella. Yiannis hovered, and she wondered if he was going to say anything.

'Were they now?' said Dean, squaring his shoulders, puffing out his chest in bravado. Stella's heart filled her mouth.

'One track mind,' said Eliana, and she gave Stella a reassuring look.

Stella looked away hoping they didn't notice her blushing. Yiannis passed by, brushing her arm gently, as if unaware she had male company, or perhaps this was a game, something he did with all the vulnerable females who came to Miramare. She sipped at her cocktail; a speciality drink prepared by Yiannis, the Raspberry Ouzo Slush, matching her cheeks which shone out under her already golden tan.

'To one track minds,' said Dean and he raised his glass in a toast. They all chinked their glasses as Prodromos waved them over to take their seats. Anton, slipped his arm around Stella's waist, guiding her to the beautifully set table but Stella caught Yiannis staring, a rising heat filled her like hot caramel sauce and prickled the skin along her arms.

'I forgot my drink on the table,' said Stella a moment later, moving away from Anton. Stella hung back a little hoping to catch Yiannis alone, but he had moved to the next table, busy serving them. She wanted to explain. She wanted him to know what happened between them wasn't a mistake. It had been perfect, was perfect, and she was confused and unsure of how to move forward.

She never meant it to be like this; Yiannis and Anton in the same space. Yiannis and Anton both in her heart at the same time, both pulling and reshaping every cell in her body.

The round table, covered in breezy linen, had been moved under the arbour heavy with grapevines, lanterns hung intermittently from the rafters creating a warm, romantic glow. The area looked dreamy in the soft lighting and the setting was perfect. Fat waxy buds and bright pink blooms filled an ancient earthenware vase in the table's centre and the glasses sparkled in the orange glow of the lit candles. Small plates filled with dips, beans and roasted vegetables scattered the white tablecloths and threw up the most evocative smells; garlic and lemon, fresh coriander, and parsley.

'*Kopiaste, elate*,' said Prodromos as he welcomed his guests to sit.

'Smells delicious,' said Stella. 'Thank you so much.'

'My Name Day, the day we celebrate Saint Prodromos. We honour our Name Day in Greece rather than our birthday. This is a day where all the Prodromoses thank everyone. I am grateful to so many for their love and for being in my life.'

'The thanks are ours,' said Stella. 'This is incredibly generous.'

Dean seized a chair, pulled it out and Melody sat down. Luke almost pushed past him to sit next to her and Stella sat on her other side. Dean and Eliana took the last two seats between Stella and Luke. With everyone sitting, Prodromos brought out two carafes of red wine and two baskets of bread.

'Round tables are so much more conducive to good conservation,' said Stella.

'Oh yes, and the bread looks good,' said Dean diving in. 'No butter then?'

'Stop it. You're so embarrassing, babe. Why do you have to be the first one to eat?'

'That's what it's here for, darling,' he said, biting into the crusty bread and scattering sesame seeds onto his front.

Eliana ignored him. She picked up the basket and handed it round to everyone in turn, before taking a chunk herself.

'Let me,' offered Anton, pouring the red wine into everyone's glass. 'A toast,' he said, hesitating. Prodromos had disappeared into the kitchens. Anton waited for him. He returned with an empty glass and Anton filled it. 'To our host and to us. Happy holidays.'

'To Prodromos,' they cheered. 'To us and happy holidays,' they all chimed, chinking their glasses. Melody spilled hers as Dean tapped his against hers a little too enthusiastically.

'Drunk already, Melody?' asked Dean, as he took a swig.

'She's fine,' said Luke, answering for her.

Melody looked embarrassed, her cheeks bursting into hot flames.

'Wait till we start playing footsy under the table,' winked Dean, laughing too loudly.

'Enough, Dean,' said Eliana as she elbowed him. 'You're not funny, babe.'

Everyone laughed, as Prodromos urged them to eat the

traditional Kefalonian cod pie, wrapped in home-made filo pastry, rice and fresh herbs accompanied by a side of *horta*, locally collected greens, and served with *aliada*, a garlic dip.

Melody seemed to curl in on herself and Luke sat with tight lips, his back ramrod straight against the back of the chair. Stella sensed Luke's possessiveness but couldn't work out what the source of it was. Melody was lovely but plain, not exactly a sexy bombshell. She hardly looked the type he would need to keep the ball and chain on.

As the evening wore on, the wine flowed, and inhibitions were lost. Dean was a great, if not gauche raconteur, confident, bold, a bit too risqué with some of his comments, but entertaining all the same. 'So, if you didn't need to wear glasses would you wear them?' asked Dean.

Eliana rolled her eyes. 'What are you talking about?'

'Glasses? Would you wear them if you didn't need to?'

'Obviously not,' said Eliana, shaking her head.

'Then why do you bother wearing a bra?' he said, peering over at Stella.

'You're such an idiot. Seriously,' said Eliana and she pushed her chair back and stormed off.

'Always making a drama out of everything,' Dean shouted after her, but shrugged his chin down into the open collar of his shirt.

Everyone else looked embarrassed and the jovial banter of a few moments before fell away and his comment landed like a wet slimy octopus in the middle of their table.

'I'll go check on her,' said Stella, already taking the napkin from her lap. She scrunched it up and dumped it by her plate. She studied Dean, toyed with reasons for the perverse pleasure he got out of being cruel.

'I'll come with you,' said Melody, pulling her arm away from Luke who had already clasped it to stop her from leaving the table. 'We'll be back in a bit,' she said, tugging her arm free, frowning at Luke.

'He's such an idiot,' said Eliana when Stella and Melody caught up with her on the other side of the pool. 'So much for sorting things out.'

'He's had a bit too much to drink,' said Stella, joining Eliana on the lounger.

'No, he's always like that. Likes to embarrass me. Makes him look like the big shot. He loves all the attention.'

'Men all have their pet fails,' said Stella.

'At least you don't have to put up with their rubbish,' said Eliana.

'Don't judge a book by its cover,' said Stella.

'Aww, that's a good one coming from an author,' said Melody, sitting opposite them. 'Still can't believe I'm here with you. Two of my favourite books are yours. If I had them with me, you could have signed them.' Stella laughed, a nervousness catching in her throat. Melody had worked out who she was, despite using a pseudonym.

'Not so funny, really,' said Stella, wondering whether to tell them, and then jumping right in with, 'Anton arrived out here later than me because something came up.'

'Something came up?' said Eliana.

'What came up which he couldn't put off?' asked Melody.

'His wife.' Melody and Eliana looked at each other and then back at Stella. Their intense expressions said it all. 'We've been lovers for twenty years. This is strictly between us, right?' The papers would have their biggest front-page story if they knew.

'Bloody hell, Stella. All those years? Longer than some people stay married.' Stella stared at Eliana. 'Me and my big mouth. Totally insensitive of me, sorry.'

'You're right and this was going to be our first holiday together.'

'This gets better and better,' said Eliana. 'And you thought I had problems.'

'Or it just gets worse,' said Melody. 'What about finding someone who can love you all the time, with all of himself?' asked Melody. 'Don't you deserve that?' and as she uttered the words, Stella stared over at Yiannis at the bar, a metal cocktail shaker in hand, his biceps pushing against his tight T-shirt sleeves, and she tingled with lusty anticipation.

'You don't exactly look happy,' said Eliana, moving the conversation to Melody. Stella noticed how she did this to save her from any more interrogation and quietly thanks her under her breath.

'Look, we've come here to see if you're okay,' said Melody, not taking the bait. 'Not to talk about me.'

'Yeah, sorry. I'm fine. Honestly. He got to me in that second,' said Eliana.

'Guessing you love him, or you wouldn't put up with all his, dare I say, vulgar comments,' said Melody.

'Let's not start about love. Did you know the Greeks have got love right? They have seven different words for love, and they all mean something and represent something different between people.'

'Go on, then. What are they?' asked Eliana.

'Well, there's *eros*. The kind of love you have, full of passion and scalding sex and wild desire. The kind that has you shaking and breaking out in a sweat.'

'Everyone has that at first, well that's what you imagine anyway. Swoony love, lusty love,' said Melody, with a wistfulness in her voice.

'Then there's *philia*. Love between friends, loyal and kind, patient and understanding. It's a soul-to-soul bond. It's a calmer love, more settled, intimate.'

'That's me and Anne,' said Eliana. 'I've known her since school, and we get each other. No need for explanations or justifications.'

'Then there's the love you would see between a parent and their child. The love the Greeks called *storge*.'

'Pretty clever the Greeks. With their civilisations and democracy, medicine, the Olympics, geometry.' said Melody. 'We studied the Greeks at school with the children. Always a great topic.'

'And here we are,' said Stella, 'Talking about love on the most enchanting Greek island.'

'Love and food. Shall we go back and join them. I'm still hungry,' said Melody.

'And I want another cocktail,' said Stella.

'Yes, let's go and eat and be merry,' said Eliana and they all hugged.

Chapter 21

After an early breakfast, Stella gathered her things, including her notebook and pen and took a walk, making sure she had her closed canvas shoes on.

'Why don't you wait for me to come with you? The Zoom call won't take long but it's important,' said Anton, opening his laptop, waiting for it to connect to the internet.

'Because I'm on holiday and I spend more than half my life at home waiting for you. I don't want to do that here too. This was meant to be our time together.'

'It's one hour.'

'And I will be back in an hour.'

'It's okay for you to write but not okay for me to take one blasted Zoom call?' said Anton, running his hand through his hair, deep lines etched on his face, frown lines marking his brow.

'It's not about that. What's the difference if I wait here

or go off?' said Stella, swatting a mosquito away. It was more than the gnat irritating her.

'Why don't you sunbathe round the pool. I'll come and find you as soon as I'm done.'

She didn't feel like sun-bathing, the heat blistering, humid, and decided to take the less-travelled path Prodromos had marked on her map. It led from behind the hotel and its little lemon orchard all the way around the base of the mountain and to a hilltop overlooking a heart-shaped alcove.

The climb was steep, and Stella stopped intermittently to drink from her water bottle, letting the water dribble down onto her chest to cool herself. As she climbed, she recognised the swooping bird above as a golden eagle, its lighter golden-brown plumage a giveaway. She sat for a moment on a rock, small mauve flowers and white flora busily blooming in the cracks. A butterfly silently fluttered by, its cerulean wings, like silk, shimmering in the sunlight. She couldn't tear her eyes away from it; so delicate. She jumped as a shade-loving lizard scurried across the rock's top and darted into a crevice, and chirping coal tits began singing to her, as Prodromos had predicted.

When she reached the top, the view was too magnificent for words, taking her breath away for a second, stunning beyond even her writer's imagination. The horizon stretched on and on... wide and open, in contrast to the mountains behind her. She drew on the view, filling herself with strength and perseverance. She had to face the challenges in her life. Suddenly frantic, a rush of something shaking her insides, she took another breath and focused.

Here.
Now.
Right this second.

On one side, looking more closely, a row of dwellings, two-houses, and three-houses deep, lined the bay; painted an array of soft hues: crisp white, washed-out sienna, peony rose and lemon yellow. Their terracotta roofs hot under the scorching sun and where the bougainvillea cascaded over the front walls and around the windows, a splash of panache pink burst out. On the other, like tiny moving pinpricks, locals had gathered on the beach, sitting in the shade of the towering black firs, or cooling down in the calm aquamarine waters. In the distance the yachts of the rich and famous bobbed on the watery horizon, the sparkling depths of the waters reflecting the day's effervescent glow, not a single floating cloud in the sky.

The air was clear. The blue of the sea, crested with the whites of the soft unfurling waves as they rolled gently across the white sandy beach, played out below her as if she were watching a film. She tried to recall the beach scene in Captain Corelli's Mandolin, a film she had enjoyed immensely but a book which she had abandoned, left unfinished. She hadn't been able to get past the deep-as-night, heavy history and the pages and pages of minutiae. She felt disappointed in herself, especially as a writer, but at the same time knew time was too short to waste on books she didn't enjoy. She wanted to be inspired and romanced, not bogged down in detail. This view was what she craved and needed to inspire her innermost creativity, to entice the words out and onto the page. *Preferably in the right order.* She smiled to herself, enjoying the freedom of being so far away from anyone.

She found a little patch of soil, shaded by a tree full of almond blossom, surrounded by scattered wildflowers, and sat down. She folded her legs up towards her and tucked her hair behind her ear, a loose strand having fallen away from the grip of her truffle pink butterfly clip. She closed her eyes and listened. She could hear the gentlest breeze and the sound of a goat scratching under a tree in the distance.

She took out her notepad and a pen and began to write, free writing. She liked the way her hand and the pen slotted together, the story filtering through her energy. Three women, three relationships, one outcome. She wrote in her neat handwriting, word after word, line after line. She didn't stop, not even for a second, her mind full of words and ideas. She filled the notebook and only stopped when her hand began to ache.

And then it came. The tiniest sound, a musical note. At first, she almost missed it. She strained her ears and listened more carefully. There it was again. She turned left and right, twisting to look. No one was around.

Out of nowhere a sheet of paper flew into her lap and she caught it before it got carried away by the wind again. She stared at the writing. A message? A love note? The words were written in Greek; she recognised some of the letters and in the background faded musical notes seemed to dance across the page. She held the thin sheet of paper up against the sky and the notes seemed to create a pattern on the paper behind each line. What did it mean? She pondered whether Prodromos would be able to help her. She scooped up the hem of her skirt from around her ankles and wandered back in the direction of the hotel, the note safely tucked between the pages of her notebook in her bag. The music tinkled as she picked up her pace, in a hurry to get back to the hotel.

***

'Prodromos, can I ask you a question?' she asked, conscious of her red face.

'Of course,' he said, his smile lighting up his eyes.

'I found a note up on the hillside overlooking the cove and wondered whether you could tell me what it says.' Prodromos took the note from her, hesitant, his hand shaking. He studied it carefully and when Stella looked up at him, his eyes were wet with tears. 'I'm so sorry. I didn't mean to upset you. What is it?'

Something powerful and unmistakable passed between them. She hadn't imagined it.

Prodromos sunk into one of the decrepit, old Cahors of his ancestors. She reached out and gave his hand a gentle squeeze of reassurance. Eventually, he spoke in a deep voice, as if scared to be heard by anyone. 'It's a poem. A love poem. So old, so precious. But where did you get it?'

'It appeared, as if flirting with the breeze. I thought someone may have lost it but there was no one around.

Is it important?'

'Where were you?'

'At the top of the hill, overlooking the cove. I took the path you mapped out for me.'

'You made it to the top?'

'Yes, it was quite a struggle, let me tell you. The note…' said Stella expectantly.

'The note…'

'We have preparations to do. The festival won't run itself tonight and Andri is calling,' he said.

He stood up, still holding onto the crepe-thin sheet. 'Let me hold onto this for now and I will explain. I promise. But now, I must go. I cannot bear to be at the brunt of Andri's sharp tongue. Not today. Not now.'

'Of course, and sorry for upsetting you,' said Stella, not sure Andri was calling him; Stella hadn't heard her, but she supposed she wasn't tuned into Andri's voice like Prodromos was.

'I will see you tonight, yes? The whole of Kefalonia will be celebrating.'

The hill and its spattering of lemon trees had always held a special kind of magic in its midst; the kind of magic which sits and waits, resides with patience over everything else, it bides its time, shows itself at the right time, the right second. But the number seven, revealed in the dregs of Andri's coffee-cup reading, encouraged Prodromos. There were five guests. The sixth and seventh would be known in time. He thought about Yiannis.

Prodromos' yiayia always said number seven was both deep and wise with a tenacity to keep going, to dig deep, while following its intuition; asking for more, listening with one's heart as well as with the eyes, researching all that life had to offer, sensing what was right and what was to come.

He sat deep in thought, twiddling his worry beads in his left hand, passing them through his fingers, the sound a soft clipping as the beads knocked against each other. A profound sense of spirituality, of the magic surrounding him, offered him a sense of mystery, and he was keen to discover who the other two people would be and how they would be presented. But he had to be patient and hoped the number seven did not hold back, hold all its glinting secrets, and promises too tightly creating suspicion and distrust.

He closed his eyes and imagined the setting sun across the ancient, temple, the golden reflection of its glory settling on the Ionian Sea and seeping into its depths, touching its bed, touching the heart of it.

When he opened his eyes, Andri gave him one of her looks, quizzical, questioning. 'What are you so deep in thought about?' she asked.

'The number seven doesn't add up,' he said, his forehead furrowed.

'But it will in time. Don't overthink it. Let the magic you are so encouraged and led by be the guide. All will be revealed. You say it always does.'

'You are right my dear. You are as wise as you are beautiful.'

'Get away,' she said, smiling, but deep inside Prodromos knew she welcomed his compliments despite being a humble, loyal, industrious woman who paid little attention to her beauty.

That's what made her ever more beautiful, in his eyes and her beauty had not faded in all these years.

'What else does your coffee cup reveal?' he asked, with a twinkle in his eye.

'I see a…' she continued, and he listened intently, his fingers working but his gaze never once leaving her face as he breathed in her gentle words, animated yet calm, and her rose perfume.

Chapter 22

Stella kicked off her dusty sandals and roused Anton from his lie in. He was getting old, and it irritated Stella.

'Hey, you okay?' he asked, through sleepy eyes. 'How was your walk?'

'Something strange is happening here. I keep hearing music. No one else seems to hear it but I can hear it so clearly.'

'What sort of music?'

'Tinkly, spellbinding… kind of romantic, full of love, the sort of music which is carried on the air like sweet pollen from the blossom.'

'Maybe it's filtered through a tannoy system?'

'All the way up in the mountains?'

'Okay. Point taken.'

'A note flew into my hand when I was on the hilltop earlier. It's like there's a magic energy at work.'

'You must be one of those mystics who picks up the

vibes of lost souls. Doomed as they live precariously between two worlds,' he said, teasing her.

'Stop it. The note upset Prodromos.'

'Why? What did it say?'

'He's going to talk to me tonight at the festival. He's got a lot to do between now and then and promised to catch up with me later.'

'And you? What do you have to do between now and then?'

He drew her down onto the bed and undid her blouse, his mouth hungrily seeking her nipples, hard and erect under his tongue. In one movement, he flipped on top of her as she widened her legs to welcome him, throbbing in anticipation of their lovemaking.

***

The air was still, hardly a leaf moved on the lemon trees. Stella and Anton walked hand in hand to where Eliana and Dean and Melody and Luke had gathered by the pool bar, ready to join Prodromos for the short walk to the festival in the *plateia* of the next town.

'The square will be full of people… dancing, singing and drinking,' Prodromos told them. 'You will experience the true hospitality of the Greeks and our culture and traditions. You will all enjoy it, I am sure,' he said, with a glint in his eye.

Stella breathed a sigh of relief as her initial reservation about Anton bonding with Dean and Luke fell away after a staccato start; he soon found his space with them and before she had time to ease him into their conversation they were all talking football and the latest embarrassing scores and penalties, they surprisingly all supported the same team and Dean proudly edged up the cuff of his short-sleeved shirt to show off his football team's tattoo, proving to the others he was a true fan. They talked on, drifting into an easy exchange from one subject to another like life-long friends meeting up after a hiatus.

Stella took a step back, lifted a brow; she couldn't help but notice Luke's dishevelled appearance, his crazy eyes, and surmised he had been drinking. Slurring his words, he appeared more animated than she had seen him before and Melody, in contrast, appeared subdued.

'Drinking without us?' asked Dean, as if reading her mind. 'Mate, that's not how we do it back home.'

'Just a couple before we headed off,' said Luke, sheepishly.

Melody looked away and tottered precariously in her clipping high heels, obviously the wrong choice for the dusty, uneven route to the town. She wore a long-sleeved cardigan despite the closeness of the evening's heat. A shiver darted through Stella. She hoped her suspicions were proved wrong. Stella slowed her pace, leaving Anton to chat with Dean and fell back in step with Melody.

'You look gorgeous,' said Stella.

'Thought I'd dress up, it's exciting to be going to the festival,' said Melody, giving a hesitant but happy twirl. The shimmer of the pleated skirt and top shone like pretty birthday wrapping.

'Looking forward to it, for sure,' Stella said, her eyes darting towards Luke, checking his reaction, but he was too engrossed in whatever men found to talk about even when they had only just met.

Stella ignored his split-second agitation when he did turn round but continued talking. 'You obviously don't feel the heat like I do. I couldn't possibly wear a cardigan. Baking hot even in this dress and it's as light a fabric as I could find in what I'd brought with me.'

'I thought it might get breezy later,' said Melody, and she stretched the cardigan sleeves down over her wrists.

'True. The travel agent said the Greek islands get windy.'

'Who's windy?' asked Anton, laughter playing round the edges of his mouth. Stella hadn't seen him this relaxed at home in a long time.

'The weather.' Stella rolled her eyes.

'I've got a cardi in my bag. You can borrow it if you like,' chirped Eliana.

'Maybe later, thanks,' said Stella.

'Wraps herself up like a mummy every night. It's like trying to break into Tutankhamun's casket to get to her,' said Dean.

'Ha-ha,' said Eliana to Dean, but he playfully slapped her bottom.

'Dean,' she said, scolding him and the jovial playful atmosphere was broken by her tone.

They continued walking, the three women together, sisters in arms, their steps keeping up with each other's pace and their arms intertwined.

'Anton looks amazing,' said Eliana, a whisper. 'Don't think I haven't noticed how he paws over you, showers you with love and affection.'

'He does, when he's with me.'

'It works.'

'We accept it for what it is. No demands. No expectations.'

'And I bet you get spoilt.'

'It's not all candyfloss and roses. I spend half my life waiting for him to come over and half my life dreading his wife finding out about us.'

'Ooh, not so great. Why do you put up with it?'

'Because I love him. He's mine when he's with me and I'm his.' Stella bit her lip, conscious of her aggressive reply.

Prodromos announced he was going to walk ahead. 'Andri and Yiannis will be needing my help for last-minute organising, and I have some preparations of my own to do.'

They bid him goodbye promising to seek him out later.

'You're attracting a lot of attention,' said Anton, slipping in next to Stella.

'Attention?'

'I've seen the way Prodromos' eyes stroke the whole of you when he speaks.'

Stella ignored his comment. Anton was not in a position to be jealous, and neither was she in the mood to deal with his insecurities. But conscious of not spoiling the evening for everyone she plastered a smile on her face and made up her mind to enjoy what she hoped would be a fun evening.

After a while, the three women stopped talking, their steps on the road echoing across the openness of the apricot and pomegranate orchards either side of the road with only the occasional car passing, their headlights illuminating the road for them.

Stella concentrated on her breathing, laboured from the talking and walking, and looked down at her feet, careful not to trip on any of the protruding, rocks of the path as it unfolded ahead of her. She saw something sparkle in the dust and bent to pick it up, falling behind the group.

As she stood, turning the piece of glass in her hand, she heard the faint yet now familiar music tinkle in the air. She caught up with the two women who had continued walking, about to ask them if they heard it too, but they were obviously oblivious. What did it mean? She couldn't wait to speak to Prodromos about the mysterious note. And a twist in her story formulated in her head.

Prodromos heard Anton's comment and couldn't believe how a man who didn't appreciate the woman he was meant to love, to be with, could justify making such a derogatory assumption about Prodromos' interest in Stella. He couldn't be further from the truth.

'That man, he arrives late and then has the audacity to claim I am making eyes at his woman. Only a man who shares his love, spreads it selfishly thin, can make such a beastly comment.'

'You fret too much,' said Andri. 'Leave the man alone. It is their business, is it not? Why are you interfering?'

'I am not interfering. I am making a comment. An observation. Is it not wise to notice? To notice even the smallest of things?'

She laughed. 'Yes, my darling. Notice but do not absorb the energy, especially if it is negative. Tonight is for dancing and enjoying the music and the energy of friends and lovers.'

'You sent a note,' said Prodromos. Andri stared ahead. 'You're as wise as you are beautiful, and yes, I know I say it often, but heed my words, Andri. Not everyone is wise.'

'Though everyone has beauty we do not see,' she said, a smile playing on her lips.

'And not all beauty can be touched,' he sighed.

'Now who's being wise,' she chuckled, and she carried on peeling potatoes, the dried clay earth still clinging to them, falling away into the towel she had spread over her lap, patterns of sunlight dancing across her bare legs, her socks scrunched round her ankles in soft folds.

Those potatoes took me an hour to dig up,' he said. 'They had better taste good.'

'With the fresh sea air and the clean mountain rain watering their baby shoots from the moment you planted them; they are sure to be as tasty as ever.'

'The gods will not fail us. They are no longer fighting each other but coming together for the good of earth, for the good of all people and Stella will find her way.'

'Don't get carried away,' she said.

'You can smirk all you like,' he said, 'but it's the truth. I swear to you. I feel it as well as I feel my own bones inside me. The gods are banging on their drums, abundantly joyful.'

'If you say so, my love,' said Andri.

'That's why you sent the note.'

'Note? Nothing to do with me.' Her chuckle pulled at his heart; her eyes glinted.

Chapter 23

The sun had quickly dipped behind the deep mahogany and russet browns of the mountain tops, the black firs silhouetted against the bouncing sparkle coming off the rocky crags. The sky streaked with the most glittering strokes of smoked-lox orange, hibiscus pink and rose-petal coral, hanging over them like a silk batik canopy; a landscape abundant with the beauty of another world. Stella wished she had her notebook with her, wanting to record the words in her head and to capture the magnificence of the landscape in her writing. By the end of the night her words would have been unremembered.

As they neared the town square, the ribbons of cobbled streets leading to the *panigiri* revealed a colourful melee of people, stalls, and acoustic music, arranged around the outside of the town square. White masts topped with limp flags marked out the main square and strings of Greek-flag bunting created a criss-cross canopy above the pretty *plateia*, a second sky sitting on the horizon of the radiant sunset.

The excitement rose a few decibels as they arrived, and the local people, with their foreign tongues and fast talking, welcomed Prodromos and his guests. He was like a celebrity; people shook his hand, others clapped him fondly on the back while women kissed him on both cheeks, full of smiles. In the distance, a shout alerted them to Yiannis waving from the other side of the square, equally as excited to see them.

Within minutes their little group dispersed in different directions. Stella put her arm through Anton's trying to stay close to him. A woman with long trailing waves and a dark beauty spot on her left cheek thrust her arm out towards Stella; it was filled all the way to her elbow with copper bangles studded with bright jewels. She chose three and slipped them onto her wrist, leaving the woman smiling as she pocketed the euros.

'Looks like we're going to be drinking and dancing all night,' Anton said, pulling her closer.

'And I'll be rattling all night,' said Stella, shaking her wrist, jingling with the new bracelets.

'Jingle away,' he said.

'Sounds perfect. But first I really do need to eat something,' said Stella, pressing down on her rumbling tummy. 'I'm suddenly ravenous.'

'Well, if there's something the Greeks do well it's food,' he said. They continued walking. 'And the food smells amazing.'

'Ooh, coriander and oregano...' said Stella, her tastebuds coming alive with the fragrant, tantalising smells around her.

'And the sizzling meat,' said Anton, pointing to a row of barbeques piled with nuggets of ash-coloured hot coals with skewers turning over them.

Stella took in the nuttiness of chestnuts roasting over split oil barrels filled with coal, the sweetness of pastries dripping in mountain honey and the savoury spices of barbequed meat.

'Looks so good,' said Stella.

They found a wobbly trestle table and two chairs and sat with their chicken *giros* and a shot of raki each.

A group of youths in traditional Greek costumes lined up in the square and a band struck up a tune, folksy, an air of romance to its beat. A bouzouki player, his plectrum moving across the strings played in turn with the *daouli*, a double-sided drum, which beat out the soothing rhythm as the dancing continued.

'Opas,' called out the tallest boy, the leader of the dance troupe.

They held hands and created a circle, took steps to the left and right and kicked their left foot out and then their right leg. They turned and formed two lines and faced each other. A group of girls appeared and took their places opposite the young men, and they held hands and twirled and turned and skipped. The girls' skirts swished over their hips and the boys looped round and round them smiling goofily; they bounced on the balls of their feet, a dance as light as a butterfly. The music increased in tempo, the girls stood back, clapping. The boys finished off with a Zorba-The-Greek type dance. The crowds clapped and cheered and whistled.

'This is delicious,' said Stella, between mouthfuls, the pungent, sulphuric garlic-rich tzatziki filling her nostrils and igniting her tastebuds, the music ringing through her.

'I can tell you're enjoying the chicken,' said Anton, wiping a blob of the yoghurt dip from her upper lip with his finger and licking the tip. 'It's what I want to do to you… right now.'

'You're insatiable,' she said.

'Aren't you lucky,' he said, and knocking back his raki he looked round, and like a teenager on his first hot date, rushed her away from the square and down one of the cobbled streets tucked away like a secret in the night. 'Let's dive down here.'

'Stop it,' she laughed. 'You're going to trip us both up.'

They stumbled further and further away; the music faded. He finally stopped, pushed her up against one of the stone walls of an abandoned house festooned with wild rose and jasmine. He nuzzled her neck, kissing her, his manhood pressing urgently into her groin.

'God, you turn me on,' he said, pulling down her panties, her dress scrunched up around her waist.

Stella, carried away by his evident horniness, reached her peak as quickly and as powerfully as he did. She rested her head back on the wall, her legs still shaking, clinging onto his shoulders for support.

Panting, Anton zipped up, and as Stella pulled up her panties, a flock of white-winged birds flew overhead. She caught a glimpse of the wings and thought of the purity of the colour. Something inside her shift; white is a promise that there is fodder to feed and nourish, that the emptiness would be filled. She wondered why the words she had read long ago had come to her then. And then, a voice called out.

***

'Melody? Is that you? Stop playing games. I'm not in the mood for your dramatics.'

'Luke?' called Stella.

'Have you seen Melody?'

'No.'

'I've got to find her,' he said, pushing her away from him.

'Mate, watch it. How much have you had to drink?'

'I'm not your mate and what's it got to do with you?'

'Stay here and I'll go back to the square and look for her,' said Stella, trying to diffuse the dangerously over-heated situation.

'I'm not staying here so you can talk rubbish to her about me.' Luke stormed off, stumbling as he shot off in the direction he came.

'What was all that about?' asked Anton.

'I think he has anger management issues.'

'What? Did she tell you that?'

'No, but the way she clings onto her cardigan, wrapping it around her like it's her protection, her rabbit-in-the-headlights look, the way she sometimes freezes when he's around.'

'It's your overactive writer's compass whizzing round and round uncontrollably,' he said.

'We've got to find her before he does,' said Stella and she darted off.

Chapter 24

Stella and Anton, tried to keep up pace with Luke, Stella puffed from exhaustion and the sex. Luke raced through the maze of streets until they all found themselves back in the main square. The crowds were dense; adults chatting too loudly, children in fancy dress, their faces painted, old men drinking thick black coffee, laughing, and talking.

'Luke!' Stella called after him.

'Where's Mel?' he shouted, turning on her, eyes blazing.

'She'll be around here somewhere. She can't have gone far.'

'I hate it when she disappears. It makes me so angry.'

'Angry? That's a bit strong,' said Stella, unable to keep the shock from her voice.

'What would you know?'

Stella spotted Prodromos bent over in laughter,

holding onto his stomach, as if he would burst, the four men standing around him, clutching at their bellies as they chuckled along with him. His chortling softened the intensity of the moment and she smiled.

'Maybe he's seen her,' Luke said, following her gaze and he walked off.

A group of children watched a man in traditional Greek costume balancing five tumblers on his head as he danced to the fiddle, and the youths sang along to the chorus. Luke pushed past the boys and approached Prodromos from behind, tapped him on the shoulder.

'Luke, my friend,' Prodromos exclaimed, turning round to face him. 'Come. Join us,' he said, introducing the other locals. 'You too Stella and Anton,' he said, as they pitched up.

'Have you seen my wife?'

'You English keep our friend in business,' joked one of the men.

'Stop it,' said another, 'Prodromos knows what real *filoxenia* is. He is the epitome of hospitality.'

'Here, have a drink,' said Prodromos, proffering a bottle of ice-cold beer.

Luke, momentarily thrown by the unexpected warmth and alcohol-induced hospitality of the men around him, accepted the beer and took a swig, a forced smile touched the corner of his eyes, glinting like a knife, the rage emanating from him unmistakable.

'My wife. Have you seen her?' he asked again, with an edge to his voice, heavy like the hull of a sinking ship.

'She can't be far. Relax. She will be having fun somewhere,' said one of the men, stretching his arm out to his side and clicking his fingers to the quickening beat of the musician's drumming.

'She should be with me. Have you seen her?'

Prodromos raised his shoulders in response. 'I saw her with the other guest. The one with the long ponytail.'

'Eliana?'

'Yes, they were at the stall near the bandstand, looking at the *amatopetres*.'

'The what?'

'The glass evil eyes... they are thought to keep evil spirits and negative energy away... like jealousy...'

'Never mind. I haven't got time for a lesson in Greek superstitions. I'll find her myself,' he said, cutting him off mid-sentence. He tipped up the bottle and emptied it. The bottle shook the table as he slammed it down and he lurched off. He pressed against the people, forcing them to step out of his way as he elbowed a walkway through them.

Chapter 25

'Tell me, what's with you and Luke?' asked Stella, when she finally caught up with Melody.

'What do you mean?' said Eliana.

'Luke's searching all over the place for you. Looks like he's going to give himself a hernia,' she said, focusing on Melody.

'It's all my fault,' said Melody.

'Do you want to tell me what's going on,' said Eliana, her face in shock.

'I know we're strangers really but sometimes it's always easier to talk to the person you don't know,' continued Stella.

'I know,' said Melody, visibly shaking.

'And to be honest if you can't be happy in a place like this, there's a problem.' Stella picked up one of the key chains, tiny white pebbles strung between glass beads with the evil eye on each one, and it tinkled in her hand.

'I, umm...'

'I know. You don't want to say anything against him. But you don't have to. I can see it,' said Stella, gazing towards Melody's cardigan.

'It's not what you think,' said Melody, her eyes open wide, as if in shock.

'I'll take three of these,' said Stella, pointing to the pretty key fobs, not wanting to waste the shopkeeper's time. She took the paper bag he wrapped them in, complete with curled pink ribbon and a little sticker bearing the shop's name. She put it in her handbag, flicking out the hair trapped under its strap on her shoulder. '*Efharisto*,' she said politely to the grey-haired lady who looked like she would be better placed in a quiet courtyard than a shop on the bustling town square.

'It doesn't matter what I think. It's what you think that matters,' Stella said, turning her attention back to Melody.

'He can be so loving. He's a good man. Looks after me.'

'Yeah, right. Like someone who cares for a puppy and then throws it out into the cold at Christmas.' Stella stopped. 'Sorry, that sounds harsh. I don't mean to judge.'

Stella waited for a reply. Melody fell into Stella's arms sobbing. 'Hey, there, there. Let's find somewhere quieter.' Stella led her off down a lane. Eliana tagged behind them. They found a dry-stone wall to sit on. Melody gently picked up the sleeping cat and placed her in her lap, sitting in the space next to Eliana.

'Talk to me. You don't really know me, and I don't really know you. That makes it easier, right? No judgement. I promise. I will just listen,' said Stella.

'He started to get controlling about a year ago.'

'What started it? Usually there's a trauma or some sort of episode which marks out their vulnerability.' Melody stared at her. 'I've done lots of research for one of my books, consulted so many sprawling non-fiction stuff,' Stella filled in, instantly dispelling Melody's surprise.

'It all began after he discovered I was having a relationship with one of the teachers where I worked.' Stella forced herself to hold her expression, hoped the shock she felt didn't show, hoped the guilt she should have been carrying didn't cloud her thinking. 'I didn't mean it to happen. Luke was always at work; I was working longer hours to avoid sitting at home on my own and one day a peck on the cheek turned into something more.'

'I didn't see that coming.' Stella spoke in a soft, subdued voice, as if calming a child after a toddler tantrum.

'Neither did I. It evolved so quickly into something deeper, something I hadn't anticipated or planned.'

'That's how it happens,' said Stella.

'It was shocking but exhilarating too.'

'I can relate to that,' said Stella, thinking about those same emotions, the incredible highs which carried her through those early months and years of being with Anton.

'At first it was talking, sharing stuff about our families, our homes, our life outside of school.'

'Friendship is how these affairs start. It takes away any awkwardness.'

'He was so easy to talk to. He understood me. He knew what made me who I am, and we soon discovered we had a lot more in common than the mundane school stuff.'

'Talking. Sharing...' said Stella, momentarily disappearing into a deja-vu hole of how she had allowed her life to slip into a routine of illicit meetups and incredible lovemaking quickly and ever-so-easily.

'It then moved into something different. I didn't sleep with him at first. We just kissed.' Stella listened, imagining how her own relationship with Anton might have been something different had they taken it slowly to start with. Love, life, and lust were complicated 'We kissed a lot, something Luke doesn't really enjoy, and did other stuff but we only slept together the once. But the once has haunted me, filled my dreams since then, all my waking hours and all the hours in between.'

'How did Luke find out? Did you confess?'

'He finished work early and decided to come via the school to pick me up, save me from walking in the rain.'

'And?' said Stella, her hand stroking Melody's arm.

'He came in all smiles, wet from the rain himself after walking across the car park and waiting for the "lazy caretaker," his words not mine, to buzz him into the building. I found out later, Luke's phone was dead otherwise he would have called me to go and meet him. He didn't see anything. Didn't notice anything. Not at first. But the empty bottle of wine and wine glasses, the lit candle dripping melted wax on the desk, my lipstick everywhere but on my lips, painted a best-selling romance novel. Told him everything. He crumpled in a heap, as if his legs had lost their strength. In front of both of us.'

'Oh, no. That must've been awful, for you, for him...'

'It was. I had never ever seen him so broken, so small.'

'Couldn't you have denied it?' asked Eliana.

'How could I? It was plain to see. It was all laid out like the clues of an Agatha Christie whodunnit. And he would've guessed eventually. I don't think I would have stopped. Being with this other man was like a drug, seeping into me intravenously, the more I had of him the more I wanted. The talking, the laughing, the intimacy. Even the danger fired me up.'

Stella listened; her heart beating like the wings of a trapped moth in a jar. Melody's revelation both shocked her and excited her; she could relate to everything she was saying.

Anton and she had been exactly like that. He was an aphrodisiac; every waking moment had been all about planning how and when to see him. But Stella didn't share any of those details with Melody and, instead, said, 'I guess that's the grasp of something illicit... the scalding secrets, the cutting lies, the energising risk, the pounding adrenalin.'

'I'd never done anything like that before. But this was different. He was different.'

'What's going on now? Are you still seeing him?'

'No, I ended it the following day and resigned not long after. Handed in my notice. I couldn't be around him and I knew it was hurting Luke knowing I was working with him, seeing him, every day.'

'It still doesn't give him the right to... do you love

Luke? Have you thought about counselling?' Stella's mind was working hard to keep up with Melody's revelation.

'He's not the kind of man to speak openly and bare his soul to a counsellor. His family are all very much "what happens behind closed doors is nobody's business." And I don't think I could talk about it all in front of him.'

'Do you still think about him? This other man?'

'Sometimes. He was so gentle. So connected to me somehow, and I don't mean the intimate stuff between us, but intellectually, physically, spiritually. We bonded.'

Melody wiped her tears away and jumped at the sound of running footsteps getting louder and louder. Out of the dark shadows and into the soft glow of the streetlamp appeared Anton.

'You okay?' asked Anton and then noticing Eliana perched on the wall said, 'Hi.'

Melody answered him, 'Yes, why? Has something happened?' She sprang up and the cat frightened by her sudden movement, mewed throatily, and jumped onto its feet, and ran off, scattering a crunch of tiny stones across the ground.

'No. Yes. Luke's looking for you and he seems pretty fired up. He's been drinking,' said Anton.

'Right,' said Melody.

'Stay here,' said Stella, panic rising in the back of her throat.

The silence between them hung like a mallet suspended over a gong... the sensual sound and powerful vibrations an exquisite anticipation.

'Are you okay? Do you need to stay with us tonight?'

asked Eliana. Stella, looked up, surprised at Eliana's gentle thoughtfulness.

'No, no… it's okay. I know how to handle him. It's my fault. Please don't say anything to him,' said Melody.

'I don't know what's going on but he's not in a good mood. He's been drinking and–' she stopped midsentence as Luke, wild eyes, and gesturing arms, appeared with Dean close behind him.

Luke threw himself at Melody, dropped to his knees and cried like a baby. Stella stood watching; tears glistened in her eyes. Eliana shocked, stroked the cat in her lap over and over, a nervousness revealing itself in her actions.

Anton and Dean came to a stop, gasping for breath.

'It's okay my love. I'm here,' said Melody. 'There, there. It's okay. I'm here.'

'Let's go,' Luke said, and he peered up at her with a pathetic, boyish but compelling expression. Momentarily embarrassed with an audience around him, he pulled himself together and said, with more assertiveness, 'Come on, Mel.'

Melody took his hands in hers and hauled him to his feet. He stood up, unsteady, swaying precariously. He leaned into her, and they walked away protected by the shadows, two broken souls, small and pathetic. They slipped silently from view, leaving four stiffly statuesque figures staring beadily into the dappled shade until only blackness remained.

'Didn't see that coming with those two,' said Eliana, nuzzling into Dean's embrace.

'Don't get involved in whatever's going on between

them. We're here to enjoy ourselves, not get dragged into everyone's problems,' said Dean, enveloping Eliana in his arms tighter still and planting a kiss on her lips.

'Pretty hard not to be involved, we see them every morning at breakfast,' said Stella.

'Eliana's more important to me than them. Luke seems out of control. Who knows what he might do,' said Dean and Stella noted the protective tone in his voice and hoped Eliana had noticed it too.

'Babe, I guess you love me, huh?' Eliana said right on cue.

'You know I do, stupid woman,' Dean said, leading her back towards the street party.

Anton and Stella, holding hands, walked a few paces behind them and Stella contemplated why love had to be so difficult and complicated.

The magic was never wrong and though it highlighted the good, the sense of light and possibility, it also sensed the dread, the cursed. Prodromos stared after the man who was disturbed, humiliated, and deeply hurt. Luke had not revealed this to Prodromos, but he knew. Prodromos trusted the magic and his own eyes, his own heart, and the vibes of those who were fighting not only themselves but the world around them. The pain in the world dimmed only momentarily when love was near, yet that love could provide the light for days, weeks, months, years.

He wondered whether Kefalonia's deep-rooted peace, resilience and unconditional love might save the man from himself and called upon the magic of the island to shower Luke with control and self-love, with a lightness of heart and forgiveness. Let it pour into him, thought Prodromos and a red light, brighter than the strongest fire, rose around him.

As the festival continued, he called upon the gods and the power of their healing, resilient and energetic music to illuminate Luke with a sense of tenacity and clarity. Clarity after all was the most coherent and intelligible of qualities, allowing all people to make decisions without stumbling over foggy emotions and dwelling on the past. Clarity opened a path to new opportunities and chances otherwise lost, ignored, unrecognised.

He drifted deeper and thought about love in all its forms. What would the magic create here, now? There were two choices: one spell to produce eros, erotic seizure in the victim, and the other used to create philia, affection, or friendship.

Love in Greece was full of the wonder of the gods and there was no escaping their extraordinary hold over the ordinary love in their lives, ever present, whether in full view or shrouded in life's complications and confusion.

The magic was brewing, building strength and momentum, already at work, he felt its energy around him and in the air, above the sound of the band's music, as it floated between the people unseen searching for the right person to plant itself into. That's how it worked, that's how it always worked, though when, and for whom, he had no answer, though he had his suspicions and held onto them, praying the right people would be touched by the hand of change. A borning was soon to come, the red appeared around him again like a hugging sunset.

As he caught sight again of Luke, he threw his hands in the air, as if in praise, and then moving his feet danced as if he was a young man again, newlywed, dancing with his beautiful bride... touching her... almost, and the image of her faded into dust.

Chapter 26

Stella watched as Prodromos disappeared behind a makeshift, tented-covered stall while the others continued to merry-make. Anton now at ease, despite the angry-filled moments of earlier with Luke, was drinking with Yiannis. Two of Yiannis' uncles had promised to show Anton how to drink like a Greek.

'Join us, beautiful English rose,' said Yiannis, holding Stella's gaze a little too long, her colour rising, a fizzing building inside her, like unexploded fireworks.

'Come on, darling. Let's get sloshed,' said Anton, already past the "let's get" stage and fully "in" that stage.

'I need a word with Prodromos about the note,' she said. 'But I'll be back as soon as I can. Save me a glass,' she said, excusing herself, unable to tear herself away fast enough.

Anton seemed to understand, too far gone to make any sort of coherent response.

'Tell me about the note,' she said, getting straight to the point, when she found their host unable to contain the excitement bursting forth from within her.

'Yes, come with me.' Prodromos handed a bottle of white liquid to one of the men closest to him and excused himself from the quartet of bellowing men, their hum a vibrating force in the small circle of chairs arranged under the tarpaulin.

Prodromos lead her through the crowds who were clapping as two young men danced to a heavy, slow tune; they kicked their legs out in front of them, throwing up tiny grey pebbles from the gravel, and then bounced down towards the ground on bended knees as they clapped, jumped back up and turned around full circle to face each other. They were like peacocks proudly strutting and preening their tail feathers with a show of agility, strength, and coordination.

Finally, they sat under a lone, ancient olive tree, a few hundred metres from the hubbub of the square's celebrations. The tree, dressed in twinkling lights, seemed to dance with the hundreds of pieces of fabric and cotton tied to its thick branches. Prodromos saw her looking and said, 'For good luck.'

'I hope this note brings some good news,' she said, giving his arm a gentle squeeze.

'This note is not what you think it is.'

'I haven't guessed what it is. But I am intrigued.'

'It is a note which binds people together in love and invites you to look to your heart for truth.'

'Can you read it to me... in English... translate it?'

He cleared his throat, visibly fighting his emotions, his

eyes glistening in the roundness of the full moon's light, and puffing out his chest, his voice quivering, he read:

"Be still, love is near.
Fear not its fragility
For the strongest truest love
Remains and never fades.
Musical notes carried on the wind.
Of love and heartbreak
Across the Ionian Sea
From the lemon groves
The mountains' crevices
Love trickles like crimson blood
From the round distant moon
Moving from place to place
Until it sits in the burning heat of a
Broken but ever beating heart.
Where it was meant to be all along."

'It's beautiful. Hauntingly so. But what does it mean, Prodromos?'

'It's a poem about love, letting go, holding on, finding truth, eternal love.'

'Who wrote it? How did it come to be flying in the air?'

'It's the magic of the hilltop.'

'What magic? I haven't read anything about magic in the guidebooks.'

'This is not to be found in the pages of trailblazing guides. It is something intangible, yet real. To be found here.' He thumped his chest with his fist.

'That must be what I hear. Do you feel it too?'

'Every time,' he said. 'It is here in the rustle of the leaves on the lemon trees, it is carried on the sea breeze, it is to be found deep under the dry, cracked earth, where roots satiate their thirst with the tiniest trickle of mountain water.'

'Why does it make you so sad?'

He hesitated, then said, in the quietest of voices, 'These are the words of a woman I used to love. She is long gone but she still plays music for me, for those who need to hear. To listen. Not only to their hearts but to the love within them.'

'She wrote this for you?'

'Yes... for everyone who needs it.'

'How does she know?'

'She feels it, as I feel it too. It is both a blessing and a curse. And...'

'And?'

'The music...'

'Is that the music I can hear?'

'Yes,' he said.

'Why can no one else hear it?'

'It draws in, connects with those who need to hear and feel its vibrations, whether for themselves or for others.'

'And why is she not here? Where has she gone?'

Prodromos shook his head, his eyes lowered. 'She died. That is all I can say. All I am at liberty to share.'

'I'm so sorry,' said Stella, squeezing Prodromos' arm gently. 'And Andri?'

He hesitated. 'She is my constant. A beautiful reminder love can arrive and endure when we least expect it. When we least deserve it. And we must be ready to welcome it, pull it in and hold it close.'

'Oh, Prodromos…'

'She is still very much here,' he said, gesturing with his arms around him. 'And here,' he said, resting his hand over his chest. Stella, moved by his gesture, felt compelled to rest her hand over his, to feel the life-affirming thrum of his beating heart.

Chapter 27

The following day was blistering and desperate to avoid the sun, Anton, nursing a hangover, persuaded Stella to visit the tiny church on the other side of the old town, built into the side of the mountain, overlooking the streets and houses below. It was a special church known for its famed crawling snakes over the icon of the Virgin Mary, the *Panayia*.

'It says here,' he said, reading from a concertina brochure on the island's places of interest, '*locals eagerly await the emergence of the snakes every year, and tradition dictates if they do not show up, something unfortunate will happen. The "Snakes of the Virgin Mary."*

'It's a bit creepy,' said Stella, shaking her head, drawing her lower lip between her teeth.

Ignoring her, Anton shook his head from side to side and continued the hike. '*They have failed to appear only twice: The first time was in August of 1940, shortly before the outbreak of World War II, and the second time was in August 1953, when Kefalonia suffered a tremendously destructive earthquake.'* Anton, a few paces ahead of her, paused for effect, but it was wasted on Stella who had spotted their new friends from Miramare; the group ambled across the town square below, too far away for Stella to attract their attention.

'According to tradition, in 1200 AD, pirates raided the island and tried to take over a convent full of nuns. Innumerable snakes then appeared, entangling the bodies of the pirates, and forming a wall between them and the convent. Understandably, the pirates panicked and fled after this occurrence.'

'Anton, stop. I'm knackered,' breathed Stella, taking a gulp from her water bottle.

'Definitely hard work,' he said. 'But my head feels better.'

'Keep drinking water,' Stella said, stopping to catch her breath.

She dropped to her knees, her hands over her ears.

'Hey, Stella. What's wrong?' Anton knelt next to her, dropping the backpack he was holding onto the ground.

'I feel faint. It's the sun.'

'Can you stand?'

'No, I don't think I can.' She took her hands away from her ears and she filled with the same music she had heard that morning at breakfast. 'Can you hear it now?' she asked as panic consumed her.

'What? Hear what?'

'The music. Tell me you can hear it now...'

'Oh my God. Stella. What is going on?'

'I don't know. That music…'

'There's no music babe. There's no one around. It's just you and me.' But Stella knew differently. And held onto what Prodromos had shared with her, decided it was a secret for her to keep.

'I can't face going in,' she said. 'I'll wait here.' Stella sipped from the bottle and perched on a stone seat, under the shade of an ancient olive tree. The heaviness in her chest lightened and she calmed down. Anton disappeared for a short ten minutes, wandered around the inside of the church.

'I lit a candle,' he announced proudly, when he emerged, shielding his eyes from the glare of sunshine.

Strolling back to the town, the decline made it an easier path to navigate. The tall pines shaded them from the beaming sun, absorbing some of its heat too. They hitched a ride on the back of a farmer's truck.

'*Ade,*' he called, rushing them to get in, though Stella wondered what there was to hurry for.

When they reached the town, Anton helped Stella jump down from the truck and they thanked the driver. Stella wiped down her skirt and shook her legs out, numb from being folded awkwardly under her for too long.

Stella spotted Dean and Eliana at the same moment he saw her. She waved across to him as he called out their names.

'Let's go over and say hello,' said Stella, only half listening to Anton babbling on about the church again. 'I need a drink and a rest.'

'Didn't know you were coming into town,' said Stella

as she and Anton approached. 'I thought I saw you from up there.' She pointed to the little church at the top of the mountain.

'Too hot to be by the pool,' said Dean. 'You trying to live like the locals?' he asked, his attention on the truck's tailgate as it sped off.

'We've walked a long way,' said Stella.

'Thought we'd never make it here alive. We had the most hair-raising taxi ride. The driver talked non-stop. He used to dream of being a professional rally driver,' said Eliana as she smoothed her dress and fiddled with the strap of her bag over her shoulder.

'Reckon he was on a promise,' said Dean. 'I handed over the euro notes, and he sped off without so much as a thank you.'

'Here we go again. Don't you ever stop thinking about it,' said Eliana, rolling her eyes and sighing exaggeratedly.

'Lighten up, I'm only joking,' he said, and took her arm and placed it through his as they began to walk towards the town square.

'Looks so different to the other night,' said Eliana.

'It does,' said Stella, 'and it's busier than I imagined it would be. Don't any of the men work around here?'

'Coffee, yes.' said Dean, nodding towards the old men sitting, bent over their coffee cups and their newspapers. 'Guess, they're too old to work.'

'Nah, it's the culture. Coffee shops, backgammon and playing with their worry beads,' said Stella. My mum's family is Greek, though little of the culture or the language has passed onto me.'

'Do you speak Greek?' asked Dean.

'A few words, I understand a little, but only when the words are spoken slowly.'

'They do speak quickly, don't they?' said Eliana.

'Talking of quick, let's go slow. Coffee break?' asked Dean, pulling Eliana by the arm towards the traditional coffee shop which had seen better days.

'Slowing down will happen after shopping,' Eliana teased, though her expression said she was serious. 'We're here for the shops, babe. So don't think you're getting out of it.'

'This heat is tough,' Dean puffed, sweat trickling from his sideburns and down his cheeks.

'And you need to lose weight, so you don't sweat like a pig,' she said.

'You're not exactly muffin-top free, woman. So, stop mithering or I'll get a taxi back to the apartment and leave you here.'

Eliana knew when to stop. The couples walked aimlessly between one striped, canopied shopfront to another, browsing the locally made handicrafts: gold jewellery, delicate lace, hardy leather bags, wooden backgammon boards, shining bouzouki instruments and the aroma of home-made breads, pastries, bottled sweet liquors and bottles of wild mountain herb-infused olive oil.

'This is just amazing,' said Eliana, taking down a lace shawl from one of the hanging rails. 'Look at the detail,' said Stella.

'Look at the price,' said Dean, pointing to the hand-written tag, '45 euros.'

'It's handmade, not a factory batch one,' said Stella, fingering the delicate edging as Eliana draped it over her shoulders. She winked, recognising the ally in Stella.

'I like it. It'll go with my strappy dress, the one from Oasis. Give me your card,' Eliana said, and Dean handed over his card, pulling out from his back pocket where it had been wedged between the taxi driver's card and a few notes, which he stuffed back.

'I think it would look better without the dress, he said. 'Nothing on, with your nipples poking through the holes.'

Eliana gave him one of her looks. 'Be quiet, they'll hear you!'

Stella had heard, but walked away, pretending to be interested in the rows and rows of worry beads hanging from a white board, punctured with little gold hooks, immediately inside the tented shop front. Eliana, it seemed, could see Dean was angry with her, and she tried to shrug her anger off too.

Eliana wandered into the shop and Stella followed her. She pushed her sunglasses onto her head; it was much darker inside and crammed with more racks and shelving to the ceiling. Towards the back of the shop, leaning against a glass-fronted cabinet an old man, looked up, sensing their presence. Next to him, an old lady, her strands of grey poking out from under her black headscarf tightly knotted at the top of her head, looked up from the crochet she worked on in her lap, the ball of silk thread wound round her hand.

'You buy?' she asked, smiling.

'Yes, thank you,' said Eliana. 'It's gorgeous. You made it?'

Stella glanced over. The old lady was smiling, and Stella breathed in her old-lady scent, with a top note of rose and a hint of bergamot.

The old man took the shawl from Eliana and with shaking hands, flecked with brown age spots and leathery from too much sun, put it into a blue plastic bag.

'Very good,' he said, passing her the credit card terminal.

'Got it,' she said to Stella as she bounced out of the shop.

'Do I get a kiss then?' asked Dean, waiting expectantly. Stella thought he looked like a puppy waiting for his treat.

Eliana gave him a little peck and pushed her arm through his.

Outside, the sun bounced off a huge mirror which rested against a tree. The patisserie had been built around the huge trunk, the tree too old, too much a part of the town's landscape, to be cut down. Stella searched for Anton and then spotted him sitting at one of the tables on the small, overcrowded patio with two other people.

They wandered over, Eliana holding onto the plastic bag with her new acquisition by the handles. Stella recognised the faces as she got nearer to the little patisserie.

'Look who else I bumped into,' said Anton.

'Hi guys,' said Eliana, with a little too much enthusiasm, and then turning to Dean said, 'This is not an excuse to drink beer all afternoon.'

'Buy something nice?' asked Melody.

'A shawl to accessorise one of my evening dresses.'

'She's going to put on a show for me later,' said Dean, winking at Melody. 'That's what the deal was with using my credit card. Hand it over ' he said and held his hand out to Eliana.

Eliana, laughed, her embarrassment high on her flaming cheeks. Stella cringed at Dean's inuendo but wasn't surprised.

The waiter, a white apron tied around his waist and a cloth over his shoulder, handed them a menu each, a smile shining out from him like a beacon of love, his whole face beaming.

'You choose. I come back,' he said, and sauntered off back inside. Melody edged her chair under the wide-brimmed parasol and Eliana simultaneously moved her chair back a foot, so her body and her face were in full sun.

'I know what I want,' said Melody. I want to try the orange cake.'

'*Portokalopita*, said the waiter, already returned with glasses and a carafe of water for the table. He scribbled on his pad, squinting in concentration and against the burning sun.

'Me too,' said Luke.

'And we'll have the same and a Greek coffee,' said Anton, ordering for him and Stella.

'Of course,' said the waiter.

'Same for us,' said Eliana, ordering for Dean too.

'I'd also like a slice of the apple cake. With ice cream,' said Dean.

Stella marvelled at Dean's double dessert order. Eliana rolled her eyes, Melody and Luke gave each other a look.

'*Milopita.* Excellent choice.'

He whistled a simple four-note tune as he strode across

213

the paved outdoor area towards the patisserie entrance, swinging his arms, menus in one hand, notepad, and pen in the other.

Chapter 28

Shaded by the pretty sun umbrellas, striped, blue, and pink, yellow, and orange, they cut into their Greek sweets with little dessert forks and sipped their coffees. A tremor followed. A thunderous sound filled the air. They dropped their cutlery and covered their ears.

Within seconds the ground beneath them shook and a few feet beyond the al fresco seating area, cracks tunnelled their way across the street like hungry slithering snakes, zigzagging viciously under the surrounding lop-sided buildings. Another vibration underfoot took them by surprise again. They looked from one to the other, their smiles faded, searching for an explanation.

The dry earth crumbled beneath their feet and seemed to cry, like thousands of women howling. The café furniture wobbled, then shook violently, seized by the ever-growing ferocity. The uncensored energy sent the crockery onto the floor with a resounding clatter. Dust and debris clouded the air, rolled over them, forcing them to cover their mouths.

Eliana grabbed her shawl and shielded her trembling lips. Stella grabbed the napkin off the table and dabbed at her own stinging eyes, her nose wrinkling, as she clung onto Anton with her other hand. Melody let out a shriek, as if in pain, tears welled behind her sparkling eyes.

'What's going on?' Stella asked, her heart thumping, her brain buzzing and her ears ringing.

Cars were lifted off the ground and then swallowed into the deep crevices, hungry jaws. A destructive scene unfolded, as if in slow motion. Motorbikes and mopeds crashed to the ground, disappearing into the widening open-mouthed craters in the street. People began to panic. Tourists scooped up their children, people pushed and shoved each other as they scrambled to safety under shop awnings, moving towards calling shop-owners who beckoned them to safety.

'It's an earthquake,' yelled Anton. 'Quick, over here.' He grabbed Stella and yanked her with all his might away from the advancing opening of a deep crack, her chair narrowly escaping its hold.

'Please don't tell me it has anything to do with the church. If there are snakes, I'm going to die of fright,' said Stella.

'Of course not. Come on, before we all get swallowed up.'

The Venetian buildings which swayed violently for a few seconds, the force breaking windows. A canopy crumpled to the ground to their left and then another to their right, an almighty crash deafening them, instilling alarm, and a hollow scream from Stella. Fear gripped her. She shivered.

The locals disappeared inside their shops and houses, calling to each other in Greek, taking each other under their arms, protecting each other from harm as they hid. This was something unfamiliar to the holidaymakers. There was an eerie calm from the Greeks; the way they moved, assuredly, with intent, no panic, and no frantic behaviour, but the atmosphere soon changed again.

An umbrella, wrenched from its stand, smacked Dean across the head. Blood trickled from the wound and down the side of his face. Eliana wrapped her arms around herself, gripping her waist. She could only stare, unable to move, rooted to the ground like the roots of the huge tree whose branches shook above her; a reminder that nothing was safe.

'Eliana,' called Stella, fighting the prickling sensation which worked its way up her arms. But Eliana was frozen still. 'Eliana, come on.'

Eventually she spoke. 'He will be okay, won't he?'

'Yes. He will.'

'I can't be without him. I love him,' Eliana whispered.

'Of course you do. And he knows that. But now's not the time to be declaring your undying love,' said Stella.

Dean tried to stand up, reached up to his face and swabbed away a trickle of blood; he stared at the smudge of red-rust brown on his fingers. Eliana stared at the blood, the deep stain, almost the colour of the wine they had been drinking the night before. The colour washed away from his face, and he flopped forwards in his chair, almost toppling out of it. The next moment she looked at him his head, limp, had dropped to his chest, his mouth hanging open.

'No,' she cried, suddenly moving, lurching towards him.

'Quick, let's get him inside,' shouted Luke to Anton. 'Eliana move inside, come on, don't waste time. We've got him,' he said, also pulling at Melody who was looking for her handbag.

The women held onto Eliana's arms, one on each side of her, and guided her limp figure, into the shop, spluttering against the rising dust, her eyes streaming from the debris already there.

Within minutes, the tremors, the ground's buckling, and the crashing of falling masonry subsided. The stillness was like a silence cutting across a graveyard. They moved towards the inside the patisserie, the only place which was free of the running tracks and falling debris.

'It's stopped,' said Luke, a puff of relief deflating his chest; he slumped down next to Dean, against the wall of the café, his hands shaking. 'Melody?' he called out. 'Melody!'

'I'm here,' she said, and she stumbled across the café, throwing herself into his arms, tucking her head under his chin. 'I can't believe it. I can't believe this is happening.'

'What on earth?' said Stella. 'OMG! Did that really happen?' And she burst into tears, clinging onto Anton. Anton wrapped his arms around her and whispered softly into her hair, 'There, there. We're safe.'

Stella, kneeling next to Anton, held onto his hand. Dean had come round and was sipping water from a glass. The waiter and two of his staff, fussing about their customers, assuring them it would all be okay.

'How will we get back to the hotel?' asked Melody, her eyes wide, saucers of milk against her even paler face.

'You will have to stay here until the emergency services give us the okay to go out,' said one of the staff, shouting above the panic infiltrating from outside. Stella looked up at him. Judging by his chequered apron and tall hat he was the chef. His bright white hat, a beacon of hope in all the chaos. He handed out patchwork blankets, their colours congruent with the dim interior of the café, and extra cushions, their seat ties hanging limply like plants thirsty for water. 'Get comfortable. You may be here for hours,' he said.

Anton tried his phone, threw it to the ground next to him. 'The network's down,' he said, his voice full of despair, one cheek glistening with tears.

'Don't worry,' said Stella. 'At least we're safe here, for now.'

'I need to get in touch with my wife − ,' he said, stopping himself mid-sentence but it was too late. Stella had heard him. 'I need to let my family know I'm okay,' he continued, but only making the situation worse.

Stella's face dropped. He was thinking about his family, not her. Something in her snapped. 'They're safe. It's us out here in the middle of an earthquake.'

'What's wrong with you?' Anton spat.

'What's wrong with me? Are you seriously asking me that?'

'You're overreacting. You're in shock.'

'Too right I am but I'm not overreacting. I'm reacting. Reacting to this farce of a relationship. You're not here with me. Look at you, even now thinking about her.'

Anton peered across at Melody and Luke who quickly looked away. Eliana hugged her body, rocking back and forth, the blanket draped across her shoulders.

'Darling, please. Don't say that. We're on holiday. We're safe. We're together.' He reached for Stella's shoulder, but she inched away, couldn't bear to have him touch her.

'I'm on holiday. You're still in London with your wife. Your heart and your head are in London and whatever you say now won't convince me otherwise.' She sounded like a petulant child, but she didn't care. This was all such a disaster.

Anton opened his mouth to speak and, to Stella's relief, thought better of it. He sighed and sunk back against the wall.

Stella sat with her thoughts. *It's over.* Why she ever thought coming away would make it better, make it more solid and real. It was a ridiculous supposition. They had spent months planning it. To fit around his anniversary, around his birthday, his wife's birthday, his work commitments. From the beginning she had made all the compromises again. She had had enough. He had begged her to reconsider, but it was too late.

She turned away from him and let the tears fall. This was the end. After two decades together. If she added the actual time physically together, in each other's company, it didn't even add up to three or four years. She had thrown away the best years of her life to a fake relationship.

An anger burst from her, like the shudder of the earthquake, and it freed her. It gave her wings and inside, though her heart was breaking, there was a warm glow, a shining light, and she knew she would be okay. And for the first time in a long time, she finally put herself and her feelings first. It felt good. It was liberating.

In one corner other patrons trapped with them, Greeks, talked in hushed conspiratorial tones, leaning into each other, sniffing into hankies and women crossing themselves looking to God for protection, their prayers evident. The atmosphere was one of doom, claustrophobic in its humming darkness, spreading like an unwelcome buzz. The heavy sighs of men trying to contain their fright did not ease the gloom; it was plainly yet delicately painted as clear as the moon in the sky on their creased faces.

Stella recognised one woman's mumblings… she spoke of the earthquake in Turkey and Syria earlier that year and taken the lives of more than 28,000 people. Stella had cried for days watching the news unfold, the horrific, agonising footage of mangled bodies and dead children. The image of the broken father holding onto his dead daughter's hand poking out from the rubble still haunted her, his tears leaving tracks down his grimy face.

The inside of the cafe was dark and dingy; the hum of the quiet chatter, the strain of stressed voices and quiet sobbing reached her ears, then fell away as she took herself somewhere else and the conversations mingled into nothingness.

She sat there for a few minutes and then shook herself

out, wanting to stay focused. On the glass-fronted serving counter an array of glasses and small dishes holding candles of all sizes shaped a shadowy light into the space, the flickering flames cast moving shadows up the stone walls, but they were not menacing they were dancing. A sign of hope. She clung onto those silhouettes, their fluidity, their swaying bodies like ballet dancers swathed in long golden skirts of silk, like life rafts.

The waiter who had served them, offered food to everyone, and bent down towards Stella proffering a breadstick and some dried apricots. She took both, her stomach growling in gratitude as she swallowed the crunchy snack, her body shaking despite the incredible heat.

She watched as he navigated the tables and chairs and the stretched-out legs across the floor, coming from all angles, as he offered sustenance to all the hostages of the earthquake. *Efharisto, efharisto...* thanks were repeated one after the other as the simple, but much-needed food was handed out. The crunching of bread sticks replaced the sobbing and the prayers.

Chapter 29

It was hours before they were finally able to contact anyone at Miramare and like captives, people clung onto one another, huddling for both the sense of security it gave but also to feel less alone. Stella knew there was a chasm between her and Anton.

She felt it pushing them apart like a split oyster shell. A numbness seeped its way into her and the harder she tried to stay connected to Anton, to hold onto their happiest memories, she couldn't. The numbness froze her.

The minibus Prodromos organised to collect them was like an angel before her eyes. Stella cried with relief, hot tears flooding her like a blazing fire, the frozen deadness of earlier thawing, the respite overwhelming. Eliana and Melody cried openly, unabashed, shamelessly transparent.

The men nodded and smiled tentatively at each other,

too terrified to show their real feelings.

The drive back, in silence, everyone too shocked to speak of the catastrophic event, was thankfully uneventful. The locals, used to living with the threat of and the sustained pounding to their towns and villages, once clear of danger, seemed to carry on. The further away from the town they drove, the less the earthquake's destruction and the landscape appeared untouched.

At the hotel Stella noticed there had been negligible damage to the building, thankfully. She caught Prodromos' sympathetic smile, and with effort smiled back, but they were all shivery from fear and shock, afraid they would not be found and shaken from the bumpy drive back.

The couples sat around the pool, shell-shocked, barely speaking. Prodromos sent blankets and bottles of water to them, and they sat, huddled, deep in their own thoughts. A guest walked past them, her feet leaving wet footprints on the stone flooring.

Stella stared at the tattered ribbon knotted in her hair, the ends floating behind her, tangled in her wet locks. It reminded her of the red ribbon caught in the branches of the tree in the movie Matilda and she shivered hoping the worst had passed. She couldn't cope with anymore; her nerves frayed, coiled like a spring; her heart weary.

Prodromos appeared with a tray of Greek coffee. 'Strong and sweet,' he said as Yiannis passed around the remaining demi-tasses with care.

'Thank you, both of you. You've been exceedingly kind,' said Stella, her mouth suddenly dry, her voice shaking with delayed shock. She stroked her arm, a graze from her elbow all the way down to her wrist burning, the wound seeping over the caked, dry streaks of blood.

'I will bring you something for your arm,' said Prodromos.

Yiannis appeared, skulking behind him, an agony filling his eyes.

'It's fine, thank you. It's a bit sore. Nothing a cool shower won't make better.'

'It's no trouble,' he said, scurrying back towards the white building where he and Andri resided, a one-storey annexe, bursting with the colours of summer, the trellis on its outer walls heavy with blooms of hot magenta, lentil-yellow and lavender purple.

'I thought we were going to die,' breathed Eliana, eventually, twisting the hem of her skirt, her eyes wide, red from crying and tears threatening to fall again as she fought to swallow them back. 'All I could do was think about the Turkey-Syria earthquake.'

Dean, next to her, his head bandaged, remained silent, the shock of his accident muting his otherwise usually free-flow chatter. He nodded every now and again, as if following the conversation, though Stella suspected he was not listening at all, hardly engaging. Eventually the chatter spiked in volume and intensity.

'Of all the luck,' said Luke. 'I'd heard about earthquakes across the Greek islands but never for a moment thought I'd be here in one. Terrifying... quite unbelievable.'

'It's surreal,' said Anton. 'One minute we were talking and the next covered in dust and surrounded by craters the size of...' His mobile, suddenly alive with the glimmer of a signal, interrupted him. He looked down at the screen and then straight at Stella.

'Aren't you going to pick it up?' asked Stella, tilting her chin up, daring him to lie to her as she wrapped her arms around her knees, protecting herself from what she imagined was to come. He seemed to want to say something, but stopped himself and instead said, 'Excuse me,' and walked away from the group, back towards the canopied corner of the bar, the twinkly lights twisted around the edge of the bar and up and across the canopy.

Stella stiffened, though she tried hard to look relaxed, she changed position, forced her arms to rest in her lap limply, but she could feel the intensity with which she held her breath, almost willing everyone to disappear. She leaned back in her chair, trying to catch what Anton was saying, her nails now digging into her sweating palms. Snippets of his conversation found their way to her:

No, the conference....
Miss you so much...
I'm safe...
I'm sorry...
Darling...
I promise...
I love you too.

Stella fought back against the tight pain in her chest. He was still lying to his wife. He would never come clean about their relationship. She had never thought about Anton's words being shared in the same way with his wife... flowing off his tongue like oil on water... no hesitation, no hint of guilt in his voice. He was such a good liar. The words, once crimped with happy edges, full and round, now gave her a paper cut. She had always known it but today she had wanted him to prove his love for her and no one else. But he hadn't and the realisation crushed her more than any falling debris could have.

She breathed evenly trying to keep the tears at bay as they threatened to escape, making her vision milky. She wiped at her eyes, trying to eliminate the blurriness with the back of her hand, frantically muttering something about the dust in the air. She caught Melody and Eliana's eye; they were both watching her. She looked away. She didn't need their pity or their sympathies. She knew what she had to do.

'Stella, please. Can we talk?' begged Yiannis, pulling at her arm.

'Not here, not now.' She shook him off, but part of her wanted to be wrapped in his arms.

'I want to be with you,' he said, 'and I won't give up. Do you hear me? I won't give up.' He gave her a pleading look; desperation filled his eyes. 'Had the earthquake taken you away from me... I don't know what I would have done.'

Anton's conversation ended, and she pretended to be engrossed in the chatter around her; calmer, lighter, now that everyone seemed to have got over the shock and soothed by the effects of the sweet coffee. But her heart raced. She was in too deep.

'It is all okay. Please do not worry yourselves. You are safe here,' repeated Prodromos. We are far away from the town, from the tectonic activity. We have suffered much worse as an island. This is nothing. And we rarely feel it out as far as here. The gods protect us. As does love,' he said.

'Thank you. It's good to be here, away from the chaos,' said Luke, tipping back his demi-tasse and then twitching his nose and scrunching his face as the bitter dregs of the coffee coated his tongue.

'If you don't mind, I'm going back to my room. I'm still a little shaky,' said Stella.

'Take the lint gauze and the antiseptic. You can apply it yourself,' said Prodromos.

Stella reluctantly conceded, accepting the first aid. From afar, she could feel Yiannis staring at her. She had to do something. She had to decide. The music tinkled. The discussion had already been made for her.

'I'll come back with you,' said Anton, pulling back her chair. Giving him a half-smile, for the benefit of their friends, Stella bid them good night.

'I will make sure dinner is something exceptional,' Prodromos called after them. 'Eight o'clock I will have a feast good enough for the gods ready for you all.'

'We're looking forward to it,' Anton called back. 'See you all later.'

'Thank you so much,' said Stella with more cheer than she held inside her.

Chapter 30

Stella showered, the door to the bathroom firmly shut, ensuring her message to Anton came across loud and clear. Thoughts of the town and the crumbling buildings crowded her mind. She had to speak to Prodromos, see if everyone had been brought to safety.

The water, though only a soft spray from the showerhead, stung the graze, now angry red. She languished in the shower, the water stripping her of the outer shell of bravery cloaking her. She buckled under the weight of what had happened; the realisation she had reached the end of her relationship. Stuffing her balled fist into her mouth, she stifled the animal-like sobs which escaped her, rendering her small and feeble, exposed, and vulnerable, as she sunk into the shower tray, the tears falling, her heart shattered.

'You okay in there?' Anton asked, knocking on the locked door gently. She didn't answer, afraid of letting him hear how broken she was. She turned off the faucet and sat, huddled for minutes... minutes which felt like hours until she began to shiver. She dragged herself up and wrapped the huge bath towel around her, shaking, weak with sadness, regret, and pain, physical and emotional; she was battered and bruised from the inside out and the outside in.

She wandered into the bedroom and kicked the door shut. She didn't want Anton near her. She didn't want him here. She had waited so long for this holiday, longed to spend more than a few hours at a time with him, and now it was over. Nothing left. Nothing beating for him.

She winced at the sting of the antiseptic against her skin as it pressed down on her, and she wrapped the lint gauze around her arm as best she could with one hand. It was a superficial graze, it wouldn't leave a lasting scar, unlike the tear on her heart, which would remain forever.

She slipped on a beach dress and slid her feet into her flipflops.

Anton was sitting on the verandah; the back of his head tipped upwards against the top of the chair as he looked straight up. She tried to fathom what he was thinking. Was he feeling like her?

'Hey,' she said, not wanting to creep up on him, fighting to hold onto her nerve.

'You okay?' he asked.

'Yeah, a bit sore. No lasting damage. Not to my arm anyway.'

'I'm sorry, Stella. Sorry for all of it,' he said with feeling.

'Don't be. We had some good times. The good times will stay with us forever,' she said, tilting her head girlishly to one side.

'Let's not finish it,' he said, turning round to face her in the seat next to him.

'I can't see a way back from this. It's reached its expiration date. It had to come one way or another. Maybe this is the kinder less painful way for all of us.'

'Less painful? I'm gutted here,' he said.

'As I am too. But I need to be selfish. I need to put my own needs first.'

'And I don't do that?'

'You know you don't. Not intentionally but with a wife and a son... your thoughts are always not too far away from them. I understood. I accepted. But now I want something different for me. I'm nearly fifty. I don't want to be creeping around. I don't want to be second best. I deserve someone who can be with me heart and soul and across time and space.'

'I can't let you go.'

'But imagine the pain if your wife found out the truth. At least this way you have a chance to patch things up with her. Make it right,' she said, losing her patience, the heat getting to her, her arm sore.

'Why would she find out?'

'Go home, Anton. It's where you should be. Where you have always been, with your family. We were playing games. Pretending,' said Stella.

'Go home?'

'You should be at home with her.'

'And you?' he asked.

'I'm going to stay and write. And I'm not your problem anymore.'

Anton turned away, she knew he was crying, she'd seen the tears in his eyes long before they fell, and she couldn't bear the thought of all the heartbreak, splintering shards between them like a thousand memories of broken glass everywhere, but she had no choice. She had to choose herself over him this time. It was her only choice.

Stella panicked. Hoped Yiannis wouldn't turn up at their room. She grabbed her bag, and banging the door behind her, swept from the room. She flipped the sign on the door handle to "Do not Disturb." She needed some air, time to think.

***

'You okay?' asked Melody.

'Are you okay?' Stella asked Melody as she took the sunbed adjacent to hers and dumped her bag on the cool tiles.

'Yes, no. It's all been a bit traumatic.'

Stella took out her suncream and smothered her face with it. 'The earthquake?'

'Yes, I suppose. It's made me reflect,' said Melody, biting the skin around her fingertips.

'Yeah, so frightening. You don't expect to come on holiday and then get caught up in an earthquake,' said Stella. 'But Prodromos said everyone was safe. No serious injuries.'

'Thank goodness.' Melody sighed.

'Is there something else on your mind?'

'Selfishly I'm thinking about my relationship.'

'It's not selfish,' said Stella. She was thinking about

her own mess of one too.

'How can Luke and I carry on like this? It's stifling. He's smothering me and I can't ever make up for what I did. I can't turn back time. I can't change the way he feels after what I did. The way I feel.'

'And how do you feel?'

'Like a prisoner. Like I should be grateful he's forgiven me and yet I'm not. I'm dying in here,' she said, poking a finger into her chest. 'I think I'm going to leave him.'

'I'm done too. I've ended it with Anton.'

'Stella, no. I'm so sorry. Looks like this holiday is making us take stock of our lives and what we really want. Love has a lot to answer for.'

'Yeah. And not what we want but what we deserve. I deserve better than stolen hours here and there. Secret messages. Sitting by the phone waiting until I'm ready to burst.'

'I guess after all these years it's not exhilarating anymore.'

'It's not even about the excitement. I want stability. I want a partner who's there for me.'

'And I want to be free of the inquisition and the suspicious looks and the spot-checks on where I am and who I'm with. I want his possessiveness to stop.'

'What are you going to do?'

'I need to go and tell him.'

'Now?'

'Before I bottle it.'

'Shall I come with you... in case he gets annoyed, lashes out.'

'I'll be fine, but thanks,' Melody said, and she grabbed

her towel, rolled it up and stuffed it into her beach bag with her magazine.

Stella lifted a palm in farewell as she walked off and hoped Melody would be okay. Luke might have been a nice guy once but clearly troubled he had anger issues. Life was messy. It was cruel. But Melody was at least facing up to the part she played in bringing their relationship to this point. She hoped Luke did too.

Chapter 31

'You didn't tell me about your husband,' said Yiannis, the following day, pulling Stella into the shadows by the arm and filling her up with the passion of his deep kiss.

'He's not my husband,' Stella said, pulling away, speaking in a hushed voice, irrational panic filling her, replacing the passion of their kiss. Her eyes darted around for Anton who had ran back into their room for his sunglasses. He would find them next to the bed and emerge any second.

'Boyfriend?' he smirked, a twist pulled at his mouth, but it was quickly replaced with a sadness which touched his eyes and tugged at Stella's heartstrings.

But then a sudden force of determination, of not wanting to be controlled, gave way and pulling her arm away from him, she said, 'Actually, Yiannis, he is my lover. We have been together for a long time.'

Confusion faded and gave way to a marked frown

of distrust. Yiannis's voice shook. 'I thought we were together.'

'Yiannis, this was a holiday romance. A fling. It can't go anywhere,' said Stella dismissively, trying to ignore her heart's thrum, her welling desire for him.

'Why not?'

'Because I am almost twice your age, and it won't work.'

'It worked with him for years and you were only half his life.'

'Well, yes, it has. It did. But not anymore.'

'Because of me?' he asked, hope flooding his eyes with a spark of light.

Stella hesitated, looking back towards her bedroom, waiting for the door to open at any moment. A maelstrom of emotions, guilt, and panic, flooding her.

'I have fallen in love with you,' said Yiannis.

'You're not in love with me. You're in lust with me. It's what you Greeks call *ludus*.'

'*Ludus*, yes. In the beginning flirting, laughing together, but not now. Now it is heading towards something more.'

'This cannot be,' insisted Stella.

'You are mistaken, my dearest Stella. Give us a chance.'

'I'm sorry Yiannis. It was a mistake.'

'Don't tell me that. We are good together, no?' Stella looked into his pleading eyes and nodded ever so slightly, unable to disappoint him.

'Yes. But it can't carry on.'

'What can't carry on? Is he hassling you?' asked Anton, taking a step towards Yiannis, and pushing him away from Stella.

'No, it's okay,' said Stella, her eyes darting to Yiannis.

'It doesn't look okay,' Anton said, taking off his sunglasses and pushing them into the front pocket of his shirt, before staring Yiannis in the eyes, unflinching, steady.

'He was talking about the... the music I hear. He doesn't want me to question Prodromos about it again.'

'She can ask him anything she wants, mate,' said Anton, squaring up to Yiannis. Stella thought he looked ridiculous picking a fight with a man half his age, agile, lighter, younger. She could see how this was going to go.

Stella's heart rate shot up, panic filling her. 'Leave it, Anton. Come on. It's a simple misunderstanding. Yiannis didn't mean anything by it, did you Yiannis?'

Panic threatened to freeze her to the spot. Diverting her attention to Anton, she grabbed Anton's hand and turned from Yiannis. She tried leading Anton away from the imminent combustion between the two men, her two lovers.

'You may leave this, but I will not,' called Yiannis after them, their backs to him as they walked away. '*Malaka*!'

On hearing the expletive, Stella knew Anton had heard it too. Seconds later, Anton leapt forward and swung a punch at Yiannis. But the younger man, too quick for him, ducked and brought up his arm, fist clenched, as he drove into Anton's jaw from below and then pushed Anton, winded and disorientated, back up against the wall, pressing his full weight into him.

Stella heard a crack and then saw drops of blood falling to the ground, curling slowly into each other, creating a smattering pool of red; it reminded her of the pressed wet-paint butterfly paintings she used to do at school and for a moment, she found herself lost in the flash of a memory.

'You don't deserve her,' yelled Yiannis.

'What the hell do you know about it?'

'I know more than you know. I know how a woman should be treated. Should be respected.'

'You are unbelievable. I am going to get you sacked, you bastard.'

'You can't touch me, you English think you are in charge of the world. You know nothing, nothing about love and loving a woman.'

'Stop it. Both of you!' she said, their shouting pulling her out of her momentary amnesia. Yiannis turned and began to walk away. Stella caught sight of the hurt tears filling his eyes and her heart pounded in her chest, with a heady concoction of love and admiration.

'You shit head!' yelled Anton out of nowhere and he came back with another swing. Yiannis intercepted it with his left arm and threw two punches with his right, one after the other, into Anton's abdomen. Anton dropped to the ground; his glasses flew out of his pocket with the second thrust. Anton gasped for air, his breathing shallow, his arm clamped over his abdomen.

'*Malaka*,' Yiannis yelled again, this time louder, and he stamped on the glasses, grinding his heel into them, shattering them into pieces.

Stella fell to her knees next to him, tears streaming down her face. Her nostrils filled with the iron smell of fresh blood, making her turn away for a second.

He straightened into an upright position, the wall now smudged with blood, imprints from his hands smeared across it as he tried to prop himself up. He moved his head left and right, trying to bring back his focus.

Seconds later, Anton had his hands around Yiannis' throat. Stella pulled and pulled at Anton's clenched hands, trying to loosen his grip but Anton elbowed her away. She fell back, sickeningly askew. The last thing she saw was the lemon tree in the pot opposite her, swaying back and forth, as if flirting with her, enticing her to dance. Her eyes closed, Yiannis' name on her lips, barely a whisper.

'The magic is wavering; it is blinking on and off. Something is happening my love, and I am fearful. Fearful of the pain and the agony of lost love,' said Prodromos, scratching his head, pacing the small kitchen. He stood by the open window, breathing in the air, but it gave him no respite from the closing heat, claustrophobic, stifling.

'Lost love is always followed by new-found love, stronger, more passionate than before,' said Andri, her voice calm, unaffected by his agitation.

'You stay calm, as if you have the answer,' said Prodromos, looking back at her.

'I have answers, but they may not be the ones those seeking love are wishing for,' she said, bent over her sewing, not looking up, not meeting his eyes.

'The air is warm, heavy with a mood that is not one I wish to welcome. It is a bad energy; forbidden, angry, cruel, egocentric. The mountain does not wish to hold onto it. It is pushing, pushing and the magic is heavy with confusion, heavy with the responsibility of it all.'

'You fret too much. Let it go. Trust the magic, my darling Prodromos, trust it, breathe deeply, let it go.'

'I cannot. I want it to work.'

'And it will, it will in its own good time, in its own way.'

'Trust…'

'Yes, trust. Trust it is moving forward with purpose. It is only then people can trust they have their own place in this world.'

'My beautiful, wise, Andri. I cannot ever let you go.'

'The time will come and when it does it will be right. Trust me,' she smiled. 'Truthfulness and its timing are one. And together they are powered and driven by something more powerful than any of us.'

'You are all I need.'

'Go and bring me some cottons. Pinks, blues, yellows, and oranges. I need to finish this sewing. This will look beautiful on our table when it is finished,' she said, holding up her handiwork, pride dancing across her features, lighting her diamond-bright eyes.

'I will go this afternoon.'

'And as you drive, look to the west and breathe in the colours of the setting sun.'

'Always my darling, my precious love.'

Chapter 32

'Oh my God. What's happened?' said Melody. 'Stella, Stella, can you hear me love?'

'It's Yiannis. He's out of control,' said Anton, but he noticed how Melody was not convinced.

'Stella, it's me. Melody.' Stella could hear the familiar voices but didn't have the strength to open her eyes, to open them and focus, she could make out the conversation around her, voices full of wild panic, heavy with tempestuous anger and relentless frustration.

Anton let out a long, exasperated sigh. 'We had a disagreement.'

Stella opened her eyes and Melody leaned in to hug her. 'Bring the water from my bag,' she shouted to Luke. 'What sort of disagreement? Why?'

'He was hitting on her. The little shit,' said Anton. Stella had never seen him so angry; the throbbing veins in his neck, his jutting chin. 'She's mine. If he's done anything to her, even so much as touched her, I will kill him with my bare hands.'

Melody held the bottle up to Stella's lips and poured a little of the cool water into her mouth, Stella reached up and tried to hold the bottle, but she was too feeble. She took a sip and coughed. 'Let's get her inside. How close is your room?' she asked Anton.

'Ours is on the next level. Let's take her to Eliana and Dean's. It's closer.'

Anton and Luke heaved Stella up and half-conscious they half-carried half-dragged her to Eliana and Dean's room.

'I'm okay,' Stella slurred, as she sunk in and out of consciousness.

When she next opened her eyes, Eliana was standing at the open door of her hotel room.

'I'm okay,' managed Stella when she realised how upset they all appeared.

Stella was propped up on the couch and Eliana brought her some more water.

'Here, you'll be okay,' Eliana said, wrapping her arms around her.

'What happened?' asked Luke, turning to Anton. 'And look at your face.'

'I'm fine, mate. An altercation with Yiannis. Nothing I can't handle.'

'Yiannis? The young waiter? Doesn't sound like him to be causing trouble,' said Eliana.

'I want to make sure Stella's okay,' Anton said, avoiding an answer.

'Ouch, it hurts,' Stella said, and she ran her hand over

her head, wincing.

'I think she should stay here for a bit,' said Melody. 'I know how disorientating it is to be...' They all turned to look at her. 'I mean, I can imagine what it's like,' she stumbled on, her face red.

'Why don't we go onto the balcony and leave the women to it, give them some space,' suggested Dean. 'You need to sort out that lip too,' he said to Anton.

'Yeah, good idea,' said Anton, with some hesitation. 'Call me if you need anything, my darling. I'm sorry,' he said and bent to kiss her forehead. 'I'll check on you in a bit.'

'What the hell happened?' jumped in Eliana once the men were out of earshot.

'Anton and Yiannis had a fight,' said Stella, avoiding the women's eyes.

'We got that much, but why?' urged Eliana.

'Because Anton became suspicious of Yiannis and me talking and went for him.'

'Why? What were you talking about?' Melody asked sheepishly.

'That doesn't sound right. Come on, tell us Stella. What's really going on?'

Stella crumpled and the tears she had been holding in flooded the backs of her eyes and rolled down her cheeks. She shielded her face with her hands, but her sobs kept coming.

'Stella, you're scaring us. What's happened? Has Yiannis been inappropriate with you?' Eliana and Melody's eyes widened with horror and in anticipation of Stella's unfolding revelation.

'It was a misunderstanding. A heat of the moment thing,' Stella said.

'Not on holiday. Not a waiter and a guest,' said Eliana.

'I slept with Yiannis.' Both women stared at Stella.

'I'm the last one to judge,' said Melody, 'but them punching the shit out of each other is not going to solve the problem.'

'Anton doesn't know. I haven't told him. He got the wrong end of the stick.'

'Wrong end of the stick? Looks like there's no wrong end and he's getting the gist something's not right,' said Eliana.

'I know. I know. I tried to fob him off. I'm not ready to admit sleeping with Yiannis.'

'You've been stuck in this long-term relationship for so long you have got used to being quiet, taking it all lying down...'

'Literally,' giggled Melody uncharacteristically, but then put on a straight face when Eliana glared at her.

'This is serious,' continued Eliana. 'How do you feel?'

'I never thought I would love anyone but Anton. It's been him for so long but it's over. He knows it. It's done.'

'But,' prompted Eliana.

'No but. With Yiannis, and I know it's ridiculous, something in me has changed. I feel free. I feel like I can do whatever I want. Can be the person I was always meant to be.'

'And?' Eliana paused, giving her time to open up.

'Anton and I don't have a future now. I can see a life without Anton. Not necessarily with Yiannis either. I think I can be on my own. Live life on my terms. Be with Yiannis or not.'

'Then you have to be clear with Anton,' Melody pleaded. 'Secrets can eat away at you and once they've burrowed so deep there's never a safe way out. No hurt-free way out.'

'You have to make Anton see it's over for your own sanity. Your future self will thank you for it,' said Eliana.

Stella looked at her. 'I will. It's over between Anton and me. I have to admit that and move on.' She sipped the sweet tea Eliana passed to her; a coil of nerves wrapped around her shaking hand as she brought the cup to her lips. 'You have to do the same, Melody.'

Melody hesitated. 'You think you know. But you don't, not really. You see me in my cardigan, covering up, but that's only one part of the story, the ugly part. And it doesn't play justly. Your eyes see what they want to see, but only I know what's behind it all.'

'Don't you dare stick up for Luke,' said Eliana.

'I'm not.'

'Why are you covering up then?'

'It's not what you think. He's just over-protective. Gets jealous.'

'So, he hits you,' said Eliana.

'No... no he doesn't. He's just passionate. I bruise easily. I cheated on him. I'm the one who has made him like this.'

'Melody, there's never a valid excuse for a man to strike a woman. Never.'

'I'm not saying it as an excuse. I'm offering an explanation. I'm not saying it's right. I'm not saying I deserve it.'

'I should hope not,' said Eliana forcefully.

'Our relationship is one big mess. I need to sort it out with Luke.'

'You're not going anywhere until you don't resemble a white harvest moon,' said Eliana.

'Ooh, listen to you,' cooed Stella.

'I know, right?' said Eliana. 'Sorry, too much trash in the magazine I got at the airport.'

'How's the patient?' asked Anton, interrupting their conversation. 'Are you feeling okay darling?'

'She's much better. We ordered a pot of mountain tea with herbs,' said Eliana.

'And the vodka?' asked Anton, running his fingers over his swollen lip.

'Duty Free. That was for us... for the shock of seeing Stella so distraught.'

Anton didn't say anything and for a second the girls let out a squeal of laughter but quickly stifled their giggles when Anton's reaction didn't mirror their own silliness.

'Do you feel well enough to go back to our room?' he asked, with concern.

'I think so, yes,' she said, and the guilt filled his eyes and the same guilt, only for a different reason, filled Stella's.

The sixth person had revealed themselves and Prodromos could not but help harbouring a little mistrust and resentment towards the man who claimed to love Stella. He was selfish, arrogant, entitled. How could she not see it? How could a woman with so much goodness, a writer of hearts, not see the sterility of the man who claimed to love her.

'Nobody knows what goes on between a man and his lover,' said Andri. 'Why do you concern yourself so with him?'

'He is greedy, he abuses the love of the women in his life.'

'*Philautia* is love of the self, associated with narcissism. It's unhealthy but it's not destructive, Prodromos,' said Andri quietly.

'He thinks he is untouchable. But the gods will not allow such a love to grow, to go unclipped.'

'The gods are too busy protecting their own to think about us mortals. Leave the English alone. Let them be.'

'There's a shift in the air, Andri and it has nothing to do with the earthquake. There will be a much needed shake up amongst our guests and I am willing to bet it will be most felt by three of our couples. Stella will be stronger for it and will find the longstanding love she deserves and has waited for. It's the love she has been writing about in her books.'

'And the others?'

'The magic will help them too.'

'It's the wildness and the wilderness within them,' said Andri.

'They will all be changed by it,' said Prodromos.

Andri nodded and Prodromos threw his hands up towards the heavens, his eyes closed. He held them shut for a few seconds, imagining the gods' fighting over who would win, but he knew they had more faith in love than they allowed to show. Love would conquer all.

He felt a whisper in his ear and the zestiness of lemons

filled his senses; there was freshness and renewal here. Love was closer than he thought. The sun would be setting over the temple now, low, and red and big, and he could see the reflection on the ancient white stone columns and cornicing. Triumphant in its beauty the magic swirled around it. Tempestuous, unyielding, waiting for something to happen. Something to say yes.

There was friction sending up sparks into the air. Something deeper and more meaningful was possible. Prodromos felt the enchanting powerful world of possibility closing in.

Chapter 33

'Oh my God. Are you okay?'

'Yeah,' said Stella, wiping her eyes. 'What are you doing here?'

'I heard you arguing,' said Eliana.

'Sorry.'

'Don't be. It's difficult not to hear everything when the doors are open and our room's below yours.'

'Anton and I have finished.'

'I know,' said Eliana, looking up from the English pages of the Greek newspaper she'd ran out with in her hand. 'I heard you shouting and then it went all quiet.'

'I've ended our relationship. We're over,' said Stella and she crumpled into tears.

'Stella, it's okay. Don't cry.'

'It's such a shock. After all this time. I don't know what I'm doing. It's like I'm this other person,' she said, wiping her tears and snotty nose with the back of her hand. Eliana jumped up and came back with some loo roll. 'Thank you.'

'It's okay,' repeated Eliana.

'I thought this was going to be the holiday of a lifetime. Put all my trust in him. Him and me, no one else. Just us and all the time we needed to be together.'

'I thought it was Melody and Luke having trust issues. I'm so sorry,' said Eliana, her eyes glazing over with tears. 'Dean said I was hearing things, accused me of playing Chinese whispers.'

'I'm sorry. I didn't realise how easily our voices carried in this place.'

'I've been listening to you for the past fifteen minutes,' said Eliana, wincing at her admission, her embarrassment colouring her face. 'And anyway, Dean and I had a row too. He told me to put my efforts into something a bit more rewarding and sat there groping his manhood, straining against his boxers, and singing, *When you're in love with a beautiful woman, you know it's hard, it's hard, you know it gets so hard...*' Her voice got louder and louder. 'I told him to suck it himself.'

'Bloody hell,' said Stella and they both fell about laughing.

'I've brought you on holiday and you haven't so much as touched me,' Eliana said, mimicking Dean.

'And then what?'

'I told him to shut up and get on with it,' Eliana said. 'I went through the motions, thinking about our afternoon of shopping later and considering whether this really is what being married is all about.'

'You must be in love though, huh?' said Stella.

'Dean would argue I'm in love with his money.' She held out her hand and showed off her sparkling new ring.

'Love before money, no?' Stella said.

'The woman at the shop said something similar. What is it with all the Greeks and their obsession with love?'

'I'd say it's what makes the whole go round and the ride worthwhile,' laughed Dean, appearing from within the shadows of the path around the pool.

'How long have you been listening?' asked Eliana, but she could see Dean was a little hurt despite the joke, and she put her arm through his.

'Not long. You okay Stella?' he said, squeezing her arm.

'Come on,' said Eliana to Dean. 'Let's find somewhere in town to sit and I will fill you in. And you can eat whatever you like, babe,' she said, with a softness Stella knew she rarely expressed.

'Will you be okay?' Eliana asked.

'Yeah, of course. You go. Have fun.'

'Don't meddle too much,' Andri warned. 'You cannot know how the gods will react and you must not go against their wishes. They are already working their ancient magic. It is something they have been practising for centuries.'

Prodromos looked over at her fair face, that of an angel's, and long golden hair like straw, her blue eyes shining like jewels. 'I won't. I hear you my darling,' he said.

'Good, because this will not serve you well. I want you to be happy. Want you to be fulfilled in all you do.'

'I have done everything the gods have asked of me. I

will not jeopardise our eternal happiness. I promise you Andri. You are the centre of all my love. Celestial. A temple between us.

'I know, my love. Now go, get ready for your day. I will be here waiting for you. I always will be.'

He reached for her hand, but she had already turned from him, busying herself with her sewing, and urging him to drink his coffee.

He drank from the demi-tasse, holding it with his left hand and leaving a little at the bottom of the cup. Then he upturned it onto its saucer and pushed the cup and saucer towards her. The gentle rattle matched the rhythm of his hands tapping on the table. She nodded.

He closed his eyes and felt the warmth of her words near him, felt, as if she were next to him, her energy, her soul at ease, entwined with his. 'This is how we were meant to be.'

'Go,' she urged.

'The reading?'

She turned the tiny cup over and studied the coffee dregs' formations... 'I see angel wings,' she said, beaming. 'And a candle, its flame burning brightly.'

'The gods are behaving themselves; they are on my side,' said Prodromos.

And in that moment a golden light shone through the tiny window in the kitchen and Prodromos knew the goodness of love and commitment and loyalty would win over. He was right. The most extraordinary situation was coming. No one would see it, but he could feel it. He shivered in anticipation.

Chapter 34

'Please Stella,' begged Melody.

'I'm not sure I'm the right person to mediate,' said Stella.

'Of course, you are. You're intelligent, you write about relationships...'

'I just don't know. I don't want to fan the flames.'

'You won't. Please Stella, but only if you feel well enough. I can't put it off any longer. I have to talk to him now. Now I have braved that awful tightening inside me. Now I have somehow freed the words and know what to say.'

'If, you're sure. I mean you're on holiday.'

'I feel like we've covered it all for long enough, the wound needs to be exposed if it is to heal, not left in the dark.'

'Won't he resent me being there?'

'I won't give him a choice. If you can do it, I can do

it too,' said Melody, her hands shaking as she spoke, giving away her nerves despite her positive words, which seemed to tumble out with a force so much bigger than her slight frame could bear.

Stella agreed and the women decided it would be best to plan it. But, one afternoon, it happened serendipitously while the three of them were coincidentally ambling across the wildflower flanks of the hills.

At the top of a ridge, looking down across the tiny white cove, the sea a deep blue, like a glistening sapphire surrounded by diamonds, shone brightly. Stella watched as the colours merged as one with the infinite blue sky; the silver-tipped clouds, as light as candy floss balls, pleasantly intoxicating. The waves, dimpling and dancing, broke gently on the shore which was hugged with drifts of dark green seaweed. Stella anxious the atmosphere was about to explode into something more sinister could hear nothing but the beating of her own heart, and she wilfully slowed her breathing.

Melody signalled to Stella. Stella had already encouraged Melody to express her concerns calmly and with as much gentleness and caring as she could muster. She didn't feel like a row and didn't want a scene and felt certain Melody reciprocated her feelings.

'We need to talk,' Melody said gently, pulling Luke down beside her, onto the dry earth. Luke's shoulders instantly stiffened. *Tread carefully, tread carefully,* Stella said under her breath, holding back a moment to let them sit.

'You're not going to start on about how great Stella is, throwing out her man like that are you? Sorry Stella, no offence intended.'

'Strictly speaking, he wasn't her man at all. He was married to someone else. Is married to someone else,' said Melody.

'Whatever way I liked to dress it up and pretend, that's the ugly truth,' said Stella and she sat, her breath bated, waiting for Luke to blow. It was all a bit too close for comfort. The heat was stifling. The light breeze's familiar sweet perfume was replaced by the bitterness of bruised fruit and did little to reduce the heat coming off her.

'I wanted to talk to you too,' Luke said, looking away, suddenly small, weak, as he lowered himself to the ground next to Melody, his shoulders hunched, rounded. Stella hoped he wasn't about to lose his temper.

'It's about us,' she blurted. 'And I wanted Stella to be here, so now that she is, let's talk.'

'In front of Stella? We hardly know her.'

'It makes her the perfect person to mediate. To listen to what we both have to say.'

'I won't interrupt. I'm here as a neutral third-party presence,' assured Stella and she sat down, legs crossed, opposite them, more assertive than her beating heart indicated inside her chest, and hoping she could sit like this for longer than five minutes. She guessed they would be here a while.

'Let me say something first,' he said, turning away from Stella, facing Melody head on.

'No, please. Otherwise, I'm going to bottle it and I've been thinking about this for a long time.'

'I can't go on like this,' blurted Luke, jumping in ahead of Melody, as if afraid of losing his chance to speak. 'Did you hear what I said?'

Melody sat motionless. It was obvious she couldn't quite understand what Luke was saying. She looked as if her mind was blurred. Stella recognised that look; unable to make sense of the words coming at you. The breeze, suddenly cooler, buzzed in Stella's ears and left a chill on her shoulders. It whipped around Melody's face as it came over the edge of the cliff.

Swallows swooped and dived above their heads, casting dancing shadows across Melody and Luke's features. Deep inside, Stella hoped, as she believed Melody did too, that Luke was about to end it, to save Melody the agony of having to say the words herself.

'What?' she said eventually, and Stella saw her swallowing down a rising panic, recognising the mixed emotions threatening to drown her as they had not so long ago come at her too.

'Us, this constant arguing, the way your affair has made me become. I don't recognise myself,' said Luke.

'What are you saying?' Melody couldn't look at him. Her expression reminded Stella of her own heart thumping against her ribs like a bird trying to escape the confines of a locked cage.

'I'm saying it's time we admitted this isn't working and I think we should separate. Go our own ways.'

'Why now?' Melody asked, and Stella noted the panic in her eyes, her face screwed up as if in discomfort.

'I don't know. Being here. Stella. Anton. Luke. Eliana... all of them. It's made me think about us. The us we used to be.'

'There's still an "us", Luke,' said Melody, looking

crushed by his words.

'It's given me time to think properly,' he said.

'It's the calm of this place.'

'Guests fighting in the hotel, banging their heads and passing out isn't calm,' Luke said, in a muffled voice and Melody looked apologetically in Stella's direction.

'I'm calm. I don't want to be angry all the time, consumed by thoughts of you with him, us no longer how we used to be.' He clenched and unclenched his fists and Melody flinched. Stella shifted uneasily; the scent of the air seemed to change with the atmosphere. What would Stella do if Luke lunged at Melody? 'See? Look at you. This is killing me,' he said.

'And me,' Melody said, barely a whisper. 'But we can work things out. If you want to.'

'How? Look at us. We are going to end up hating each other.'

'We can try. See a relationship counsellor, a couples' therapist.'

'No. All they want is your money. And we don't have money to waste.'

'We can work it out,' said Melody. 'I'm ashamed of myself for putting us in this situation, a tug of war, our hearts bruised.' She stopped, wiped her tears, took a breath. 'I realise you're bruised too, from the inside out, but I couldn't see it. I see it now.'

'I am working it out. Working it out for me. I can't be responsible for you, your mess, the repercussions, the aftermath of your affair.'

'What do you mean? Working them out for you?' she asked. Again, Stella noted how Melody had a tell-tale expression of betrayal shadowing her demeanour; hunched shoulders, bowed head. Melody was ashamed.

'These past few months I've been going to therapy.'

'You said it was expensive,' Melody said, her head darting up.

'Work paid for it. I was losing it at work too,' he said, his voice dropping to a whisper.

'You've always been against counselling, said it was a load of codswallop,' said Melody, the shock of his revelation pink on her face.

'I didn't tell you because I wanted to work out what to do. What to do about the anger in me.' He stood up, took a few paces towards the cliff edge, looked down. 'I am not an abuser. I am not a man who controls and coerces. You turned me into this monster. This person I don't recognise. I can't live like this.'

Melody jumped up and took a tentative step towards him. 'Luke, please. Come back from the edge.' Her hand involuntarily trembled for a few seconds over her mouth.

'Don't tell me what to do!' Luke's jaw tensed visibly as he yelled; his body swung precariously close to the overhanging ledge.

'Okay. Okay,' was all she could say, the shock of his revelation etched on her features, hot tears streaming down her cheeks, snot running over her mouth.

He looked back at her. 'I hate myself. I need to go,' he said, eyelids clenched, his face crumpled in despair.

'Luke, please,' she begged. 'Don't do this. Please.'

Stella edged towards him. 'Luke, this isn't the answer. Come away from the cliff edge. It's not safe. Don't do this. You're scaring Melody.'

'I have to leave.'

'Have you been told to leave me?' Melody asked, wiping the wet from her face.

The wind picked up, the waves seemed to rise higher and faster towards the shore, crashing further inland, higher, and higher up the beach, battering the alcove, dismissing its protection. Stella stood a few feet away from Luke, taking in his profile, the deep hurt etched in the fine lines around his eyes.

'No. It's my decision. I've thought about nothing else for weeks.'

'I'm sorry, Luke. Really, I am.'

'Don't turn this around and make it about you,' he said, and turning towards her, his eyes momentarily flashing, glaring at her, he stepped back, closer to the edge of the cliff.

'I'm not, you're right,' she said. 'Luke, please. Come here.' She stretched out her arms towards him, her eyes pleading.

'Luke, you can't solve this if you're smashed into a hundred pieces at the bottom of a cliff,' said Stella. He twisted round and looked over the cliff's edge. 'Luke, come on. You're scaring Melody. You're scaring me.' A chill crept up Stella's arm.

He stepped back, away from the edge, with reluctance. He dropped to the ground, his hands shielding his face. A heart wrenching cry flew from his chest. Melody startled, moved towards him, quick as a flash. She knelt next to him, stroking his back. She comforted him until at last he looked up. 'I can't do this anymore.'

They sat there for a long time, half an hour, an hour.

Stella sat close by, not daring to leave them. Both fragile. Both broken. The love between them beaten. It was excruciating.

And then she heard the musical notes as they unfolded on the breeze, carried like confetti, this time, their rhythm slowed, echoing the group's sense of anticipation.

Luke stopped howling. A vast silence closed in around them, prolonged, uncomfortable. Eventually, he said, 'I'll book a flight home.'

'You don't have to go. Let's talk. We can move on from this. Don't walk away. At least stay to the end of the holiday. It's only a few more days.'

Luke stared at her in shocked disbelief. 'If, you're sure. I'll move my things out when we get back and we can then make plans for selling the house, work out our finances.'

'Sell the house? Luke, no,' wept Melody.

'It's the only way. The only way to save the goodness that might be left in us.'

'What will you do? Where will you go?' Melody asked, a note of panic in her voice, a film of perspiration breaking out on her forehead.

'What do you care?' he yelled, suddenly up on his feet and then, more calmly, 'I'll sort it out. Work has a flat they use for our visiting partners from abroad. I'll use that for a few weeks until I sort something more permanent.'

Melody fought against another flood of tears. Her heart sank like a wilting flower. 'If that's what you want. You can always stay until…' she trailed off.

'No,' said Luke. 'Clean break. There's no point

churning over it. It's too painful.' And then, calming down, he said, 'What did you want to say?'

'Nothing,' she whispered. 'You've said it all.' She threw herself at him and wrapped her arms around him. He sat there momentarily, unresponsive, stiff, and then he relaxed, his strong arms wrapped around her, and Stella knew they would both come out of this better, happier people.

'It'll be okay,' he said, as if reading her thoughts. 'We will both be okay,' he said with a flourish of returning courage and resolve. He walked away, not once looking back, leaving the two women together.

'It wasn't meant to end like this. I feel broken. My heart hurts. My soul hurts,' said Melody through her streaming tears as she desperately tried to brush them away.

'I'm so sorry,' said Stella and she wrapped her arms around the trembling frame of the woman she barely knew but who had shared one of her most vulnerable moments with her.

'It wasn't what I wanted, not really, even though I've wished it hundreds of times over the past few months, even wishing him dead. But now, watching him walk away, leaving me here, on the cliff, alone…'

Stella looked at her, surely, she wasn't thinking about ending more than just their relationship. Stella shivered; her eyes widened.

'You know what I mean,' said Melody, picking up on Stella's panic as she looked over the edge of the cliff and then back at Melody. 'I feel the loneliest I have ever been. I still love him.'

'Of course, you do. It will feel strange without him.'

'I took that love and threw it away for a fling. Now I'm paying the price, I have paid the price and so has Luke. He shouldn't have had to. It was all my fault.'

Fresh tears flooded Melody's eyes, and she threw herself onto the ground. The scent and taste of the sea filled Stella's lungs as she breathed deeply, taking in what had happened. Stella watched, feeling the wrench of what was happening. Melody was confused. She gently tugged Melody up onto her feet, but Melody had succumbed to weariness, the golden colour of her tan gone from her. The sea salt clung to Melody's hair and stained her tear-wet face.

'Let's get back to the hotel,' Stella said. 'Tell him how you feel.'

Tomorrow was another day. Tomorrow was the chance to start again. But did Melody really want that?

Stella put her arm through Melody's and the music, now with a steady rhythm comforted Stella, like the ticking of a clock.

Chapter 35

'What's really going on?' asked Stella when they were back at the hotel bar, cocktails in hand and a bowl of pistachios between them. 'Luke has made splitting up easy for you. He has made the decision you were dreading having to make, to tell him.'

'It's not as straight forward as that.'

'I know you still love him. I'd be a fool to think you can just stop loving someone, even if they have treated you atrociously and irrelevant of who deserves what. But this is your chance to be free, to live your life on your terms.'

'I found a lump,' said Melody and she suddenly looked small, vulnerable, and childlike.

'Oh, my goodness. Melody. You have to tell Luke.'

'Maybe,' said Melody.

'He has to know.'

'I need to wait on the biopsy results. I'm praying it

will be nothing, but I'm honestly not sure. I can't do this on my own.'

'What a mess. But don't make it even messier.'

'I know,' Melody said. Stella couldn't stop the tears from falling and as fast as she brushed them away, they kept coming. 'Last time, it was nothing in the end. A cyst but I had a miscarriage two weeks later.' Stella stared. Swallowed. 'You okay?' Melody asked.

'Yeah, I had a scare once and I… I didn't tell Anton. We were arguing about commitment and bringing up a baby together. I was a few weeks pregnant. I couldn't imagine bringing up a baby on top of fighting cancer and I didn't want him to feel sorry for me. It was a terrible time and in the end the decision was made for me. I lost the baby. It was a lonely time. I was so out of my depth, drowning in the loss and the heartache.'

'I'm so sorry. How long ago was that?'

'Seven years ago. I won't ever forget the guilt I carried. Like I had willed the baby to die in me.'

'That's tough. And the cancer?'

'Luckily, a tiny tumour, initial stages, which was easily eradicated with a few sessions of chemotherapy and surgery. All clear now.'

'I'm so sorry.'

'It never goes away. The fear, the dread.'

'And did you ever try for another baby?' said Melody, biting round her thumb nail until it bled.

'I would never have been able to bring up a child on my own. And we weren't trying for a baby in the first place. Some things are never meant to be. So will you tell Luke?'

'I can't think straight. I don't know. See what happens between us. I still think now that he has admitted he is at fault too, recognises his behaviour is poisoning our relationship, at least what's left of it, I think we could make a go of it. I really don't think I loved this other man. It was lust. Attention. An infatuation,' said Melody.

The word infatuation snaked its way into Stella, like something rifling through the chambers of her heart and she thought about the other evening with Yiannis. *Was that infatuation?* She shifted from side to side on the bar stool and avoided Melody's gaze.

As if reading her thoughts, Yiannis appeared behind the bar and their eyes met. Her stomach flipped and as he leaned over the bar to refill their glasses, she caught a whiff of his aftershave and swallowed it as if he had poured the nectar of the gods into her mouth, honeyed drop by honeyed drop. She turned away, vulnerability forcing her to shrink from him. *What was going on here?*

Chapter 36

'Ouch,' that hurts complained Anton as Stella, recovered other than the bump on the back of her head, dabbed at his still broken, swollen lip with a warm flannel.

Anton was lying on the bed, hugging his ribs. The bedroom doors were propped open onto the veranda and the crying cicadas disturbed the still air, piercing the quiet savagely with their shrieks. The sound ripped at the soft chambers of her heart.

'I think we should call a doctor,' said Stella.

'And you might have concussion.'

'It's not a competition, Anton. And I'm fine. You're the one who might have broken a rib.'

Anton laughed. 'I think it's more like two or three. He threw a couple of good 'uns there.'

'Then let me call Prodromos. His wife might be able to help you.'

'The only person who can help me is you. Here, come

and lie next to me.'

Stella slipped off her sandals and tying her hair up in a ponytail, sat next to him.

'Ouch,' he grimaced again. As he drew her in closer to snuggle into him, an overpowering guilt and trepidation filled her. Only a couple of nights ago she was here with Yiannis.

'Teach you to come charging in,' she smiled sympathetically, but inside she was raging anger, guilt.

'What was that really all about?' he asked, turning onto his side to face her.

'Nothing, I told you.'

'I know when you're lying, Stella.' Stella tried to look away, but his expression told her he had seen the look of shame cross her face before she realised, she had already exposed herself. 'Tell me you didn't sleep with him.'

Stella extricated herself from his arms. She sat up, jiggling the mattress with her movements, and Anton flinched from the pain. 'I'm sorry, Anton.'

'You are joking, right. Please tell me this isn't happening.'

'I'm sorry.'

'I was going to leave my wife for you.'

'What?'

'You heard. I can't lie to her anymore. I was ready to leave my wife, my home, walk out on my boy. How else do you think I risked coming here with you?'

'You didn't tell me.'

'I was going to… bloody hell. This is fucked up.'

'It's too late. The time you should have done that has gone, it's passed.' She reached out to touch Anton, but he edged away, and she carried on, 'I was lonely. Upset you hadn't come here with me. All our plans of the last few months. I was let down. He was here for me… I needed someone to love me,' Stella said.

'I don't believe this. You've slept with that slip of a boy? What, he must be half your age or younger.'

'I was disappointed. Can't you understand why? Disappointed our dream holiday had fizzled out, leaving me here on my own when I'd dreamed of the fullness of the potential, of being together, no thoughts of anyone or anything else.'

Stella felt her guilt and shame shift inside her like a boulder in front of a cave moving to let in the light. Anger and resentment, pride, and regret filled her instead, pumping into her to the point she thought she might explode.

'Just tell me.' Stella shook her head, unable to look at him. 'Well say something,' he said, glaring at her.

'Do you honestly think I wanted this? I didn't plan this, any of it. But you let me down. You didn't come.'

'One thing I never let you down on,' he boomed. 'I always come and so do you.'

'Stop being so gauche. This isn't about the sex. It's about a relationship. I have never ever cheated on you.'

'Until now,' he said, tears rolled down his face, trickled into his sideburns and into the creases of his neck, where his pulse, she saw, pounded with sorrow.

Chapter 37

The following morning, Stella woke before Anton. It had been a late night. Melody's heartfelt revelation, as well as their own mess, had kept them both talking long into the early hours. As dawn seeped across the sky, pale and warm, they both whispered, pleaded, cried. One of their rules, from the outset of their affair, had been not to talk about Anton's wife but seeing Luke's pain the night before had opened an abyss of overwhelming emotions for Stella which she could not ignore.

Sitting on the balcony, Stella watched the sun rise; her splintered emotions tinged with tangerine oranges and then aubergine purples. Stella had voiced her guilt, sometimes too heavy to bear, over Anton's wife and his son. She also expressed, for the first time, her feelings of dejection, her waves of exhaustion, her moralistic compromise, her acute and painful loneliness, at always coming second.

'How can you say you're second best? You're the one here with me.'

'Not now. But every other time. We have never spent a whole New Year's Eve together or Christmas Day snuggled in front of the fire. You have never ever called me on a whim. Don't you get tired of all the restrictions our affair is putting on us. On our lives?'

'No. I love you.'

'This isn't about whether you love me or not.'

'Then what's it about?'

'It's about whether you're loving me the way I deserve to be loved, the way I yearn to be adored.'

'Are you saying you doubt me?'

'I'm saying our love, this, this long, long affair, is exhausting. I'm exhausted. It's too big for me to carry any more.' Inside, her true feelings were plagued by doubts, and she tried to dodge them, afraid of what they would reveal.

'You're my baby doll, my best friend,' he stroked her teach with tenderness.

'And she's your wife. The mother of your child.'

'You knew that from the beginning.'

'I did. But I don't want to be squeezed in around your work schedules and your meeting agendas, I don't feel as important as anything else in your life.'

'I am always available for you. Stella, come on. Why are you being like this? Now of all times. I'm here with you.'

'And this is where this will stay. A secret between us. I can't talk about my holiday with my friends, my family. It's so lonely. I'm lonely,' she said, crushing with the exhaustion of it all.

'Stella, darling. I'm here. I'm spending every single moment with you. I want to be here.'

'You say every moment but you're texting your wife… you're still only partly here.'

'She is my wife; how could I not call her in that bloody mess of an earthquake? What if I had died? What if I died and she didn't know?' he spat out his words, his voice shaking, his lower lip trembling. 'This is awful. This is how I never imagined it being. At the end of the day, I have to show her some respect. She's the mother of our son.'

'I'm not saying you can't call her. I'm just saying you are meant to be with me, after all this time you're finally here, and yes, you talking to her, messaging her, that's a problem for me.

I can't share you anymore.'

'Oh, my God. You're really ending it? After all these years?' said Anton.

She hadn't meant for it to come to this but as soon as Anton said the words, she knew that's what she needed to do. She needed to free herself of the shackles she had allowed, and at one time welcomed. She wanted to be set free. In a tiny voice, she answered, 'Yes.'

Anton had gone to bed shortly after. She didn't follow him to the bedroom. There would be no make-up sex tonight or ever. She was numb. In shock. Yet her stomach flipped tingling with a kind of excited frisson; a bubbling fizz of freedom, electric and alive, shot through her.

She finished the bottle of wine they had bought at the *panigiri* and sank into the lounger on the verandah, opened her laptop. She was fired up with a passion so great she thought she would burst. Though part of her was sad the other part felt light and free, like a floating helium balloon drifting further and further away from what held it down.

She tapped away, her fingers moving with an almost silent lightness across the keys. The tension of the day dissolved. The story took on a new thread, but not unexpected. This was the story she had been waiting all her career to write. She stopped to rest her aching fingers and cocooned in the vast quiet and seclusion, heard the music she alone seemed to hear. It had a different beat today; unfolding its beat like a soft lullaby. She strained her ears, a prickling sensation ran through her; she was the music's only audience, the music's only auditorium.

Chapter 38

Stella sat in the same spot she had done almost two weeks before. Andros came out of the little coffee shop and kissed her on both cheeks, a warmth only the Greeks managed to share so genuinely, without it feeling strained or over the top.

'Hello again. Miss Stella.'

'Hello, Andros,' she said, 'I couldn't leave without saying goodbye.'

'It's a pleasure to see you.'

'And I'm glad the earthquake didn't cause you any damage,' she said, waving towards the pretty buildings.

'Thankfully not. It was a blessing from God not to have been affected. We have been collecting clothes and toiletries, small items, to help those who may have lost their homes.'

'I would like to donate something too if you are taking monetary contributions,' said Stella. 'I can't imagine what devastation some of your people are going through. It was terrifying for us. Thank goodness we stowed away inside a coffee shop. The owners were so calm. So kind to us all.' She shook off a shiver pulsating under her skin and pushed back the tears which were threatening to fall like raindrops clinging to the surface of a leaf after a downfall.

Andros acknowledged her kindness, and her emotions with a nod of his head. 'Did you write your story?' he asked, changing the subject.

'Another few chapters,' she said, throwing her arm into the air in a victory salute, smiling again.

'Prodromos told me about the music and the note. It's beautiful but haunting. I hope he too finds peace...'

'I'm saving that for another story,' she said, squeezing his arm with affection.

Andros trembled, as if consciously fighting off an unwelcome emotion and said, 'Yiannis is on his way. He telephoned to tell me to save the best table for you, overlooking the harbour and the jetties, but I can see you already have the best table.' He deftly pulled out the chair and positioned it for Stella to sit.

Stella reddened at the mention of Yiannis' name. She turned towards the lapping water, hoping it was not obvious and lowered her face. She let her hair cover her hot, blushing cheeks, hiding her self-consciousness.

Within minutes, Yiannis appeared, and he gave Stella a long kiss. Stella, preoccupied, was momentarily taken aback. What was she doing? What was she getting herself into?

'Yiannis,' Andros said, returning with a bottle of

water, 'I will leave the menus and come back for your order. There's no hurry,' he said, and Stella caught the flick of a smirk at the corner of his lips.

'Stella, you turn heads wherever you go,' said Yiannis. 'But I know you are mine and I am yours.'

'It's easy to feel like that when you're warm with the sun,' she said, nervous of upsetting him yet wanting to be open.

'Look, I know lunch was meant to be just the two of us but...'

'Don't tell me. You've invited the whole village to meet me,' she said.

'No, no... but I have invited my parents.'

'My goodness. I never expected that. Is this what they call *proxenia*?' Stella stifled a giggle.

'Stella, please. I'm serious. I want them to meet you and it's the only opportunity before they go back to Athens.'

'I'm nervous about meeting them. It feels too soon. And it makes me feel like a schoolchild all over again.'

'Stella, they will adore you.'

'Perhaps I should go and leave you to enjoy lunch alone with them. You don't need me here.'

'I don't need you here, but I want you here. I want you to meet everyone I know,' Yiannis said.

'And your parents?'

'Prodromos has seen to it that celebrity status comes before you. He cannot stop talking about the famous author from England.'

'That's all very well, but we've known each other a mere few days,' Stella said.

'Time… what does time matter. It's an illusion to most. There are those who think they know each other after years yet sit in the same room, at the same table, looking at each other as they would a stranger.' The words cut her. Her breakup was cruel yet liberating.

'And have you told them how old I am?'

'My stepfather is twelve years younger than my mother. Do you think that bit of detail answers your question?'

'I don't know…' Stella said, and she gulped down the last of her wine regretting it instantly, her head beginning to throb in the heat, and she strained, cocking her head forwards trying to catch the tinkle of notes in the air. She wanted to say something but before she could fathom what Yiannis began speaking again.

'They will fall in love with your beauty too much to worry about your age. And anyway, they have often said to me educating the mind without educating the heart isn't education at all… Aristotle.'

'We are but dust and shadow,' said Stella, pressing down on her temples. 'Dust and shadow,' she repeated.

'Exactly. Horace had the right idea.'

'Horace always had the right idea,' said a tall man, in a pair of dark chinos and a head of slick-backed dark hair peppered with a streak of grey. 'You must be Stella.' He bent down, took her hand, and kissed it in showy yet most adorable way.

'Enough with the antics, *baba*,' said Yiannis, giving him a clap on the back.

'Come here,' said his stepfather in Greek, pulling him in for a hug.

'And *mama?*'

'Your mother's bumped into an old school friend. I left them chatting outside the patisserie.'

He took the chair next to his son and poured a glass of water first for Stella, then for his absent wife, and then for himself and Yiannis.

'Started without us?' he asked, gesturing at the bottle of wine already open, his English holding only the tiniest Greek accent.

'An aperitif,' said Yiannis.

'Why did you choose here?' asked his stepfather.

'Stella's choice,' said Yiannis, 'and it's owned by Prodromos' cousin.'

'It's good to support our friends and family.'

'His mother prefers to sit inside but the umbrella may afford her some shade.'

Stella, uncomfortable, with the way the conversation was going, took a sip of water and welcomed Yiannis' squeeze of her hand under the table.

'Sorry I'm late,' puffed a medium-height, pear-shaped woman with the longest, darkest lashes Stella had ever seen on an older woman, though Stella surmised she was closer in age to Stella than Yiannis was. Suddenly she felt vulnerable, exposed, a fraud. Everything sat heavily on her shoulders. She couldn't mention her affair, her part in breaking up a marriage. She was too old. Too old to be dating Yiannis. Just as a sliver of certainty had entered her life, she was uncertain about it all now. The future out of reach somehow, too grey, too washed out.

Thankfully as their afternoon progressed, they proved to her that the age gap between Yiannis and her didn't matter to them one bit.

'We visited Kenwood House many years ago and took photos in the love tunnel,' she cooed, her eyes on her husband. She took out her wallet and from inside the back flap pulled out a photograph. She handed it to Stella. 'Our Notting Hill moment.'

'It hasn't changed a bit,' Stella said, fingering the faded photo, its edges crinkled with age and the top corner torn away.

'I remember the beautiful stone of the house, soft yet solid, as it shone in the most wretched of British summers.'

'The old house and grounds are quite marvellous,' said Yiannis, steering away from the not-so-generous comment.

'You're quite right, of course,' said Stella. 'Unlike the sun here. Proper summers to die for.'

'We ate lemon tart with a dollop of whipped cream and drank coffee all afternoon. Such a magnificent day. More than made up or the non-existent sun.'

They chatted to her, eager to learn more about her life, her home in England and her writing. He was a professor of philosophy at a university in Athens and his mother managed their seventeen-room hotel a few kilometres outside of the city.

'You must visit us in Athens. It's not as quiet as here but you're sure to find the architecture and history an immersive delight,' said his mother as she chatted away, placing her hand on Stella's as she spoke. 'But, of course, we love coming here for the summer.'

They talked until the sun set across the bay, pinks,

purples, oranges, and yellows painting the sky. Stella looked as far as the eye could see and smiled; the gods in this wonderful world were looking down on her and everything seemed encompassed in peace. So why did her heart not feel it too?

Chapter 39

Stella, the last to arrive, conscious of looking like she had just lost her virginity, smiled tentatively. 'Before anyone asks,' she said, 'I want you to know Anton and I have separated. Probably for good and he left for the UK late last night… to be with his wife. Now, let's not wait any longer to tuck into Prodromos' cuisine.'

Eliana leaned across the table and gave her hand a squeeze and Melody walked around the other side to give Stella a hug, whispering, 'You're so brave, but you'll be okay, I know it.'

'I will be. And there's something else, but I will save that for later.'

'You can't say that and then make us wait.'

'Let me say this: It looks like I might not be going back to England on my own.'

Both women shrieked and jumped up to hug Stella, almost knocking over the wine glasses. 'And how about you?' Stella whispered to Melody as she took her seat.

'I've persuaded Luke to finish the holiday with me. I am hoping some of the magic here might work on us.' Stella squeezed her hand under the table.

The men looked at each other, unsure of the announcement and what to make of it but then Dean picked up a carafe and generously overfilled Stella's glass with the red nectar. 'I'm guessing you'll need this,' he winked. 'And for what it's worth. You deserve the best.'

Eliana gave him a look and then glancing towards Stella, said, 'Sorry, he got the other bit out of me.'

'It's fine. It's not a secret. Not anymore.'

'Babe, you've got such a big mouth,' Eliana said to Dean, swiping him one across the arm.

'Thank you,' Stella said. 'I don't want this to spoil our night or your holiday. No tears… looking forward to new beginnings.'

'New beginnings and friends,' said Dean, making a comeback. He picked up his drink and they all clinked their glasses together.

'New beginnings and friends,' said Melody, searching Luke's eyes as she chinked her glass with Stella's and drank the whole glass in one.

The dinner Prodromos had promised did not fall short of a banquet. The table was lit with lanterns, which lit up the small space under the most sparkly star-lit sky. An oval platter filled the centre of the table: roasted potatoes, chunks of lamb on the bone infused with bay leaves and crushed garlic heads. Carrots and whole onions, oozed with the meat juices. A basket of bread and a heavy bowl, filled to the brim with a Greek salad, invited them to sit and eat. The black olives glistened and the feta cheese, creamy white, drizzled in a traditional dressing of olive oil and freshly squeezed lemon, lured them in. Small plates, scattered at intervals and heaped with beans, vegetables, and cheese, created another layer of enticement; foods to tantalise the tastebuds.

The meal was scrumptious. Prodromos served and Yiannis hovered to refill the breadbasket with the local-baked bread; its inside fluffy and the crust hard. Leaning across Stella to pick up the empty basket, Yiannis touched her lightly across the shoulders, she shivered, the sensation thrilling her, a throbbing between her legs making her squirm in her seat, awakening her lust for him again. She crossed and uncrossed her legs, wiped her sweaty palms on her dress. The friends, chatted and laughed into the descending starry night, eating and drinking.

'We should get an early night if we're out hiking tomorrow,' announced Luke to Melody, as he knocked back another glass of wine.

'Of course,' said Melody obediently, but, Stella noticed, with a spark of something explosive behind her eyes. 'We'll see you soon,' she said, getting up and placed her napkin neatly on her empty plate.

'There is still dessert,' said Prodromos. He cleared the plates with professional competence, balancing the stacked dishes between his flat open palm and his wrist; his little finger directly beneath the rim, his thumb on the rim's upper side steadying the pile.

'Have dessert and then go,' said Stella. 'You know

you want to.'

Luke glanced at Melody, and with a softness said, 'Ten minutes and then we really should be going.'

The friends all clapped and cheered. 'Knew you wouldn't be able to resist dessert,' said Dean. 'Though I'm guessing you had your own dessert of a different kind planned back in the bedroom, if you know what I mean.'

'Always have to lower the tone of the conversation,' said Eliana. 'Honestly, mind like a sewer.'

'And you, my darling, will get extra helpings tonight if you're a good girl.' Dean winked at Eliana, but she looked away, not bothering to reply.

Dean looked awkward, left dangling until Luke broke the ice and said, 'Lucky you, Eliana!'

Everyone broke into raucous, uninhibited laughter and the situation was diffused.

Stella could feel Yiannis watching her, and she hoped he wanted her like she wanted him. She began to fantasise about him, undressing for him, showing him what she liked. She felt herself becoming more aroused and her body ached with the memory of him and the anticipation of having him again. She took a swig of her wine to try and alleviate her swaying senses, but it only intensified her growing excitement.

Prodromos emerged smiling, carrying a tray. He handed out the golden cake on glass plates and passed them tiny dessert forks with yellowy cream ceramic handles.

'I know what this is,' said Eliana. 'It's the orange cake we ordered but didn't eat when the earthquake hit.'

'It is. My friend told me about the English who didn't eat their dessert the day the earthquake hit, and I guessed it was you, my friends. So here you are.' Prodromos pushed out his chest, pride showing in his posture.

Chapter 40

Stella, Eliana, and Melody paced the hotel's foyer. They waited impatiently for the bus to pull up; it would take them all to the town's pop-up art competition in one of the churches.

Both Melody and Eliana's paintings had been selected by the town's Mayor, the priest, and one of the most prominent businesspeople in the area, to be exhibited in the competition. The friends were excited about the forthcoming debut showcase of their art and chatted excitedly as they waited for Dean and Luke to join them. They had both disappeared to the bar for a quick pre-celebration bevvy.

'Any excuse to down one,' said Eliana. 'But at least we don't have to listen to Dean prattling on.' She laughed at her own joke.

'His teasing can get pretty lively,' said Melody.

'Slight understatement,' said Eliana.

Ten minutes later, the minibus organised Prodromos hooted, its faint honking dancing gently on the wind.

'The bus is here. It is waiting at the bottom of the road,' announced Prodromos with a flurry of his hand. 'Quick, quick. We cannot be late.'

They trailed down the pebbly decline to where the bus waited. Stella gripped her sunhat which threatened to be carried away on the twirling summer breeze and smiled to herself. Melody and Luke, arm in arm, walked a few paces ahead of her. Stella filled with joy and hoped they would be able to find a way through their ordeal when they got home. She had grown to love them both, warts, and all.

No one was perfect. Stella knew that more so than most and a bolt of melancholy momentarily shadowed her otherwise contentment.

'Come on, slow coach,' called Eliana as she waltzed past her with Dean limping two paces behind her. Eliana's light pace in contrast to Dean's heavy thump with each step he made.

'She will never understand,' he smiled.

Stella gave him a sympathetic smile and offered her arm. He took it and they walked together. 'Not one, but two slow coaches,' said Eliana as she looked back at them.

'Is that everyone?' asked the bus driver. Stella recognised him as the man who had driven them here on their first day. A day only two weeks before which seemed like a lifetime away. So much had changed, for all of them.

They all nodded in agreement, and he set off. The bus

trundled down the road towards the town centre, the sheer drop to the deep valley below first on their left and then on their right as the bus navigated the bends.

'Imagine if one of us wins,' shrieked Eliana.

'You deserve to win,' said Melody. 'My painting's too plain. I don't think I've captured the true essence of this place at all.'

'Nonsense,' said Luke, uncharacteristically supporting her. 'That painting's sea is so real. You could reach out and feel its spray on your hand.'

'Aww, thanks my darling,' Melody said, and she beamed a huge grin across at him, reaching over the seat between them to grip his hand.

Twenty minutes later they parked up outside a little church; the whitewashed walls, blue painted windows, and door, and a rich, orange terracotta roof, sparkled in the glint of the midday sun. A colourful melee of people outside the church and the many conversations' high volume reflected the excitement surrounding the competition.

The next two hours drifted by and with each ticking minute Stella felt the intensifying nerves of Eliana and Melody as they pondered, heads together, what their chances would be of being featured in the final run up of selected winners.

'You're both already winners whether you are chosen or not,' said Stella. 'To have been selected in the first place proves your work is valid and worthy of its place in the competition. 'To have painted in all this heat and produced something so beautiful is incredible.'

'Stella,' said Eliana. 'You're such a darling. Honestly.

Thank you.'

'Yes, thank you Stella,' said Melody.

'Will you stop chatting,' said Dean. 'They're about to do a minute's silence to remember those who lost their lives in the Turkey-Syria earthquake.'

They stood in silence and Stella remembered how they all too, had experienced the terror of an earthquake only a few days before.

With great reverence and respect all the invitees bowed their heads, some of the locals making the sign of the cross, while others held onto the crosses around their necks.

Moments later, the atmosphere changed. The mayor of the town thanked the participants, the judges and all the visitors, for their attendance. He proceeded to announce the winners.

'Melody,' called Stella. 'You've got second place.'

Melody, in a trance, smiled. 'I have?'

'Yes,' said Luke. 'You've done it.'

'Melody Cleverly. Please come up and collect your prize,' said the mayor and everyone clapped and cheered.

'Thank you so much,' said Melody and she quickly waved to Luke from the front of the hall as she passed along the row of judges shaking hands and thanking them in turn. Eliana screamed and Luke threw a victory punch in the air with one hand, the fingers of his other hand in his mouth as he blew a shrill whistle.

Melody posed for photographs with the other winning artists. The photographs would be featured in the local paper and on the island's tourist webpage.

All the while Stella and Eliana clicked away with their

mobiles trying to get as many photos as possible of their newly famous artist friend.

Eventually, the friends made their way to a tiny bar where raffia shades hung limply and lopsidedly around naked bulbs, casting patterns across the small courtyard. They celebrated late into the night with some of the other entrants, and a lot of local wine, and then stumbled, singing, and propping each other up, as they made their way back to Miramare.

Chapter 41

It was their last night in Kefalonia. This place had brought a new dimension to the way Stella saw things, everything she had once relied on as constant, had changed its tone and rhythm, changed its steps, quick and fresh, danced to a different beat, one which excited her, set alight her senses, and fanned a fire in her soul.

The friends agreed to meet at the bar by the pool for one last merry-making evening before leaving; the end of their two weeks with the magic of Miramare already slowly slipping away.

The stars sparkled transparently in the untouchable night sky, the thrumming of the cicadas filled her ears, and further out the barking of stray dogs reached her ears. The beating life punctuated the peace in a welcoming blanket of familiarity and comfort, no longer intrusive as it had once been.

Dean and Luke had disappeared into town on the

pretext they wanted to buy souvenirs to take back home.

'The only souvenirs they are looking for are the cheap bottles of raki,' laughed Eliana. 'But it gets him out of the way for a bit. Honestly, he does not stop touching me.'

'Be glad he's like that around you. There are so many women who would kill to have the sort of relationship you have,' said Melody.

'I know. And I'm not being ungrateful,' said Eliana.

'Not much,' smiled Stella.

'But seriously, I can't believe it's our last night here,' said Melody.

'Our last night here but the first of many delightful nights to come,' said Stella. 'And I have an announcement to make.'

Eliana and Melody looked at each other and back at her. 'Spill it, then,' said Eliana.

'Anton and I have agreed to end this farce of a relationship. It's been built on a million little lies, his and mine, and I don't want to be doing life like this anymore. It's exhausting and I deserve better. His wife deserves better.'

'Wow!' they both chimed.

'I think it's been a long time coming. The lies and the deceit have been weighing us down, and we're still going to be friends. And as friends we can see each other without the guilt.'

'Guilt is a horrible emotion,' said Melody.

'We can bump into each other and not worry about being seen by someone, we can stop and have a hug in the street without the angst of being recognised. My publisher announced a record-breaking sales tally for my books worldwide and things can only get better. And that means no messy complications, no skeletons in the closet.'

'And Anton? Is he okay?'

'He's accepted my decision.'

'He must be heartbroken.'

'I'm heartbroken too, but he was never ever going to let go of his family.'

'I'm so sorry.'

'This is about accepting things must change. It's not about me punishing him.'

'Wasn't he ready to leave his wife?' asked Eliana. 'That must have been a difficult decision for him to come to.'

Melody shifted, twiddled with her hair. 'I suppose that came too late.'

'I never asked him to leave her though a few months ago, even a few weeks ago, I would have been the happiest woman alive at his declaration of love for me. But it's come too late. Yiannis and this place, have shown me what life is all about and what life should be about. Honesty. Love. Passion. Openness. Gratitude. I want to live a whole life not a half-life.'

'What are you going to do?'

'I'm going to finish my book, I'm almost there and get it off to my publisher as soon as I can and then Yiannis coming to spend some time with me.'

'Stella! That's amazing,' yelled Melody, almost toppling off her bar stool.

'Good for you,' said Eliana.

'It feels right. It's the first time anything like this has happened to me and I want to see where it goes but with a clean slate. No more lies and hiding behind closed doors.'

'Yiannis must be thrilled,' said Melody.

'He is and so are his parents. They are such lovely people. I think I would even consider living here if the UK isn't right for him, for us. Live right here amongst the olive and lemon groves.'

'And in the arms of Yiannis,' laughed Eliana.

'Yes, I think I can. I have felt content here despite the way things have turned out.'

Prodromos appeared behind the bar with a twinkle in his eye and a little skip in his step. He filled their glasses, and they extended their thanks as he quietly went on with serving his other guests.

'And what about you,' asked Eliana directing her gaze towards Melody.

'Oh, you know,' said Melody and she rested her open palm over her tummy.

'OMG! You're not! You are! OMG!' shouted Stella.

'Am I missing something,' said Eliana, blushing with confusion.

'I'm pregnant,' smiled Melody, her palm still across her tiny bump, evidently there now Stella looked more closely.

'Congratulations,' they chimed.

'Probably explains your queasiness,' said Eliana. 'Gosh, how exciting for you.'

'Luke is as excited as a boy with a new puppy at Christmas and he has booked us into couple's therapy.'

'I bet,' said Stella.

'That was quick,' said Eliana.

'Someone he found on LinkedIn. We've got our first session in two days' time.'

'You're amazing. You both are. I'm so pleased you've found each other again,' said Stella.

'It's taken a while and I think I've got you to thank. Your patience and guidance have helped a lot,' said Melody. 'You have made me realise how it's what we have that gives us the magic and not the what ifs.'

'I just gave you some advice,' said Stella, squeezing her hand while at the same time squeezing the tears back.

'This place has really helped us all,' said Eliana.

'It's the magic of Miramare,' said Stella and she raised her glass and tapped it against their filled glasses with a crystal-clear clink echo matching the lightness of the joy suffused on their faces.

'To the magic of Miramare,' said Eliana, and they all repeated her toast.

And, in the distance, barely audible, Stella caught the gentle notes of the familiar music which she had heard on the first day of her holiday and her feet tapped to the beat as her heart pumped to the same beat, with joy, with hope and love.

'It's time to let go…' Andri whispered, tears clinging to her dark lashes, a faint blush across her cheeks.

Prodromos knew this moment would come and though he had dreaded it, it came with a peace which lightened his heart and a heavy weight which suffocated him.

The music, once as clear as the ringing of a crystal

glass, began to fade. Prodromos strained his ears, but so faint was it now he could hardly catch the single vibrating note.

'I don't want to. I want to hold you forever, my darling Andri,' he said, hot tears stinging his eyes, his boiling cheeks wet with their streaming.

'And you will, deep in your heart.'

'And the magic of this place, of Miramare?' he asked, sniffling, the tears unashamedly falling.

'That will always be here too; in the waxy zest of the lemons, you will pick next summer. In the mountain breeze that will ruffle your hair. In the dregs of the coffee cups, you will continue to read, though I'm guessing you still aren't sure of what they say,' she laughed. 'Deep under the cracked soil where the roots of the lemon trees and the olive trees reach for water. In every sunset and every sunrise. In every full moon and every moon phase that comes between.'

'I will be lost without you.'

'You will never be without me. I will always be near, and the music will keep us together.'

'The notes are fading.'

'They will fade as their energy guides me to where I have to go... but they will come back strong again... in time.'

'Promise?'

'I will send them as often as I can, but I am tired of being between here and there, Prodromos mou. It is time.'

'So, you are saying goodbye?' he asked, his voice a squeak as the tears continued and his emotions clogged him.

'I am saying until we meet again.'

'Stay a little longer,' he said, choking with emotion, his arms reaching out for her, wanting to feel her close one last time.

'I will stay and watch the sunset with you.'

'And watch the moon rise, full and white over the mountain.'

'And the moon,' she nodded, as she nestled into his side, his arm protectively across her back and tucking her in at the waist.

'I love you,' Prodromos said.

'And I love you… forever and ever.'

Prodromos sat, watching the moon's gentle trajectory until it hung, suspended high above the rugged mountain's silhouette, a disc of gleaming silver, its light ever present in the nearing midnight of the brilliantly star-lit sky. He sat rooted, and only when he could no longer smell Andri's rose-scented sweetness did he dare to look for her, dare to look at the empty space beside him.

'I will always love you, Andri,' he called out, and his voice, though his heart was breaking, danced on the breeze. He was free.

October 2023

Eliana

Eliana danced around the kitchen, Moscow lazing in his basket, while she brewed the tea.

After a cooked breakfast of bacon, eggs and hot, buttered toast, Dean gulped down the dregs of his tea and rubbed his stomach in appreciation.

'That was really nice, darling.'

'You're welcome,' said Eliana, planting a kiss on him before clearing the table.

'I'll get dressed and we can go for a walk.' Moscow jumped out of his basket at hearing the word walk and wagged his tail impatiently, walking round in circles and yapping excitedly. His tail wagging.

She heard him shuffling up the stairs, she too almost wincing with every step he took.

'You okay, Dean?'

'Stiff, but I'm not complaining,' he called back.

'You have to wait, Moscow,' said Eliana. She splashed about washing the pans and loaded the dishwasher with their breakfast dishes and cutlery.

She dashed upstairs to get changed out of her pyjamas and found Dean waiting for her on their bed with his puppy-dog eyes.

'Feeling horny?'

'Always,' he said, pulling her towards him.

'I'll have to make breakfast more often,' she said, feeling happiness bursting from her.

And Eliana didn't resist; she allowed herself to go where Dean took her with passion. She knew this was the glue to their relationship and it was a good glue; constant, true, and came from a place of love.

'I love you more than ever,' she said, and tried to hide her worry over his health though it was something they would have to face up to sooner rather than later.

As she showered, she thought back over her past controlling nature; the sheet, the withholding sex, the nagging about Dean's eating. She felt a sense of release, and relief, knowing she had managed to change, looked at things between them, their relationship, with a unique perspective. It was as if she had released herself from a glass jar that she herself had screwed the lid onto, and only she could loosen it. Their loving gave her more joy and far less anxiety now she saw it as a mutual way to express, and share, their love for each other.

An hour later, with her Kefalonia scarf wrapped tightly around her neck and her coat buttoned up, she opened the front door and waited for Dean to pull on his boots.

'Come on Dean. Moscow's getting impatient.' Moscow strained against his lead, his tail flicking back and forth with excitement. He dragged her along the garden path a few feet closer to the open gate.

'Coming darling, my knee's taking its time loosening up,' called Dean.

'Take your time. There's no hurry. Stop it, Moscow. Wait for Daddy,' said Eliana, looking back towards the front door. Dean emerged a few seconds later, stepping over the threshold and onto the path with a strain, his footsteps dislodging a few pebbles in the cracks.

'Looks painful, babe,' said Eliana. 'I can always take him for a quick run around the park on my own.'

'I'll be fine once I start walking,' said Dean, wincing as he took another step. 'I might need to go ahead with the knee op.'

'Let's make an appointment at the doctor's, babe, and see what she suggests,' said Eliana, in a soft tone.

'I don't think I will have much choice.'

'I don't mind if you want to stay indoors and do your daily stretches instead.'

'It's all good. I took my CBD oil this morning.'

They walked off arm in arm and Eliana smiled, crinkling her eyes against the bright November sun. Her heart swelled, her mind full of only love, for the man she used to find annoying with all his attention-seeking and sexual remarks. Now she welcomed his banter and attention, recognised it as Dean's way of loving her the best way he knew how. It was good between them, and she thanked their summer vacation to Kefalonia for their renewed closeness and intimacy. They had grown as a couple, were doing so much more than merely co-existing.

'Lean on me,' she said, and she meant it with all her heart, though for a second, she daren't look at him, for fear of giving herself away.

She let Moscow off his lead, and he scarpered off, sniffing around patches on the grass and under trees. She read somewhere dogs expended as much energy sniffing around as walking and running, so if Dean looked like he was struggling, she would find a bench and let Moscow sniff away his energy today. Dean needed to be careful.

'You okay?' asked Dean.

'Yes, sorry babe... miles away.'

'Somewhere away from me?'

'No, never.'

He pulled her to a standstill and faced her towards him. He tipped up her chin and kissed her on the lips.

'What's that for?'

'To say I love you.'

'And I love you,' she said. It felt good telling him she loved him. No more hiding behind her own insecurities and doubts that he would leave her or hurt her. He was here to stay, and she felt it in her heart and embraced the moment of deep contentment.

They walked a little further and Eliana dropped onto the next bench. She threw the ball into the distance for Moscow and tapped the space next to her, prompting Dean to sit down.

'I might not be able to get up once I sit down.'

'I'll pull you up,' she said, and feeling emotional she hanged the subject.

'I heard from Stella and Melody first thing.'

'Oh, yeah? What did they have to say for themselves?'

'Melody's worked it all out with Luke, the baby is only a few days away from coming and she's been offered a commission to work with a little gallery; they love her paintings.'

'Great news. What a turnaround.'

'I'm thrilled for her.'

'Still can't believe she had an affair. So mousey...'

'That's all in the past, Dean, so when we see them don't you dare mention it.'

'I'm the soul of discretion,' he laughed.

'More like a bull in a China shop,' Eliana sighed.

'And Stella?'

'She got her story to her publisher and secured another multi-book signing with a new publisher. Some big US publishing house contacted her unexpectedly and she said yes.'

'Good for her.'

'She's already panicking about whether she can drum up enough inspiration to write another three books.'

'She'll do it. She's done it before.'

'Yeah, that's true.'

'Yiannis should be inspiration enough,' said Dean.

'I know. Lucky her,' said Eliana, pretending to swoon.

'You're not looking for a Greek waiter, are you?'

'Not ever. I've got you and you're all the man I need right here. Muffin top and all,' she teased and softly kissed the creases around the edges of his mouth.

'Glad she got rid of Anton. Nice guy but cheating on his wife? Nah,' said Dean.

'I think they're still friends.'

'I think she should tell him where to go... out of her life for good.'

'It must be difficult to let go after all those years. For some people that's a lifetime,' said Eliana.

'She sounded happy.'

'And what about Yiannis? Has she been back to see him?'

'Still together. But long-distance relationships are hard to keep going. She didn't say much when I prompted her.'

'Likely fizzled out. Shame.'

'I didn't get the same impression. She'll hold onto him. She seemed jubilant around him.'

'And are you happy around me?'

'You know I am you silly sod. And in a funny sort of way Stella and Melody's messy relationships highlighted how good ours really is. But you still want sex too much…'

'And you don't want it enough,' laughed Dean.

'But at least we have an understanding. We are loyal and love each other in our own unique way.'

'We do.'

'I love you, Dean.'

'I love you, Eliana.'

Melody

'Thank you darling. A lovely meal as ever. 'How was your painting class today?'

'I got another painting finished to add to the collection.'

'That's amazing. So proud of you. Proud of your talent and your amazingness.'

'Let's hope the gallery sells enough of my work to warrant renewing the hire space. Without those sales they won't want my art taking up space that could be showcasing more lucrative art,' said Melody, biting on her bottom lip.

'That won't happen,' said Luke. 'Let me wash up and you can have a soak. I got you a surprise. I left it by the bath,' he said, hugging her, careful not to squash her baby bump.

'Aww, thank you. I'm aching all over and this little person has been fidgeting inside me all day,' she said, rubbing her belly and off she staggered.

Twenty minutes later, Luke came up and knelt at the side of the bath. He lovingly sponged her belly which poked out the water like a mountain island.

'The bubbles are amazing,' said Melody. 'Thank you, Luke. That was thoughtful.'

'I did my due diligence too. Babybathmagic products are safe for mummies-to-be.'

'The lavender is gorgeous,' she said. She sank further back into the bath and rested her head on the lilac bath pillow. She closed her eyes and Luke continued to soak the sponge in the water and squeeze it over her belly.

She was the happiest she had been in a long time and as she lay there with her eyes closed, she gave thanks to the magic of Miramare which had helped mend their marriage.

'So, it was never about not loving me?' she blurted out, later that night as they sat on the couch, with her legs raised on two cushions. They had been watching a soppy Hallmark romance movie and her heart began to race at one point thinking about how close she had been to losing Luke.

'I always loved you. I just forgot how to show you,' he said.

'And now?'

'It was like another bit of me took over and you made it easy Melody. I know it's no excuse and I'm not making excuses. You made it easy for me to be a tyrant. You were so desperate to please me. To do what I wanted to ease your own guilt.'

'You're right. That was my guilt. I wanted to make you happy again.'

'It made me sick, made me so bloody angry. When the only thing I wanted was to go back to having my beautiful, loyal, loving wife.'

'I guess I was trying to make up for what I did.'

'I know. But it didn't help. It made me feel more anger and more loathing.'

'Loathing?'

'It all frightened me and the more it scared me the more I wanted to hold onto you, control you. Control that part of my life. You at home. Me knowing your every move.'

'I see that now. I'm so sorry Luke.'

'It doesn't matter anymore. Not now we have our baby coming in a few days.'

'To be a family is all I've ever wanted. Losing our other baby, our first chance of being a family, is something I will never forget. The affair was my way of trying to take back control and to dampen the pain I held onto. The pain I didn't realise was still there, tainting me.' Melody placed both hands over her bulging belly and spread her fingers, each one like the bar of a cage protecting her baby.

'I understand. I see that now,' said Luke, tears welling behind his eyes. 'And I pushed you away. I kept you at a distance by burrowing myself in work and the office. But from this point, moving forward, it's about us three, our future and our little family.'

'We have healed, Luke, and I'm so grateful to you for that. We both needed to deal with the past trauma, and we have come through it.'

'We will be amazing parents and you'll be an incredible mother,' said Luke, his voice trembling with emotion. 'We will have a lot to celebrate.'

'Talking of which I think the girls are planning on descending upon us as soon as the baby arrives, and they have bought tickets for my exhibition.'

'They might even buy one of your paintings,' said Luke.

'Can't wait to see them,' said Melody. 'They've become good friends.'

'They'll be more than welcome, any time. And Dean.'

'Shame Yiannis won't be here, but it will be like a

holiday reunion anyway.'

'Knowing Stella, and from what she's told you she will video call him.'

'True,' tittered Melody and she felt the happiest she had in a long time.

'I'll build the cot tomorrow and the baby-changing unit. The walls look lovely painted yellow,' he said. 'The mural of the sunset and the tiny storks flying around looks great.'

'Yeah, glad I finished it. I was beginning to wish I hadn't started,' she said.

She moved closer to him and cuddled up to Luke as he put his arm around her, the other resting gently across her belly. A gentle, comfortable silence wrapped itself around her and she let out a breathy sigh. She had found her peace, her equilibrium and her happy ever after with Luke. And with this new baby she was sure she would find her happy ever after moving forward.

They had survived the turbulent, stormy black sea of their relationship. They had come out stronger and more in love than ever. They had found a way to navigate the waves and guide their flapping white sails, like freshly laundered sheets, to calmer waters, which tugged at her heart and made the veins in her blood run strong and hot and enthusiastic for the man she had always loved.

She thought about Miramare and its mystique and believed Kefalonia, and the Greek magic of the island, had saved her marriage. Saved her from making the biggest mistake of her life and she thanked her guardian angel for looking over her.

Stella

It had been six weeks since her publisher made the multi-book offer and as she signed her contract with a flourish using her new ink pen, it's nib gently scratching the paper, she smiled at how things had turned around. She remembered signing her first ever properly legal document at age twenty-eight when she bought her flat. It had been bittersweet. Moving out from her parents' home permanently, leaving all her childhood memories behind, but a flutter in her chest had given her the reassurance she needed that it was the right decision.

She did a little twirl in front of the full-length mirror in her bedroom. Her long winter skirt swished around her ankles as she sang a little tune, made up from the notes she remembered from the Kefalonian music she had heard so many times dancing on the breeze of the Ionian Sea.

She had flown out to Kefalonia with no man, no book and had returned with a book which her publisher loved and a man who she loved intensely. She had flown out with a heart wanting to be filled with love and inspiration and had returned with a heart overflowing with love and a mind full of beautiful writing inspiration and immensely romantic stories.

She gathered her long blond hair, bleached from the summer sun, into a bun and then tied it with a band. She added a dusting of blusher onto her cheeks and smothered her favourite pink gloss over her lips. There she was ready.

She took one last look at the contract and folded it, placed it in the envelope and sealed it. It was done. The next few months of her life was to be guided by how strong her inspiration was and how her creativity played ball with her. She was at ease. She was calm. She had insisted her own clause regarding timing of delivery of the work was included in the contract and with the success of her past books she had more leverage with the terms and conditions of delivery.

Her editor had already sent back her comments on the love story inspired by her Kefalonia holiday and confirmed a tentative publication date for spring of the following year. The cover, with the multitude of Ionian whites and blues, peaches, and creamy yellows, was divine. She absolutely loved it.

A flutter of dancing butterflies reminded her she was only a few hours away from seeing Yiannis again and a little shiver up her spine sent her into a tizzy fantasy; she wanted him, and she longed to be in his arms.

Since returning they had been in contact every single day and he had not failed to call her even once. He was passionate and attentive; romanticism was in his blood, and he continued to woo her and cherish her from a distance.

***

The arrivals hall, noisy and overcrowded, closed in on Stella whose heart beat faster by the minute. She peered over the heads of the two men in front of her, their heads conspiratorially lowered and close together. A family of

Chinese people stood with a banner welcoming home their loved one and a little girl with a ponytail held a silver balloon with daddy written across it. Further along taxi drivers waited for their corporate and VIP arrivals. Stella smoothed back the wet strands of hair from her face and tiptoed as more passengers swept out through the hissing sliding doors into the main hall.

'Stella *mou*. My Stella,' he breathed into her ear as he clasped her round the waist. He lifted her and twirled her around until she thought he might drop her. All the time he repeated her name. Stella, overcome with emotion, felt the sting of her tears and when she looked into his eyes, when he finally dropped her gently to the floor, his eyes reflected the same tears of pure love and joy.

'I can't believe you're finally here,' she said, planting kisses all over his face, clasping both his hands in hers.

'I keep my promises,' he said.

'I've got so much to tell you.'

'Since yesterday?'

'Since yesterday,' she said, pulling him towards her.

***

At home, Stella thought her heart would burst; as imagined fireworks crackled and burst in her chest, lighting up the chambers of her heart one by one.

Before she even had time to shake off her wet scarf, Yiannis was pulling at her coat, his mouth on hers, his hands undoing her blouse. She followed his lead… and leaving a trail of tangled clothes from the hallway, up the stairs and into her bedroom, they landed on her bed. They quickly found their rhythm, desperate to please each other. Stella gasped in anticipation as he burrowed his tongue in the scent of her, her softness. They devoured, and sucked, licked, and shared a crescendo of release as Stella called out his name over and over, like an echo filling the room.

They lay in each other's arms, staring into each other's faces; Stella taking in every smile line around his glittering dark eyes and his full lips.

'Kind of surreal, you being here,' she said eventually, her heavy breathing abating, much quieter now.

'I'm definitely real, Stella *mou*,' he said, moving closer and kissing her deeply, his tongue finding its way across her collarbone and down to her breasts, her erect nipples.

'Before we do anything else, I need to eat something,' she said, her stomach rumbling low and loud.

'I will cook,' he said. 'I know where everything is.'

'There's salmon in the fridge.'

'I will bake the finest salmon in all of England for you,' he said, kissing her again before jumping out of bed, his bottom looking good enough to eat.

'I'll help you,' she said. 'Just give me a minute to check whether my publisher has emailed the book promotion they're running. I'm hoping to have hit the top one hundred in the Amazon charts.'

'You are always number 1,' he said.

She lay back and lit a cigarette. This was surreal. Yiannis here again. Her partner. No lies, no hiding, no rushing off. She looked at the alarm clock: 10.20pm and smiled. He was here. He didn't have to rush off anywhere and they had a whole week together.

'Woo-hoo!' she yelled and then grabbed his pillow and burying her head into it, she hugged it.

'You okay in there,' he asked, popping his head around the door.

'I am,' she laughed.

'And the pillow?'

'I'm having a squidgy-kinda-love moment.'

'With the pillow?'

'Yes!' she screamed with joy and launched the pillow at him.

In the kitchen, they flirted and kissed over the chopping board, the onion stinging their eyes. They hugged while the salmon sizzled in the pan and they giggled like teenagers, their giggles bouncing one after the other into their throats, as the asparagus hissed in the vegetable steamer. They sat next to each other as they ate, their arms touching, sending a heat through Stella, and they shared a bottle of white wine sent by Prodromos with his compliments.

The week came and went, every night the same and filled with more passion and urgency than the one before. They swallowed each other up, desperate for their bodies to be one, skin on skin. Their time together was on a timer, but not the restricted, controlling timer of the life she had with Anton.

This was different, it was heady, all-consuming and Stella already counted the days until the time Yiannis would return to be with her again, and eventually come to stay. Her passion for him mirrored his and they talked late into the night of her books, her writing, his dream to run his own hotel and stories of growing up in Greece.

Last Chapter

It was a cool but blue-grey May Bank Holiday weekend with a drizzling sky which threatened a downpour. Melody had organised a Kefalonia reunion and "Meet Little Miss" evening at her and Luke's home. Stella couldn't wait to meet the little one and had arranged with Eliana to go over a couple of hours before the men so they could have their girly catch up and get their cuddle fix in without them around.

Stella had been tempted to decline last minute; Yiannis had only flown in the night before. The last time they had seen each other was at Easter a few weeks before. But she wanted to meet Melody's baby and to see her friends; the weekly video calls had dwindled and their once regular meet ups for dinner had dwindled.

'Helena Victoria, meet your Aunty Stella and Aunty Eliana,' whispered Melody, as she scooped up the baby girl from her Moses basket and rested the tiny bundle against her shoulder.

'She is so tiny,' said Stella, shaking off her damp raincoat, a pull of the mother she would never be tugging at her heartstrings.

'What a little treasure,' said Eliana, who had arrived a few minutes after Stella.

'Thank you. She is amazing. I never thought I could love anyone as much as I love her. From the minute I laid eyes on her. I fell in love. She has given life a new meaning.'

'Incredible,' cooed Stella. 'That's *storge*.'

'Such a special love between a parent and child. And can you believe it? Me. A parent. A mum,' shrieked Melody, her delight evident, almost tangible in its joy.

'As it should be,' said Eliana. 'I bet Luke's a brilliant dad too.'

'He is besotted… with both of us.'

'So glad for you. For both of you,' said Stella, giving her arm a squeeze.

'You've turned things around,' said Eliana, her eyes glistening.

'We're doing better than ever. We've overcome so much, and we've learned a lot about each other, about our life together,' said Melody.

'We can see it. The change in you is wonderful to see,' said Stella.

'I read something the other day which really struck deep with me… it was something like slow mornings, freedom to choose, peace of mind, people you love, people who love you back,' said Eliana.

'And a good night's sleep,' laughed Melody. 'Funny how things can sometimes work out better than you ever imagined.'

'Gosh, I love my sleep,' said Stella, yawning.

'And things do work out.'

'Right, you can each have another cuddle and then I'm going to wind her and put her down for a nap after her nappy change.'

'I haven't come all this way for a quick cuddle. I want a whole afternoon of cuddles, don't I?' cooed Stella as Melody gently eased the baby into her arms. Stella and Eliana cuddled the baby, each clearly in awe at how little and perfect she was.

'I will be all yours for a couple of hours once she falls asleep. We have so much to catch up on. Help yourselves to a glass of wine. It's in the kitchen.'

Melody disappeared and Stella and Eliana grabbed a glass of wine each and then settled back into the couch.

'How are things going between you and Dean?' asked Stella.

'Surprisingly good. The holiday, though I didn't realise at the time, did us the world of good. You don't know how much you and Melody helped me look at things a different way, my reaction to him, my understanding of him. You might not realise it, but you did.'

'Talking about things is always a step in the right direction. Sometimes we are too close to the situation to be able to work it out.'

'We took the time to really listen to each other and to consider what we each want and need out of our relationship. You'll be pleased to know I don't think I nag at him as much as I used to.'

'You didn't nag,' said Stella. 'You consciously, or subconsciously, reacted differently.'

'Well, maybe. But he's got his op coming up in a couple of weeks. He's been for the pre-op assessment, and everything is going ahead as planned with his knee surgery.'

'Brilliant news. That must be a relief.'

'For both of us,' laughed Eliana.

Melody was back and with shining eyes announced, 'That's Little Miss out for the count.'

'Gosh, she's good,' said Stella. 'Can't believe how quickly she's fallen asleep.'

'Really lucky. Most days she eats, sleeps, poos and does it all again a few hours later.'

'Motherhood suits you. You're glowing,' said Stella. 'And you've stopped biting your nails.'

'I stopped without even thinking about it not long after I went to my GP. One day I looked down and my nails had grown. That's what all the angst was doing to me. Dermatophagia is a compulsive disorder. I'm lucky I stopped. Some people suffer with it for their whole life.'

Eliana agreed. 'And how are things between you and Luke now?'

'As smooth as ever. The counselling sessions helped, and we both, you know, acknowledged our own flaws, and failures, which contributed to all the mess we ended up in.'

'Relationships and the love around us change over time. The Greeks have got it right. They recognise the changing love and accept it and go with it...'

'We've got to that stage of love the Greeks call *pragma*. That kind of practical love which holds you together out of understanding and commitment... because there's more to lose by breaking up than staying together. It doesn't sound romantic but there's *storge* there too, family love and bonding.'

'Sounds like a level-headed way to look at how things are between you and with Little Miss in your lives now too you will find yourselves again for sure. Slow steps,' said Stella.

'And how about you and Yiannis? He is coming later, isn't he?'

'Yes, of course. He arrived yesterday so we haven't seen anything outside of the bedroom yet,' said Stella, surprised by her openness.

'Glad we were able to entice you along to our little soiree,' said Melody, stifling a yawn. She reached over for her mobile phone and put on some Greek music. 'To get us in the mood,' she said.

'He would love to see you all.'

'And have you heard from Anton?'

'No. Nothing. He's drifted away. He's not a part of my life anymore and this might sound crazy, but I don't miss him. The hole I imagined he would leave behind isn't there. It's too full of me and work and Yiannis and writing.'

'That's because Yiannis is so great,' said Eliana.

'Lots of *eros* I'm guessing,' said Melody. 'You don't need anything but Yiannis to get into the mood.'

'Haha.'

'All the passion and the lust and the can't-wait-to-get-you-into-bed love,' said Melody, with a twinkle in her eye.

'Okay, okay but there's a lot of *ludus* between us which

is how it should be,' laughed Stella a little embarrassed at admitting this to her younger friends. 'But the Greek music does take me back. Kefalonia was an incredible island. And it helped infuse my writing with a hungry passion again!'

'And my painting,' said Melody.

'Talking of which… I don't know if you know this but my publishers in New York happened to see my social media post about your exhibition and…'

'And?' said Melody, her eyes bright.

'They have bought the triptych art pieces for their new headquarters. And that's not all. They are expanding with offices in London and have asked me to act as their UK literary agent.'

'No! Bloody hell,' said Eliana. 'This is amazing. To new news and old holiday memories,' she said, letting out a whoop.

Both women raised their glasses, 'To Kefalonia,' said Stella and she dashed to the kitchen to pour Melody a glass of wine.

'A small measure,' she said, I'm breastfeeding, though I've expressed enough for tonight's middle-of-the-night feeds. I will pay for it by the morning,' she said, rubbing her left boob.

'And what about the love in your life, dearest Eliana?' asked Stella. 'How are things with you and Dean?'

'If you're talking which Greek word for love we most fit into, I haven't got a clue,' said Eliana. 'But I'm guessing it's *pragma*, love built on commitment, understanding, and long-term interests, like sharing our lives together.'

'So, the magic of Miramare has shown you how to honour, respect, and cherish each other, accepting your differences and learning to compromise.'

'Okay, okay, yes Stella. Exactly. And it's so good for us. We're so much calmer now.'

'Glad to hear it,' said Stella. 'Some of your disagreements were pretty uncomfortable for us to listen to.'

'I know that now. Sorry... but it can't have been that bad or you both wouldn't have kept in touch,' smiled Eliana.

'Let me just get that,' said Melody, rushing to the front door.

She came back in a few seconds later. 'Look who I found on the doorstep,' she said. Both Dean and Yiannis walked in behind her and a few minutes later the front door key went and in walked Luke.

'Good timing,' said Melody.

They all hugged and kissed and beamed big joyful smiles at each other.

'I brought this for you,' said Yiannis, handing Melody a package with a red bow around it. 'It's a gift for the baby's crib.'

'Aww, thank you, Yiannis. That's so kind,' said Melody, placing the neatly wrapped present down on the coffee table.

'Prodromos sends his love. He says you are all welcome to come back to Miramare any time. He is waiting.'

'We'd love that,' said Melody. 'His place made everything between me and Luke good again. Such a magical place.'

'Prodromos believes the magic is from the gods, from the love they hold true, and comes from a place of joy that new beginnings bring to us and allow us to foster and carry in us. It's aligning with it that creates the reality.'

'So profound and true,' said Stella.

The men all shook hands and clapped each other on the back, pleased to see one another and the women kissed and hugged them in turn. Stella was pleased to see them all getting along so well despite it being the first time they had been together since their holiday and a happy, quiet peace washed over her and for a moment she had to fight back the tears, as an overwhelming emotion, one of contentment, took hold of her.

'You okay, Stella *mou*?' asked Yiannis, pulling her close.

'Of course, yes.'

'You are happy to see your friends, yes?'

'I'm delighted to see them and to have you here too,' she said, kissing him.

'Get a room, you two, eh?' said Dean.

'Friends, food and all the love in the world,' said Stella.

'Give me a bit of loving any day of the week,' said Dean.

'Love and a lot of food. Don't forget the food, babe,' smirked Eliana, as she rolled her eyes. Melody fell about in hysterics and Eliana joined in within seconds.

'I know I said I'd cook, but Little Miss has kept me extra busy today, and my Greek cooking isn't so great, despite the Greek cookery book I brought back with me. So, we're going to order Greek kebabs from the takeaway down the road. It's a restaurant too and so we've ordered a whole banquet… probably not as amazing as the ones Prodromos created for us, but their food is surprisingly good,' said Melody.

Luke got the beers out and the men talked about work and football. The women huddled together cooed around the baby who had woken up. Melody was busy discussing baby nappies and the best way to relieve sore nipples and engorged breasts, Stella checking the pros and cons of breastfeeding on her mobile phone.

Within half an hour the food arrived, and they all piled into the kitchen diner to eat, the conversation and the joking around flowing as if they were on holiday all over again. Stella surveyed the group as they bustled together passing plates, knives, and forks around.

Helena Victoria, back in her crib, went down without a murmur for the night.

'Thank you for the beautiful *mati*,' said Melody, as she bounced back into the kitchen.

'You're welcome. It was Stella's idea,' he beamed.

'It's beautiful. Thank you both.'

The couples made a toast and tucked into their meal; pork and chicken kebabs garnished with freshly chopped parsley and coriander, *klitharaki* baked in the oven with sliced onions and tomatoes, Greek salad with crumbly feta cheese and shiny black olives glistened with olive oil and lemon dressing. Houmous, taramasalata dips and warm pitta bread added a delectably welcome accompaniment to the main dishes.

'This is amazing. Thank you,' said Stella.

'You're all welcome and you're all welcome any time,' said Luke.

'To us,' said Dean, making another toast.

'To us,' they repeated.

'And to Prodromos and Andri, his forever love,' said Yiannis.

'To Prodromos,' they toasted.

'And the magic of Miramare,' said Stella, her voice twinkling, and, in the distance, she was sure she heard the same familiar notes of the tune she had heard in Kefalonia on her first day there. Yiannis squeezed her hand under the table and Stella squeezed it back. She had found her way back to her writing, found a wondrous new love and found a new, magically authentic way to live.

As the evening wore on, Stella looked around her and rested her eyes on each of her friends, each of them a bright jewel in a never-ending, beautiful sky. Women with gumption, tenacity, and a whole lot of life to live and love to share in their own distinct way: Melody with her second-chance love, newfound love for her daughter and for her nucleus family of three. Eliana with her clumsy, reserved love, which reached the very depths of her own fragile heart and the man she loved, however much she tried to hide it.

Each of them, wrapped in a blanket of love singing a special sonnet for them and only them. She thanked her lucky stars for all the phases of love, seasoned sequences that taught each soul how to love another deeply and well. She thanked the Greeks for their recognition and celebration of love in all its forms and its presence in her life, the past, the present and the future.

THE END

Note to my readers

I hope you loved reading this book as much as I loved writing it!

If your mouth was watering at the thought of eating mandolato, why not try making your own. Email me at soullaauthor@gmail.com for a free downloadable recipe sheet and you too can enjoy your own sticky dessert.

It felt only right to include the mention of a Greek Cypriot poet in the story and hope you will check out Eftychia Panayiotou's poetry for yourself. She was born in Cyprus, in 1980, and not only is she a poet, but also a copy editor and poetry translator (Anne Sexton, Anne Carson, English Romantics). Her own books of poetry are: μέγας κηπουρός (great gardener, 2007), Μαύρη Μωραλίνα (Black Moralina, 2010, third prize for best book by young poet), and Χορευτές (Dancers, 2014, shortlisted in Cyprus and Greece).

She studied Philosophy and Modern Greek Studies and has completed her Ph.D. in Modern Greek Poetry. She also teaches in creative writing programmes and workshops and is engaged with video poetry and song poetry.

The earthquake in this story was written in and researched as part of Kefalonia's natural history and plotted long before the devastating earthquake hit Turkey, Syria and Lebanon in February 2023. The story here, by no means is intended to glorify or dampen the impact the untimely and natural, but horrific, disaster has had on the communities affected.

And lastly, why I wrote this book and dedicated it to my family. My family and I visited Kefalonia in August 2014, and it was a milestone holiday for many reasons. My mum had gone through multiple chemo and radiotherapy treatments and surgeries for bowel and liver cancer. She was finally coming round to being herself again, her energy was returning, and she was smiling after years of gruelling hospital appointments, lengthy consultations, and invasive treatments.

We chose a beautiful hotel in Xi and we had the best time which is why my book is dedicated to my family who made this one of my fondest holidays.

Surrounded by the white clay cliffs, we caked our bodies in thick layers of clay on Xi beach, we drove down the steepest paths to the quietest coves and we danced to Greek music in the car park of a supermarket in the middle of the afternoon. One evening we took over the hotel bar and danced like no one was watching. We breakfasted and dined together. We laughed. We cried. Another night a wonderful doctor sensitively treated my mum for excruciating pain in her back and soothed our fears and sorrows with the kindest, most heartfelt words of wisdom and love. We sunbathed on the shores of a crystal blue lake. After driving for a while and avoiding huge cracks in the roads damaged by an earthquake a few days before our arrival, we eventually stopped at the top of a cliff and surveyed the film spot where Captain Corelli's Mandolin was filmed. We discovered a beach called St Helen's (my mum's name) where we swam in its waters. We did a surprise 70th birthday dinner for my mum, complete with balloons and a special birthday cake on a little terrace on the harbour overlooking the Ionian Sea. It was a truly magical experience from start to finish and the magic of the island made our love for each other stronger, deeper, and brighter. I will always remember it with great fondness and love in my heart.

Acknowledgements

Thank you to Maria Karamitsos, Maria Antoniou, Corinne Schurink, Lia Seaward, Maria Amoss and Elaine Graham-Leigh for your beta reader notes, feedback and encouragement. The time you took to read and thoughtfully comment will always be greatly appreciated. Thank you to Loukas Georgiou, an incredible artist and dear friend, for looking at one sentence which had me stumped and procrastinating for far too long than is sanely acceptable.

Thank you to Kingsley Publishers for their continued support and attention in bringing this book to my readers.

Thankful for the insightful information and relationship advice I came across during my research for this book which I gleaned from the podcasts, books, and social media posts of Brené Brown, Esther Perel, Julia Cole, Gretchen Rubin and Susanna Abse.

And the biggest most heartfelt thanks go to Alan, for always giving me the time and space I needed to write, to procrastinate and to spend endless hours on my social media (sometimes for research purposes and other times because it was the only place I could escape the insecurities I was feeling about this book, and where life was going). Eternally grateful and love you forever.

About the Author

Born in London to Greek Cypriot parents, Soulla Christodoulou was the first in her family to go to university and later retrained to become a teacher. She has been writing since 2015 and has many more books in her.

Her novels, *Broken Pieces of Tomorrow*, *The Summer Will Come*, *The Village House* and *A Palette of Magpies* are available on Amazon alongside *Alexander and Maria* which was nominated for the RSL Ondaatje Prize 2021.

The Summer Will Come, a book club read in the Year of Learning Festival 2019, London Borough of Barnet Libraries, has been translated into Greek and is currently being queried with Greek and Greek Cypriot publishers.

Soulla is working on her next novel, *The Pastry Girl of Malta* and writing her first non-fiction book on the craft and magic of writing. She is consulting on the movie project inspired by her book *The Summer Will Come* and is learning a lot about the world of filmmaking. She is happiest writing and reading in her pretty garden Writing Room while drinking tea infused with cinnamon sticks and cloves.

Connect with Soulla on her website
https://www.soulla-author.com/
Instagram: @soullasays
X: @schristodoulou2
She loves to hear from her readers.

The Village House

"Romantic, descriptive, and evocative… The Village House captures the authentic spirit of a Cypriot village."
- *Nadia Marks, best-selling author of Among the Lemon Trees.*

Katianna receives a solicitor's letter summoning her to Omodos, a mountain village in Cyprus.

What is at first an inconvenient trip quickly becomes more attractive as she spends more time there. Flooded with many childhood memories, she falls in love with her roots and relishes in the relaxed pace and warmth of her cousin and the Cypriot people she meets. And then there's the simmering attention of the builder tasked with renovating the village house Katianna has inherited from her maternal grandmother.

Grappling with yo-yoing emotions, she returns home. But in London all is not well for her award-winning dating agency; her world is threatened, turned upside down, forcing her to question everything she believes in and has worked so hard for.

She travels back and forth and has to face the fact she has to sell the only connection left to her family.

But can Katianna have everything? Will she find a way to hold onto her business? Or will the pull of her heartstrings and the village house entice her to start over in a place closer to home than she ever imagined.

The Village House

SOULLA CHRISTODOULOU

KINGSLEY
PUBLISHERS

Chapter 1

The building, in the heart of London, screamed success. Katianna relished it. Her patent heels clipped across the marble flooring, the echo bouncing across the bright, open space. She took the green coded escalator to the double-decker lifts, leather laptop case in one hand and designer handbag in the other.

The glass doors pinged opened, closed immediately after her. She pressed the button for the twelfth floor, the location of her dating agency, *Under the Setting Sun*. She looked straight ahead at the control panel; the buttons lighting up the company names as the elevator whooshed past each floor: Investment Management PLC, Kew and Press Lawyers, ARC Project Management, Cyprus Property Portfolio... her eyes stayed locked with the word Cyprus... the letter she had recently received on her mind, still sitting on her desk, but she shook the niggling, invasive thought away, refocused.

In her office, she tucked her handbag under her desk and smoothed out her black pencil skirt. She plugged in and switched on her laptop. She sat facing the glass-walled partition which afforded her with a view of her team and the open-plan workspace beyond. At eight promptly she went through the day's key activities with her PA.

'That's great, thank you Angie.'

'I'll get your coffee,' Angie said, her tight ponytail and wide-legged culottes swinging in time with each long step. Her yellow flat pumps coordinated nicely with the mustard of her trousers and echoed the colours of an uncharacteristically warm July. At almost six-foot Angie didn't need any more height. She towered over Katianna, who at only five foot four considered her own heels necessary, especially at work.

Angie was in her early thirties, a few years younger than Katianna, but her mature attitude and commitment shone through from the moment she said "anything it takes" in her interview five years before. Katianna recognised a kindred spirit in her and despite Angie's patchy work history hired her instantly never regretting it.

A real asset to the company, Angie was efficient, productive, proactive and loyal. She had become a good friend over the years and with life very much tipped towards work, genuine friends were hard to come by for Katianna. The glitz and glamour of award nights and ceremonies were just that and Katianna snubbed her friends' comments.

'Slow down,' they urged. 'Not everything which

shines is made of gold.'

But her circle shrunk as she rebuffed their comments telling them everything did in her world.

Katianna's sole purpose to be successful was all-consuming, her single-minded ambition her steed. Eight years before, she had won the court case against her business partner, also her ex-fiancé, to keep the business name. She had since spent every waking hour and every ounce of energy making the business a leader and had vowed never to be indebted to anyone ever again, especially in business. But in love too.

Judged by the UK and European Dating Awards' independent panel on reputation, success rate, approachability, and customer service, *Under the Setting Sun*, had been favoured many times over.

Framed awards hung in a perfect line across one wall and gave no room for doubt: UK Matchmaking Agency of the Year 2015 and 2018, International Matchmaker of the Year 2015, European Matchmaking Agency of the Year 2016 and 2018.

But achievement had come at a price; the ensuing months of working long hours and at weekends had pushed away the university friends Katianna had in her inner circle. The odd text or phone call was all she had time for now. She recognised a shift once they had husbands, wives, families of their own. She pushed aside the split-second prickle. She had her empire, didn't she?

She swiveled round in her seat to face the London vista laid out before her, the leather squeaking against the fabric of her skirt. This, all of it, she breathed, was worth every minute of working past midnight, waking at dawn, and missed lunches with friends. This is what made life worth living.

Every day she breathed in the success of the dating agency and her innovative approach had kept her ahead of the ever-growing competition and away from negative press increasingly associated with dating agencies and relationship apps.

Hers was different; clients plugged into a network of high-calibre, aspirational, professional singles. Supported by an assigned matchmaker, they worked towards the ultimate goal of a long-term relationship. Their sign-up package included professional photography, Myers Briggs-type indicator assessment which provided information on who each client really was and ID-checks on all members which ensured safety and security. Her matchmakers had backgrounds in psychology, counselling, and life coaching. Her newest recruit was a chartered psychologist and Associate Fellow of the British Psychological Society.

She took a call from John, her full-time accountant and finance manager. Running any business effectively relied on the owner's understanding of costs, money in and money out, and John handled that side of the agency for her; she preferred the company of people to figures and spreadsheets and she was instinctively yielding around him, trusting his knowledge and expertise implicitly.

John had been working with Katianna for almost seven years and he had been one of the first people she consulted with in terms of growing the business. It took off in its second year, more than tripling her forecasted income.

They rescheduled their monthly meeting around another appointment that had moved for John and said goodbye.

Katianna checked her emails and looked over the schedule of client photo shoots and website update meetings planned with her team; she kept a keen eye on the competition and read the main broadsheet newspapers and magazines every day. She followed trending hashtags, Instagram stories and LinkedIn news, including trends in the USA, Canada, and Europe.

She turned around, a knock-knock at her door.

'Come in,' she said, already gesturing to Warren, one of her advertising sales team.

'Have you got a minute?'

'Of course,' she said, nodding towards one of the black leather club chairs.

'I've got good news and bad news,' he said. 'The Mayfair Inn, Sherlock Mews and Devi Ahilya India have confirmed their online advertising for another year. I've increased the ad fee by 10%.'

'And the bad news?'

'One of the new restaurant accounts has paid for the key spot on our home page for twelve months.'

'Bad news because?'

'The Broadgate Hotel & Spa has already confirmed that spot for three months and paid-up front.'

'Use your negotiation skills to keep them holding on until then... offer them something else for the first three months and then the nine months, or even the year, on the home page.'

'I did that already. They're not biting.'

'Leave it with me. When did you last speak to them?'

'Day before yesterday.'

'Email across the details, your conversation notes, files.'

'I'll do it right now,' he said, making for the door. 'Thanks Katianna.'

She smiled at his retreating back. Warren was good at getting the advertising in but not so good with what she called "being cute"–keeping all sides happy when a pickle arose which thankfully wasn't often.

Her laptop pinged, Warren's email. She read the attachments, nothing to worry about. She was sure she could keep both accounts happy.

She pushed the laptop away and the letter caught her attention; the letter that had been mailed three times to her previous address. It was quite by chance she had bumped into her old neighbour who mentioned she had been holding onto post for her.

Katianna had hated sharing a letter box with Nosy Rosy, as she not-so-affectionately nicknamed her, who never missed an opportunity to ask why Vodafone were sending so many letters or why she received discount offer cards when everyone did their shopping online; her own daughter and three nieces did. Katianna had forced a smile and tightened her lips holding back on what she had really thought of her nosiness even though it was cloaked as neighbourly concern and kindness.

She took the envelope in her hand, felt the weight of it, in more ways than one, ran her fingers over the perforated edges of the Cyprus stamp and slipped out the thick cream sheet. She read the three short paragraphs again. She needed to book a flight to Cyprus when all she wanted was to stay in London, enjoy the rare hot summer and get on with running her business. She didn't have the time to take the four-and-a-half-hour trip to a country she hadn't been back to for years and recalled a client, two years ago, who the agency had successfully paired with a French lawyer. She believed they now lived happily in Paphos.

'Look at it as a well-deserved break,' Angie had said, 'on the island of l-o-o-o-v-e.' Katianna smiled, remembering how Angie had drawled the word.

Katianna had tried dismissing the unexpected wave of wistful affection. Her *yiayia* Anna had been the only grandmother she had known in her life and memories filled her; *yiayia* hugging Katianna tight, pinching her cheeks each summer in exaggerated awe of how much she had grown, plucking juicy purple figs, and picking grapes together.

Was going back to claim her *yiayia's* house a good idea? Her grandmother's passing had been painful, a shock, yet Katianna had not returned for the funeral still reeling from the deaths of her own parents; a stab of guilt poked at her, even more so now that the village house had been bequeathed to her and her parents were no longer here to know it. For a moment, tears threatened to fall but she pushed them away. There was no time for silly sentimentality and regrets. Living in the moment was all she had, and this is what she had right now; a house in the village waiting for her to what? Breathe new life into it? Connect with a life and a culture she had negligible ties with?

Her cousin Savva, who had linked up with her, after more than twenty years, put on the pressure, begging her to fly out.

'You can stay with me,' he said. 'I'm all grown up now.'

She had to go. She could not get out of this. Savva wouldn't take no for an answer and, of course she had to sign the legal documents for the house. Cyprus, it appeared, didn't recognise technological advancements and the solicitor insisted she visit to sign the paperwork in person with her identification: 'We have to have the original documents in front of us,' he repeated, though she wondered whether Savva had anything to do with their lack of enthusiasm to do things online.

Saying goodbye to her team was bittersweet; part of her looked forward to a break, a change of routine, and she had solved Warren's issue, with charm, so she was leaving on a high. Her team was the closest she had to family, yet she held them at a distance, preferring not to blur the lines between her work and their private lives. But she was admittedly going to miss them all as well as the buzz of the day to day in the office. As she left shortly after seven, she quietly relished the idea of disappearing for a few days, remembering her mother's words: *Rest is not an indulgence, it is essential Katianna. How can you be your best self if you don't treat yourself well?* Cyprus was going to bring her the rest she needed, she reassured herself.

Chapter 2

Katianna arrived at Larnaca International Airport exhausted and crampy; the pains in her tummy twisting her intestines with anticipation but her exterior façade portrayed nothing of her inner anxiety. It was nearly midnight by the time she exited the airport even though passport control had been efficient, and the queues had moved quickly. She hoped Savva was still waiting for her.

The flight from Heathrow Terminal 5 had been delayed by two hours because of "mechanical issues". The announcement had left her uneasy and anxiety consumed her entire flight despite the luxury of flying first class. All the while the whiney antagonistic voice in her head said: "You should have stayed at home. Leaving your business and gallivanting to God knows where…"

Katianna marvelled at the modern, bright airport remembering how she used to arrive with her parents and have to queue on the tarmac; the airport building too small to accommodate a full plane of arrivals. She walked out of the air-conditioned building with a renewed bounce.

The muggy heat of the night enveloped her and conscious of a sheen of sweat she brushed her hand across her forehead and upper lip. August, the hottest month of the year. Her clammy hand slipped against the suitcase handle as she dragged the oversized luggage behind her. Trying to keep it upright, she crossed the tarmac, no longer riddled with potholes and cracks as it had been years before, though the intense summer heat was the same. Her ankle doubled over as she caught her red stilettos on the edge of the raised walkway and her designer jacket slipped off her arm. Looking down at the heel, the leather had been shredded. Damn, she thought and gathering the jacket draped it over her shoulders despite the heat.

'Katianna,' Savva called from where he leaned against the shuttered kiosk, the streetlamp casting a harsh light.

She carefully navigated her way between the rows of parked hire cars and minibuses. As Katianna neared him, she took in his dishevelled appearance, yet his stance oozed a quiet, sexy confidence which took her by surprise. He was unkempt yet surprisingly attractive. He seemed bolder, more mature, in real life, not the soft, baby-faced man she saw on their video calls.

He threw his unfinished cigarette to the ground, grinding the stub into the tarmac and leaned in to kiss Katianna's cheeks, exhaling smoke over her shoulder. Katianna, taken by surprise, felt a blush of colour fill her cheeks. She had forgotten how kisses and hugs were nothing to shy away from in Cyprus, especially when greeting friends and relatives.

'I thought you said you were quitting?' she grimaced and then smiled as she waved the tendrils of Savva's cigarette smoke away.

'I was, until a week ago when the thought of my English cousin visiting stressed me out.'

'Very funny. You can't blame me. What's the real reason?'

'Lack of will power.'

'That's it?'

'That's it. Now come here and give me a proper hug.' He pulled her close.

'You stink like an ashtray,' she said, pulling away and giggling, surprised and delighted with the familiarity between them.

She liked the way she was able to connect with him even though her Greek was inferior to his fluency in English. But the closeness between them, there since childhood, was evident and flooded back like a ribbon-like flow of water, comfortable moving with the force of gravity, unperturbed by any babbles or ripples. They were almost twins; their birthdays only three days apart and it didn't take long for Savva to tease her about being older and therefore demanded respect.

'You haven't really changed at all,' she said.

As children they had been thrown together every summer holiday; they danced together, swam out to the floating raft at Santa Barbara beach despite words of warning from their parents, and as a teenager Savva had escorted her to clubs, keeping a close eye on anyone who dared approach her, ready to pounce with the protectiveness of a lion over his pride.

*****

The drive to the village from the airport took just shy of an hour and a half; Katianna took in the silhouetted view of tall buildings and huge lit billboards, almost unrecognisable to the landscape she remembered as a child.

The peaks of the Troodos mountains loomed darker still behind the buildings, with the stars twinkling like Van Gogh's *The Starry Night. S*he recalled a specific camping trip to the Kykko Monastery, a royal, Patriarchal Stavropygian Monastery located in the western part of the mountain range, twelve miles from the highest peak of Cyprus' Mount Olympus.

All those years ago, lying side by side with Savva, sharing the same sleeping bag, the same splintered stars had dotted the inkiest blue expanse which felt so close it was as if she could pluck one from its blanket. Savva had tried to grab one for her, huffing and puffing, exaggerating his efforts. The other campers had been woken by her laughter followed by the smack of the thrashing slaps from their parents; both had hidden inside the lumpy sleeping bag till they almost couldn't breathe, holding hands, their bodies squashed against each other's in innocence, as any brother or sister.

'Almost there already,' she said, disappointed when the car indicated at the final E-road exit for Omodos.

Omodos, she thought, coming from the Cypriot word "modos," meaning "taking your time," with tact, carefully. She had found the snippet of information on the in-flight magazine. She hadn't realised how popular a destination her ancestral village had become and felt a sense of pride shadowed by a sting of guilt at not having known it.

As a child, the drive from the airport seemed to take forever, the journey made almost in complete darkness with no lighting along the poorly tarmacked roads, pot-holed and rutted—dirt tracks—unlike the roads now, the majority brightly lit and well-maintained.

They arrived in the village, built at the slope of the mountains, the winding roads narrower than she remembered and the pretty stone village houses, with their tiled roofs and terraces and picturesque upper floors, glowing in the amber light of the streetlamps; those replaced at intervals with brighter bulbs shone at a sharp downward angle and she scrunched her tired eyes against their harshness. The sweet smell of grapes carried on the mid-night breeze as it swept over the vineyards towards the village. A stray cat, not straggly or emaciated like the strays used to be, ran out in front of the car, her shiny coat glinting in the headlights. Savva slowed down and the cat's eyes seemed to stare at Katianna.

Katianna shivered against a little tremor running through her, but she looked upon the cat crossing their path as a good omen and her black fur even more so. She slinked away and disappeared under a parked pick-up truck; battered and missing a back bumper.

*****

So where do you want to start today? I've taken three days off work to be your translator, chauffeur, whatever you need.'

'You're a real good sort. How comes you haven't been snapped up?' Katianna wiped her brow, already sweaty from the rising temperature.

'Who says I haven't?'

'Because your house is still a house, not a home,' said Katianna, pointing to the stark walls and clutter-free surfaces of the open-plan kitchen and sitting room.

'How is that observation going to help you sort out your *yiayia's* house?'

'Sorry. It isn't. It's a habit of mine… comes with the job.' She smiled, hoping to take the sting out of her comment. 'Let's start with breakfast and then you can accompany me to the house.'

'Sounds good. I want to know everything that's been happening. There's something different about you I didn't catch on our video calls. I can't put my finger on it.'

Chapter 3

'Black tea with cinnamon sticks and cloves, and a halloumi and mortadella toastie for me, thank you.' Katianna placed her order after Savva introduced her to Sofia.

Katianna had spotted the little café *stafilia kai meli* which translated as "grapes and honey" as they walked arm in arm across the village square and though Savva had tried to persuade her to walk further, Katianna's puppy-dog eyes had won him over.

'How delightful. I haven't been asked for a cinnamon and clove tea in years.'

'It's how my *yiayia* Anna made it. It seems right I should drink it now I'm back,' said Katianna.

'She was a wonderful old lady, so kind,' said Sofia.

'You knew her?'

'She was a grandmother to all of us growing up in the village,' said Sofia.

'I guess she would have been, yes. I wish I'd known her better, especially these last few years.'

'Well, there are many around here who can tell you about her,' said Sofia.

'Just a coffee for me, Sofia,' said Savva, interrupting them.

Katianna gave him a look; one she had perfected in the days of child minding to pay her university fees. Memories flooded her: piles of ironing, scrubbing shower doors until they gleamed, tidying endless toys, sleeping on her side on the edge of a single bed until her arm went numb while Jessica and James fell asleep, working with her laptop balanced on crossed legs on the sofa until after midnight, reading Eric Carle's *The Very Hungry Caterpillar* and Michael Bond's *Paddington Bear* Books over and over until she almost knew the stories word for word. She sighed, and then recalled the heavy hardbacks of J.K. Rowling which the family gifted her when she finished working with them two years later together with a generous bank transfer which put her in the black for the first time in four years.

'What?' he asked, cutting across her thoughts.

'You've taken me back to my nannying days… and not the good ones.'

'What d'you mean?'

'No smile. No please. No thank you.' She paused. 'You could at least acknowledge her. She's lovely and no wedding ring.'

'That's because she's not married,' he said, folding his arms across his chest.

'How come?' teased Katianna. Her lighter tone eased

the tension she picked up on and Savva gave her a half smile.

'I don't know. She's always lived in the village, never left. Opened the coffee shop when her parents died,' he said, avoiding eye contact.

'She looks happy.'

'They say happiness can come from the deepest sorrows, don't they?' said Savva.

'You're right. Kahil Gibran said something like, *when you feel joy, look to your heart and you'll find it's only that which has given you sorrow that is now giving you joy.*'

'I guess that's kind of true.'

'And she owns this place?'

'She spent all her inheritance breathing new life into the once derelict building abandoned by the previous owners. She's always here. Working.'

'Working but happy,' said Katianna, Sofia's situation closely mirroring her own.

Katianna sat a while, didn't say anything but her mind was already ticking with anticipation, an idea forming. Back in London and across the industry she was inevitably known as *The Matchmaker* and even though she was single herself she had this knack of pairing single hearts together and matching them fruitfully. With a first in psychology, she knew what made people tick and *Under the Setting Sun* had become more than a simple dating agency. It attracted clients serious about partnering and with a view to getting married, finding a life-long partner and it worked.

Sofia returned with their order served in a mishmash

of crockery.

'So pretty,' said Katianna, fingering the pretty floral teacup and saucer.

'Thank you, it meant a lot to my mother who received it as part of her dowry when she married. My intention was to use it temporarily and replace it once the business began making a profit but I'm glad I didn't,' she said, with a faraway look in her eye.

'I'm here refurbishing my grandmother's house and when it's done, I'm hoping to have a little celebration in memory of her life. I wonder...' she said, turning an idea around in her head. 'Would you cater for it and, of course, join me as a guest.'

'I'd be happy to arrange anything you need food-wise, but this place takes up all my time. But thank you for the invitation, that's sweet of you.'

'Don't say no to joining us just yet. Let me get sorted and once I have a date you can decide then.'

'She said, no, Katianna. Leave it,' said Savva.

Sofia's cheeks turned a fiery red. She grabbed the empty plates from the next table and scuttled off towards the serving hatch where Petros, her part-time chef, was already lining up the next round of breakfast orders.

'You embarrassed her,' said Katianna and slurping her tea she focused on its sweet, spicy fragrance to take away the sourness in the air.

'Me? You're the one going on about the catering and the invite,' he said and pulling his mouth with both fingers, stretched it wide, and waggled his tongue at her.

'You're not ten anymore,' she tutted, 'but I guess that's what so loveable about you.'

'Enough of me and how immature I am. Let's talk about you. What are your plans with the house?'

'Spruce it up and sell it. It's not convenient to keep it. I'm like Sofia with work leaching my time. And my life's in London.'

'The house is in pretty bad shape so sprucing may realistically need to be translated as refurbishing and even rebuilding in places.'

'It's been old and run down for as long as I remember,' she said, taking a bite of her toasted sandwich. The nutty aroma of the toasted, sesame-seed bread filled her nostrils. 'This is so good. The bread I buy from the bakery back home is good, Polish bread, but this is just heaven.'

'I'll tell George when I next see him. He's very proud of his baking skills.'

'And so he should be,' Katianna said.

'Eat and then let's get the solicitor out of the way.' Savva took the last swig of his Greek coffee as Katianna picked at the errant crumbs on her plate.

She wondered what the story was between Savva and Sofia, and she knew there was one; she felt it.